GOODBYE NEVER

by
PRESCOTT LANE

Copyright © 2022 Prescott Lane
Print Edition

Editing by Editing4Indies
Cover Design by lorijacksondesign.com
Cover Photos by: istockphoto: PeskyMonkey (ribbons)
Deposit Photos: solandzh (letters)
mcornelius (dogtags)
belchonock (background)

This is a work of fiction. All characters, organizations, and events portrayed in this novel are either products of the author's imagination or used fictitiously. All rights reserved. This book or any portion thereof may not be reproduced or used in any manner whatsoever without the express written permission of the author, except for the use of brief quotations in a book review.

TABLE OF CONTENTS

Prologue	1
Chapter One	3
Chapter Two	11
Chapter Three	16
Chapter Four	20
Chapter Five	30
Chapter Six	37
Chapter Seven	49
Chapter Eight	53
Chapter Nine	62
Chapter Ten	66
Chapter Eleven	71
Chapter Twelve	74
Chapter Thirteen	77
Chapter Fourteen	78
Chapter Fifteen	85
Chapter Sixteen	90
Chapter Seventeen	95
Chapter Eighteen	98
Chapter Nineteen	101
Chapter Twenty	104
Chapter Twenty-One	108
Chapter Twenty-Two	110
Chapter Twenty-Three	116
Chapter Twenty-Four	121
Chapter Twenty-Five	129
Chapter Twenty-Six	135
Chapter Twenty-Seven	139

Chapter Twenty-Eight	144
Chapter Twenty-Nine	149
Chapter Thirty	156
Chapter Thirty-One	163
Chapter Thirty-Two	168
Chapter Thirty-Three	174
Chapter Thirty-Four	178
Chapter Thirty-Five	180
Chapter Thirty-Six	184
Chapter Thirty-Seven	193
Chapter Thirty-Eight	202
Chapter Thirty-Nine	207
Chapter Forty	212
Chapter Forty-One	219
Chapter Forty-Two	224
Chapter Forty-Three	229
Chapter Forty-Four	239
Chapter Forty-Five	245
Chapter Forty-Six	250
Chapter Forty-Seven	255
Chapter Forty-Eight	262
Chapter Forty-Nine	266
Chapter Fifty	270
Epilogue	272
Also by Prescott Lane	277
Acknowledgements	278
About the Author	279

PROLOGUE
PRESENT DAY

LENNON

Some loves last a lifetime, but they all end the same way—with a goodbye.

Life is a series of goodbyes. Some are short. Some are long. Some hurt more than others. But there's no way around it. Life is one long goodbye.

It doesn't matter how long you live or how much you love. It doesn't matter if you're a good person or a terrible asshole. In the end, we all must say goodbye to everyone and everything we love.

Which is what I'm trying to do now—say goodbye to you.

Looking down at your headstone, I never dreamed I'd have to write an epitaph in my twenties. I also never dreamed that I'd be the reason you are buried in that ground.

I wipe my cheek. The weight of your death rests squarely on my shoulders, and my heart starts to ache.

No two heartbeats are exactly the same. It's true. Everyone's heart beats differently depending on its size and shape. All any of us can do is try to find the heart that beats in time with ours. But what do you do when that heart stops beating?

A cool Virginia breeze blows through the cemetery, and I bend down, placing fresh sunflowers on the ground in front of your grave. But getting back to my feet isn't as easy as it used to be, my six-month baby bump getting in the way.

This is wrong. A pregnant woman should not be standing at the foot of her baby's father's grave. It's not the natural order of things. It's not how things are supposed to be.

Rubbing my belly, I'm sad that our little bundle of joy will never know you. You will only ever be a ghost to her. You will only be a goodbye.

CHAPTER ONE
ELEVEN YEARS AGO

LENNON

High school is hell.

That goes double when you're the new kid, the scholarship kid, the girl whose mom is an ex-convict.

"Jail baby." Some guy laughs as he walks by.

Taking a deep breath, I stare into my locker—binders, notebooks, textbooks. Maybe if I look hard enough, the tears in my eyes will dry up. I should be used to this. It's October of my sophomore year. My mom insisted I stop homeschooling and go to a "real" school. When I got accepted into the local private college prep school, there was no getting out of it. I started in August and quickly became known as "jail baby."

Yep, my mom gave birth to me in jail. Yes, an actual jail. Normally, they might transfer an expectant mom to a local hospital or even the jail's infirmary, but I came quick. There was no time. I was born on the floor of my mom's jail cell. Hence the nickname.

"Aw, is jail baby gonna cry?" another guy leans in and whispers in my ear.

The entire hallway erupts into laughter. Grabbing a book, I hug it to my chest. These kids all come from money. Their parents pay a huge tuition every semester, so I have to keep my mouth shut. If I got into a beef with one of them, it would be me who took the blame. I know that. And I'm not going to let these assholes blow my shot at the best education in Virginia.

Suddenly, the laughter stops. "Hey, Lennon," Duke says, leaning up against the lockers. "Everything all right?"

I don't have any siblings, but if I did, Charles Duke III would be my Irish twin. We aren't related by blood, but we were born on the same day of the same month exactly one year apart. Throw in the fact that our mothers are the best of friends, and we were pretty much destined to be together, or at least that's what I secretly tell myself.

Duke never liked his first name. His grandfather was Charles. His dad is Charlie, so from the moment he could talk about himself in the third person, he referred to himself as Duke. It stuck.

His mom gave my mom her first job when she got out of jail. Gardening. And somehow, they just clicked, and Duke and I became each other's first friends. It's rumored that my first steps as a baby were toward him. I guess I've always wanted him.

To understand our relationship, you first must understand our mothers. Our bond is generational. We were literally born to be friends. Our mothers wouldn't have it any other way. Since they were always together, so were Duke and I. When we were little, it seemed like every weekend, either I stayed the night at his house or he stayed at mine. We were always together, and once we were too old for sleepovers, we were still always together, listening to music or watching movies. My memories are his memories, and his memories are mine.

"I'm good," I lie.

His steel-gray eyes scan the hallway, and everyone scatters like ants. No one messes with Duke. The most popular boy in school since he started freshman year, he plays baseball and football, gets good grades, and is single-handedly the cutest boy I've ever laid eyes on—those eyes, dark-blond hair, and muscles for days. Add in the fact that he's also a complete sweetheart, and my heart didn't stand a chance.

His family consists of some of Montclair's finest citizens. My mom and I might share a zip code with them, but nothing we have is "fine." Still, Duke's family is good to my mom and me. We love them. They love us. And I know we wouldn't have half the things we do without them—including my admission and scholarship into the area's best private school.

I don't want to tell Duke what the other kids are saying. One day pretty early on this year, some boy teased me about a skirt I had on. My mom had made it for me. She makes most of my clothes, including the pink sweater I'm wearing today. She can make just about anything, and she uses the leftover material to make ribbons to tie up my long brown hair. And the clothes we can afford to buy come from discount stores. Name brands are not in the budget, but I don't really mind. I don't like to stand out, and wearing the latest fashion trends makes a statement.

My statement is more—leave me in peace.

Anyway, this boy flipped my skirt up in the middle of the hallway. I'm sure anyone within eyeshot saw my panties. When Duke found out, he gave the shithead a bloody nose. Duke got suspended for three days because violence is not tolerated. The shithead was at school the next day. I guess sexual harassment is tolerated.

I can't have Duke getting in trouble for me again. Besides, what's he going to do? Beat up the whole school?

"Here," Duke says, and I look up at that boyish grin on his handsome face. He whips off his letterman jacket, holding it open for me. "Put this on."

"But your mom said you can't give your letterman jacket or class ring to a girl, ever!"

"Trust me, she won't care that I gave it to you," he says.

"But . . ."

"Lennon," he says, causing my skin to heat, "no one will bother you if you're wearing this."

"So wearing your jacket is saying what, that I belong to you?" I say in my lame attempt at flirting with him.

He laughs. "That you're under my protection." He raises an eyebrow at me, motioning for me to slip on the jacket.

Placing my book down, I turn around, moving my long brown

hair tied in a simple white ribbon to the side. As my arms slide in, the fabric is still warm from his body. I pull it tight to me, lifting it to my nose. He reaches around, helping to pull my hair out from the jacket. God, he's cute.

He grins at me as the bell rings. "Want me to walk you to class?"

I shake my head, smiling at him. "I've got my armor on now."

As I start to walk off, he calls back to me. "Wait for me after football practice, and I'll give you a ride home."

Sitting on the bleachers, I spot Duke on the field. It's not hard to find him. He's a grade above me, but even at only sixteen, he's well over six feet tall, broad-shouldered, and ripped. He runs his fingers through his dark-blond hair, which is slightly long. I wonder what it would be like to run my fingers through it.

Even though it's not winter yet, I pull his jacket tighter around me. Maybe he was right. No one messed with me for the rest of the day. Smiling to myself, I grab my sketchbook and open it. I love drawing. Every school notebook I have is filled with sketches. You'd never know it by my barely passing art grade. Only because I never let my teacher look at any of my work. I do all the assignments. I just don't turn them in.

Duke's the only one I've ever let see any of my art. He keeps telling me to apply to art school when I graduate, but that would involve letting other people see my stuff, and I'm not sure I'm brave enough to do that.

I'm not sure how my love of art began. It probably had something to do with the fact that crayons and paper were pretty cheap compared to other kids' toys like video games. Of course art can be an expensive hobby with fancy computer graphic programs and various brushes and paints, but even now, I prefer simple colored pencils and plain sketch paper. My mom swears I came out of the womb doodling. My favorite subject to draw—anything. I will literally draw a phone book if that's the only inspiration in front of me.

A group of girls starts up the bleachers and surround me—Duke's current girlfriend included. "What are you drawing, jail baby?"

I flip my pad over, ignoring them.

They start to laugh. "Jail baby instead of jail bait!"

"Yeah"—Duke's girlfriend laughs—"have to be pretty to be bait."

Suddenly, I feel small even though I'm already five-eight. The pediatrician told my mother that I'd only grow an inch or so after I got my period. Well, I got my period two years ago, and I've grown twice as many inches since then.

However, my boobs didn't get the message that I'm well into puberty. I'm still waiting on them to show up. Basically, I'm a tall, flat-chested brunette still donning braces. The complete opposite of all these pretty girls, with their perfect skin, teeth, and nails. All of whom seem to be born with the gift to know how to flirt.

"I seem to have baited Duke," I say, turning around and facing her. "Got his jacket."

I shouldn't goad her, and I shouldn't use what Duke told me in confidence to antagonize her. But I know she threw a fit when he wouldn't give her his jacket on orders from his parents.

Her nostrils flare, and for a second, I wonder if she's going to slap me. "What did you do for it?" she asks. "Spread your legs like your momma."

"My mom did not . . ."

"Maybe you stole it," she says. "Your mom's a convicted thief, right?"

"He gave it to me," I say. "And I didn't have to spread my legs or get on my knees. I'll leave that to you."

Her mouth drops open. Duke and I are close, but he would never tell me what he was or wasn't doing with other girls. He's a gentleman. But from the look on her face, I can tell he's at least gotten a blow job from her. And I'd be lying if I said that didn't hurt me.

"You little bitch!"

"What's going on here?" Duke asks, jogging up the bleachers to us.

"Did you hear what she just said to me?" his girlfriend asks.

"No, but I heard you call Lennon a bitch."

"You gave her your jacket!" she cries, feigning some tears.

Duke glances around. Practice is over, but now everyone is staring at us. This is my nightmare. I was born to blend in, not be the center of attention. Reaching into his backpack, Duke hands me his keys. "Could you wait in my truck?"

Mascara running down her face, she clings to Duke's bicep as he attempts to walk away. Right then and there, I vow that I will never be a clinger. God, she looks pathetic.

He shrugs her off, walking toward the truck, and I quickly pretend I haven't been watching the drama unfold. The door to his truck opens, and he hops inside. "Well, that's over."

"You broke up?"

He slips on his Aviator sunglasses, starts the truck, and pulls away. "Yep."

"Because of me?"

He looks over, grinning, his cute dimple coming out. "Yeah, pals before gals." I can't help but laugh. "Lake?" he asks, already turning his truck that way, and I nod.

It's a short drive. Montclair, Virginia, isn't that big of a place. It's somewhere between a small town and small city, but living here does come with a premium price tag. My mom and I can only afford to live here because Duke's family rents a small house to us cheap.

The lake and golf course make Montclair special—that and the short commute to Washington, DC. Still, the lake is where all the big community events occur, but today, it feels like it belongs to Duke and me.

The bright Virginia sun reflects in the water. A cool breeze blows, rustling the leaves that have already started to change colors for the fall. The stress of family drama, school, bullies, and everything else melts away when I'm here. It's my favorite spot. Duke and I played here as kids, hung out here as teenagers, and shared our secrets on these shores. It's our place.

My mom had me when she was young, only twenty. I've never met my dad. Maybe that's why I never felt like I fit in. Maybe it's that I'm naturally shy. Either way, the one place I have always felt I belonged was beside Duke.

Barefoot, we walk one of the man-made beaches that surround the lake. The water ripples with a deep blue, the autumn hues from the trees reflecting on the water. Even though the lake is the site of many local events, I still find it quaint and peaceful. There are benches and enough space to spread out, so you don't ever feel like you're on top of someone else.

Duke picks up a rock and skips it across the water, doing it over and over again. Then he hands me one, and I attempt to do the same thing, only my rock just sinks. We both laugh. He's been trying to teach me that trick for over a decade.

I love him.

At fifteen, I know I love him. And I know it's real. How could I not love a boy who comes to my rescue? Ends his relationship for our friendship? And looks like he does? Did I mention those steel-gray eyes, those biceps?

"Sorry about you and . . ."

"Don't be," he says. "What did she say to you?"

I shrug. "Nothing I haven't heard before."

"More of that jail baby shit?" he asks, but he's still wearing his Aviator sunglasses, so I can't see his eyes.

"You know about that?" I ask.

"Found out today," he says, a slight disappointment in his voice. "Why didn't you tell me?"

"I didn't want you to get into trouble. You already got suspended once because of me."

"Off of school," he teases. "So terrible."

"It is if you want to get into the Naval Academy," I say, reminding him of his dream.

"The military is about protecting people. That's what I did." He stops walking, looking down at me. "What did she say?"

"Nothing that I didn't give right back to her," I say.

A proud grin covers his face. "What did she say that started it, though?"

"Duke," I playfully whine, turning away, but he takes hold of my hand. I'm putty. Fifteen-year-old girl putty. "She made some cracks about my mom. Accused me of sleeping with you to get the jacket."

"Oh," he says quietly, like the thought has never crossed his mind.

"I'm used to it. People think because my mom made some bad choices that I will too. But what happened to my mom made me want to do the opposite. I'm not having sex until I'm married, and I'm . . ."

He smiles again.

"What?" I ask with my hand on my hip.

"Nothing."

"Duke?"

He pulls me under his arm, starting to walk again. "You're so young."

"I'm one year to the day younger than you."

"That one year makes all the difference," he says.

CHAPTER TWO

LENNON

"Didn't Thelma and Louise die at the end of that movie?" I ask, looking at my mom and Duke's mom dressed up for Halloween.

They both roll their eyes at me as Mrs. Connie holds her phone up, her forty-something lame attempt to take a selfie.

Mrs. Connie came over to our house to pick up my mom. They're going to some charity costume party. Since Duke's dad refuses to dress in costume, my mom is Connie's plus-one. Duke's dad is a doctor. Mrs. Connie was a lawyer until she had Duke, and they are utterly devoted to each other. Watching them might be why I believe in love. Duke's parents are my example of a healthy relationship.

"They were the OG ride or die chicks," my mom says.

Now it's me rolling my eyes, but I still laugh. My mom using the term OG is ridiculous. Bless her heart, she tries to be cool, but she's about as successful as I am.

"No costume?" Mrs. Connie asks me.

"Nope," I say, grabbing a piece of candy out of the Halloween bucket. "Staying in to pass out candy to the kids."

"You know you can go out," my mom says, pushing my hair behind my shoulders. "You really should try to . . ."

"I'm good," I say.

My mom starts to object when Mrs. Connie interrupts. "Iva, are those new curtains? I love them." When my mom starts to tell her she made them, Mrs. Connie turns to me, giving me a little wink, and I mouth a very grateful, "Thank you." Anytime you can avoid a lecture is a good time.

Plus, my mom takes a lot of pride in this house. We don't own it. Duke's family rents it to us for less than they should, so my mom always keeps the place looking nice, and she takes care of all the maintenance herself. If the stove goes out, she pays to repair or replace it. I know Mrs. Connie doesn't expect that, but my mom doesn't want to take advantage of their friendship.

The place has only two bedrooms and two bathrooms, but it's enough for us. And it's the only home I remember. I guess, technically, my first home was the penitentiary, but I don't remember that, thank God.

Luckily for my mom and me, the prison she was in had a program that allowed pregnant inmates to keep their babies with them if they had only a certain amount of time left on their sentences. So the first few months of my life were spent in lockup. When she got out, we went into a halfway house. My mom got a job working at a garden center, and one day, Mrs. Connie came in with Duke. They got to talking, my mom gave her some plant advice, and the next thing they knew, my mom had her hands in the dirt at their home while Duke and I played in the grass.

From the beginning, my mom was up front with Mrs. Connie about her past, and I don't know what possessed Mrs. Connie to hire her, to trust her, but she did. She changed our lives. A neighbor complimented their garden, and Mrs. Connie recommended my mom, then another and another. Mrs. Connie is single-handedly responsible for the life we have—my mom's job, this house, my education, and my friendship with her son.

"Iva, we should go," Mrs. Connie says.

They each kiss my cheek. "I love you," my mom says.

"Love you more," I say with a grin on my face.

She hates it when I do that, and always says the same thing. "Never love someone more than they love you, especially a . . ."

"A man." I finish her sentence, having heard it a thousand times. "I know, I know."

She shakes her head at me, steals a piece of chocolate from the bucket, then they fly out the door. Blowing out a deep breath, I grab the candy bowl and plop down on the sofa, my mom's advice still ringing in my ears.

I've heard it all before. I know she's trying to protect me, but at my core, I'm a hopeless romantic—my crush on Duke is proof of that. And I'm quite sure I love him more than he loves me. I don't think he loves me much beyond friendship. Still, I know where my mom is coming from. She's been burned. That's how she ended up in jail.

She grew up in the foster care system with no family. To hear her tell it, she was starved for love, any kind of love. The kind of love that came packaged in the form of my dad—the ultimate bad boy, and not in a good way. She loved him, so she overlooked a lot of things, including his inclination to take things that didn't belong to him.

It was commonplace for her to be walking right beside him when he'd shoplift something. She knew it was wrong, but she overlooked it in the name of love. And she fell into the trap of thinking she could try to save him, taking him to church one day, only to find him stealing from the purses of the old women when they went up to the altar to take communion.

One day, he got sloppy, and the police were called. Apparently, he'd slipped some jewelry into my mom's purse without her knowing it. When he and my mom attempted to leave the store, the alarm was activated. He got away, and my mom was left holding the stolen merchandise and holding me in her belly. That was the last time she ever saw him. There was no way to prove she didn't know what was in her purse. Still he had a list of priors a mile long, and she'd never even jaywalked. So she pled guilty, got a reduced sentence, and that's how I ended up being born in lockup, and how my mom ended up never loving a man again.

Never love a man more than he loves you.

That phrase became the code by which she lived her life, and she's drilled it into me for as long as I can remember.

Flipping open my sketchpad, I start with the eyes, wondering if my dad has blue eyes like mine. My mom's eyes are brown, so I always figured I had his eyes. My dad is an off-limits subject in my house. I've known from a very early age not to bring him up. Therefore, I know next to nothing about him. I've attempted to draw him a thousand times, but I always rip them up when I'm done. God forbid I actually draw someone who remotely resembles my father. I don't want to do that to my mom. I don't want to make her relive the worst time in her life. So I doodle and wonder.

The doorbell rings, and I get to my feet with the candy bucket. I always let the kids take a handful. It's more fun than handing out just one piece.

As I open the door, I prepare to bend down to see the cute little kids in their costumes, but what I find is a certain tall, handsome sixteen-year-old wearing a brown trench coat that clearly belongs to his father.

"Trick or treat?" Duke says with a flirty smile.

"Treat," I say, smiling back at him.

With a chuckle, he steps inside. "Our moms gone?"

I wonder exactly what kind of treat he's looking for. "Yeah, why?"

"Because I'm taking you to the Halloween party at the lake with me, and I don't think either one of them would approve of the costumes I have planned."

"Duke, I'm not going to the lake party."

"Yeah, you are," he says. "With me. Thought we just covered this."

Shaking my head and laughing, I place the candy bucket down. He reaches in and grabs a miniature candy bar. "Let's hear it," I say.

"Well, I've got a plan to shut those assholes at school up for good."

"How?"

"This!" he says, ripping off the trench coat in a dramatic fashion.

My mouth falls open. He's standing there wearing a black and white prison jumpsuit with a huge fake diaper on. He looks ridiculous, and I might actually laugh if it wasn't such a sore spot for me. "I've got a big fake baby bottle in the truck and a matching costume for you."

"Me?"

"Yeah," he says. "Don't you get it?"

"Jail baby," I say, my voice cracking a little as I try to hold back my emotions.

The grin fades from his face, and he reaches out to wipe a single tear from my cheek. "Lennon, no. Don't cry. I'm not making fun of you."

"It sure looks like you are."

"Don't you see," he says. "If you and I show up at the party dressed like this, it takes the ammo away from those assholes. They'll stop if they think you're cool with it, and it doesn't bother you."

"You think?"

"I'm sure of it," he says, holding his hands out to show off his costume. "This will work."

CHAPTER THREE

LENNON

I'm lying on my stomach in Duke's bed with my sketchpad in front of me. Duke's sitting on the floor with his back up against his footboard, playing the latest video game on the television in his room. He runs his fingers through his dark-blond hair, his eyes fixed on the screen. The scenes of the video game play out before me, and I pick up my pencil feverishly trying to capture the game.

Cartoons and graphics are in my wheelhouse. That's where my artistic passion lies. But Duke is good at this game, so the scenes change quickly, making it hard for me to keep up.

"Shit," he mutters, the screen flashing a few times. I guess that means he's been hit or is losing a life. Like most teenage boys, Duke loves these games. He and I play sometimes, but I'm not very good. That never stops him from trying to teach me, but I'm content to just watch him play.

I think that's how you know a friendship is real. You don't necessarily have to always like the same things. It's more about being open to the other person's likes. Duke doesn't know crap about art, but he still loves to see my sketches and ask me questions, giving me positive feedback. You might think what he has to say isn't worth much since what he knows about art couldn't fill a thimble, but you'd be wrong. His opinion means the world to me because he's my best friend.

He glances up at me. "I want to see that when you're done."

Smiling, I say, "I make no promises."

He rolls his eyes and turns back to his game. For a second, I lay my head down on his bed. I know this house like I know my own. Every nook and cranny has been home to our childhood hide-and-seek games. We've skinned our knees on the driveway out front more times than I can count. Running through sprinklers, riding bikes, listening to music, watching movies, building pillow forts—our friendship is marked by shared memories. Every holiday, every birthday has been together.

We've shared our fears, our tears, our hopes, and our dreams. I wish I could add a kiss to that list, but no such luck.

My eyes land on a small model of a spaceship. His mom bought him that on one of our trips to the Smithsonian National Air and Space Museum in Washington, DC. Our moms used to love to take us into the city to the museums. We spent days building that thing together and eating the astronaut freeze-dried ice cream my mom got for us to share.

His house, his room is filled with little memories like that. A pennant from the U.S. Naval Academy hangs on his wall, a reminder that our life spent together is coming to a close. Soon he will be off to college, and I'll be here for at least another year. Then who knows how far apart our lives will take us.

I won't be seeing his cute face anymore. I'll have to rely on the memories.

Turning back to my sketchpad, I eye my work. "Hey, kids," Mrs. Connie says. "What are you up to?"

"Playing some games," Duke says. "Lennon's sketching." I hold up my pad, making sure to keep it angled away from her. His mom comes over and tousles his hair. "Thought you and Dad were going out or something."

"We are," she says. "I didn't think you'd be here."

Mrs. Connie smiles over at me, but it looks unsure. Suddenly, I become acutely aware that I'm lying in her son's bed. His parents have never had any rules about me being in his room. He always leaves the door open, which I assume is at their request, but the look on his mom's face right now makes me wonder if more rules are coming soon—probably one about me being horizontal in his bed.

"We won't be here long," Duke says, not taking his eyes off his game. "Ms. Iva's making chicken spaghetti, so we're going over there."

Mrs. Connie smiles again, but this time, it looks like she's up to something. I wonder if my mom making Duke's favorite meal is simply a ploy our moms cooked up to get us over to my house where we will be supervised. That's totally something they'd do.

When we were little, Duke and I always spent the night together. We even slept in the same bed. That all stopped around the time we turned ten or so. But even then, when our parents would go out and one of us was going to be left alone, the other would always come over. Now as teenagers, they don't seem to ever want us to be alone.

I know what they're afraid of, but Duke would have to actually realize I'm a girl for them to have anything real to worry about.

"We're going to watch *The Amazing Race*," I say. We both love that show. We don't hate where we live or anything, but both of us dream of seeing the world and having a bigger life than our little corner of the globe, so we became addicted to that series.

"Would you play with honor or cheat?" his mom asks.

"Honor," Duke and I both say at the same time.

I sit up, excitement filling me, and say, "We have it all worked out if we ever get on the show. Duke will do all the physical tasks because he's strong and fast."

Duke tosses down his game controller. "And Lennon will do all the psychological stuff. The head games, overcoming your fear crap. She's the strongest person I know, so she'd kill those competitions."

My eyes dart to his, having no idea he thought of me that way. I always considered myself more of a wallflower. I guess wallflowers can be strong. The strength is just a quiet one. "She's definitely that," Mrs. Connie says.

Duke turns so he's facing me more and says, "It's my favorite thing about you."

Feeling my skin warm, I look down. Just when I think I know

everything there is to know about Duke, he surprises me.

"Don't forget I want a list of other colleges you're going to apply to," his mom says. "I'd like to set up some tours."

Duke promises to make one, but I know he's lying. One more glance at us both, and Mrs. Connie leaves.

"You better make that list," I say. "You have to apply to more schools than the Naval Academy."

"I will," he says. "And in my application essay, I'll write that I'm only applying because my parents forced me and to please deny my application."

Playfully, I swat his shoulder with my sketchpad. "You need a safety net."

"Don't want one. Annapolis is it," he says, snatching my sketchpad from me and flipping it open.

A glint appears in his gray eyes as he sees my sketch—a helicopter.

CHAPTER FOUR
TWENTY-TWO MONTHS LATER

LENNON

My mom and I step out of our car. The street in front of Duke's house is so crowded we had to park a block away. If we'd been earlier, we could've gotten a better spot, but I didn't want to be early. I want to avoid this night. His last night. The night before he leaves to go away to college—the US Naval Academy, to be exact.

Since we were little, he's always wanted to join the military. While other kids played cops and robbers, Duke played soldier. I'm not sure where his devotion to our country comes from. His dad didn't serve. Maybe it's because we live so close to Washington, DC. I'd look at the Vietnam memorial and cry, but Duke would see it and think that if he had been there, he could have saved some of those men. At his core, he's a protector. God knows he's always tried to protect me. But now he's going off to learn to protect the world.

That's the pitfall of Duke being one year older than me. He's leaving me behind in our Virginia town to head to Annapolis, Maryland. Tonight is his going-away party. At least he already goes by his last name. I hear all those military types call each other by their last names.

My mom and I walk the sidewalk toward his house. The street is clean, picturesque, just like his two-story red brick colonial house with green shutters and the best garden on the street, thanks to my mom.

We make our way to the backyard, where the party is. It's a humid August night, making me glad I wore the sundress Mom made for me and tied my hair up loosely in a red ribbon. Music and laughter lead the way, and my mom opens the back gate.

The yard is full of people, food, balloons, and what looks like the entire high school. But my eyes immediately land on Duke. He runs his fingers through his dark-blond hair. He's got one more day like that because I know it will be shaved off as soon as he gets to the Naval Academy.

"Lennon," my mom says, noticing I'm frozen to my spot. "Go see your friends."

"None of those kids are my friends," I say. Aside from Duke, my only other real friend is Brinley. She transferred to our school last year. She's the type who will talk to anyone, and lucky for me, I was included in that bunch. We became fast friends. But she's not here tonight. Her parents are divorced, and she's spending the summer break out of town with her dad. So Duke is the only person I care to see. My mom really has no idea how much high school resembles hell.

"Duke is your best friend," she says, rubbing her lower back. Clearly, she's overworked herself again. I don't know how she does it, bending over all day, on her hands and knees, carrying bags of soil and mulch. "Don't you want to say goodbye?"

I don't. I really don't. I don't know how I'm going to get through senior year without him. He's been my constant friend and protector at school. I suspect he's the only reason those kids don't pick on me. His Halloween costume idea, just as he thought, did the trick.

After that, hardly anyone ever messed with me, and I've spent the past couple of years wandering the halls in solitude. Duke tried to get me into his friend circle, but they were a year older, popular, and I didn't want to bring him down. I didn't want him to think he had to take care of me. I'm hoping that jail baby doesn't get resurrected with Duke's absence. I guess a part of me will never really trust those kids. Did they actually grow to like me? Or were they simply afraid of Duke?

He drove me to school and home every day. I'm going to miss that. Even when he had practice, I'd do homework and wait for him. Those drives were the best. We'd talk, and cut up, and I'd daydream about what it would be like if he saw me as a real girl, not his friend.

Guess I'll never know. He's leaving, and my mother's right. I have to say goodbye to him.

"I just need a minute," I say. She gives me a small smile before joining Duke's mom by the dessert table next to what looks like a pile of going-away gifts. My mom's already got a piece of chocolate cake in her hand. She loves anything chocolate. She blames me for her love affair with chocolate, saying she hated it before she got pregnant. It was the one thing she craved during her pregnancy and hard to come by in jail. I'm seventeen, and the "pregnancy" craving hasn't left her yet. Maybe once I'm legal age.

Eyeing the gift table again, I rub my empty hands together. I've been trying unsuccessfully to make a sketch for Duke to take with him to school, something that captures our friendship and how I feel about him, but I haven't been able to fit all of that onto one page. I wanted him to have something he could fold up and carry with him if he ever had to go into battle.

I hate that he's leaving, but it scares me more. An education at the US Naval Academy comes at the price of at least a five-year commitment after graduation. Five years is a long time. A lot of battles and wars can happen during that time. I wanted him to have a piece of me with him if that happened. I spent hours at the lake, trying to come up with just the right thing. I tried doing a self-portrait, but that sucked. I tried drawing a picture of us together, but I got stuck focusing on those intense eyes of his. Besides, I prefer illustrating to drawing portraits, landscapes, or stills. So I have nothing to give him.

Slowly, I wander around the yard, not ready to walk over to Duke yet. Usually, I can't wait to see him, but not tonight, because I'm not sure when I'll see him again.

"Lennon, I swear you've grown since I saw you yesterday," Mrs.

Connie says. She's not only my mother's best friend but also my *de facto* second mother, so doting on me comes with the job.

"Mrs. Connie, I hope not," I groan.

She smiles, wrapping her arm around my waist. "As strong and beautiful as your name."

Mrs. Connie insists that my mom named me after John Lennon from The Beatles, but my mom says that's not true, insisting she was naming me after the fabric linen, but the nurse at the jail spelled it wrong. My mom has also assured me that my name has nothing to do with the founder of the Russian communist party, Lenin—and I'm certainly grateful for that. I also know that my name has nothing to do with my dad. I have my mother's last name, Barlow. I don't even know my father's name or anything about him.

"Iva!" Mrs. Connie calls to my mom, who comes walking over, embracing her friend like they didn't just see each other two seconds ago.

"Our little boy is leaving," my mom says.

Yes, they refer to us each as their children. It's a little weird, considering the size of my crush on Duke.

Searching the yard, I find him again, smiling and laughing and being the life of the party. He's the guy every other guy wants to be. The guy every girl wants—including me. But Duke doesn't have a clue.

He smiles at me across the yard, and my heart warms in my chest. I know his eyes are gray, but he's too far away for me to see the specks of steel in them. He nods his head to the side, motioning for me to join him.

I turn to say something to our mothers, but they are still chatting. Even after over fifteen years of friendship, they never run out of things to say to each other. I leave them to it, heading across the yard, dodging circles of people. It's pretty easy to do when you're invisible. No one is looking to pull me into their conversations.

Duke and I keep our eyes locked on each other as we make our way toward the gate that leads out of the yard. Occasionally someone stops him, but he always makes it brief, continuing his journey to me. I reach the gate before him, and right as he gets to me, Mr. Charlie places his hand on his son's shoulder, stopping him.

"Sneaking off?" his dad asks, giving us a knowing grin.

"Lennon and I . . ." Duke starts, but his dad holds his hand up.

"You know your mother wants to toast you leaving for college."

"Dad," Duke begs. "I told you guys I didn't want anything like that."

"It's not just about you," his dad says. "You're our only child. This is about your mom and me, too."

"Yeah, and you and Mom will be driving me to Annapolis. Tonight, I want to be with my best friend."

Mr. Charlie looks over at me. Yep, I'm the best friend. Don't get me wrong, I love that Duke thinks of me that way. I wouldn't want anyone else to fill the position. But I'm a dreamer. And I dream of Duke thinking of me as something more.

"Lennon," Mr. Charlie starts, "do you want to spend this evening with my son?"

Duke's gray eyes go to me, and he gives me that boyish grin of his. His dad has always had a soft spot for me. I'm not sure why exactly, but I think he secretly wants the same thing I do—for his son and me to end up together. Of course, I think he wants that to happen in a few years, not while I'm still in high school.

I shrug my shoulders. "I don't have anything else to do."

Mr. Charlie bursts out laughing, urging his son to me, then whispers, "Okay, I'll cover for you with your mother. Have fun, you two."

"Less than twelve hours," I say, looking up at Duke's handsome profile in the moonlight.

We escaped the party and have been at the lake ever since. It's a pretty warm night. Every star in the sky seems to be out, but the thick, humid air weighs us down.

He looks down at me, whispering, "Promise you'll write to me."

He's given me his school email address, and we've already made plans to talk on our birthday in a few weeks. We've never spent a birthday apart that I can remember. You'd think birthdays would be a sore spot for me—after all, I was born in a jail cell—but honestly, I love my birthday. Duke and I always celebrated together. It was always a good time. Some of my happiest memories are our joint birthday, which is odd considering the day of my birth. But that's about to change because we won't be together for our next birthday.

We've been preparing for this moment for months, but that doesn't make it any easier. "I promise."

He draws a deep breath, looking up at the night sky. I know he's nervous and scared. He won't say it, but I know. He used to get the same look in his eyes when he had to go get shots at the doctor. So I do the same thing I used to do then and wrap my arms around his waist. I can feel his muscles. He's always been ripped, but he's been doing extra workouts to prepare for what's coming.

His chin rests on top of my head, and a few tears roll off my cheeks. There hasn't been a time in my memory when Duke hasn't been in my life. Most of my laughs have been with him. Most of my tears have soaked his shirts. All my good days and bad have been shared with him.

This is no different. This is my first big goodbye.

Since I don't know my father, and my mother doesn't have any family, I've never lost anyone close to me. We've never moved. I've never been to a funeral. Heck, I've never even had a pet that died.

It's fitting that I share this first with Duke. But it's my job as his best friend to make this easier on him, not harder. Pulling back slightly, I say, "I'm proud of you, Charles Duke III." He hates it when I use his full name, but he smiles anyway.

"I'm going to school. I haven't saved the world or anything."

"Not yet," I say. "But you saved me from the hells of high school."

He shakes his head at me, and we take a seat in the sand, letting the water lap at our feet. "Lennon, I need you to promise me something else."

"Anything."

"Apply to art school," he says, and I playfully fall back on the sand with a groan. We've had this conversation so many times. "Just trust me on this."

He lies down beside me, looking over at me, and his gray eyes weaken my resolve. "I'll think about it."

"Not good enough," he says.

"I'll seriously think about it," I say, tossing him a smile.

He rolls his eyes. "So how much trouble will you be in if I keep you out all night?"

"Whatever it is," I say, "it will be worth it."

"See, you are brave," he says. "Because I've seen your mom mad, and no art school admissions person could be worse than that."

I laugh. He's totally right. And I know he's being brave, where he's going to college, then devoting years of his life to serve our country. If he can do it, I should at least try, right? "I wanted to draw you something for your dorm room, but . . ." I sit up, looking out at the water. "I don't have a gift for you."

He sits up, gently turning my chin so I'll look at him. His eyes study my face. I know he's kissed girls. My guess is either he's no longer a virgin, or he's come really close to going all the way. I've never even kissed a boy, always wanting Duke to be my first kiss. And as he leans forward, I'm convinced my wait is coming to an end. My eyes close, the feel of his hands in my hair making me dizzy. He unties the red ribbon in my hair, causing my hair to fall loose around my shoulders. I've wanted this for so long. I can't believe it's finally happening. I can't believe he's leaving tomorrow. I'll want to do this for days on end.

Suddenly, he pulls away, his lips never touching mine.

"I'll take this," he says, holding the ribbon in his hand, his voice sounding low and needy.

My heart sinks a little, but I have to smile. A piece of me is going with him. Still, I want to give him so much more. "As long as you promise to return it someday."

Music blares through the house. My mom loves old music. I'm talking music even before her time, like Frank Sinatra and Nat King Cole. I would never admit it, but some of it is better than what's on the radio today. But when she's pissed, she always cranks it up. Normally, the volume lowers as she gets calmer. She must still be pretty pissed. And I'm the reason.

I stare at my email on my computer and re-read my words to Duke. I want to make sure I get it right. This is my first email to him away at school. This is how we will maintain our friendship from now on. I know there are holidays and breaks, but I also know his family travels a lot during those times, and it would be entirely too easy for our friendship to fade away. I'm not going to let that happen. Besides, the Naval Academy isn't like other colleges. You can't just leave campus and go out whenever you feel like it. It's basically the military. Leave is a privilege.

I promised him I'd write, and that's what I'm doing. He only left two days ago, but I miss him. So I write that. Normally, I might not say something like that out loud, but it's easier behind the safety of my computer screen. I tell him about my day, my college applications, and how I've decided to take the ACT one more time. I don't really have anything else to say, but now I'm stuck. How to end it. *Your friend* just seems silly. *Love* is out of the question. *Sincerely* is too formal. I could sign it *yours*, but I'm not his.

From my bed, I look up from my computer screen, glancing around my room—my prison for the foreseeable future. My mom has grounded me and not even bothered to tell me for how long. At least my room is cool. Posters of famous artwork alongside my own drawings cover the walls. For some people, the internet is a rabbit hole they get lost in, but art does that for me. It transports me. I can be in the countryside landscape one minute and a dreamscape the next. It's what I love most about art. It's not always how it appears at first glance—kind of like me. At first glance, you might make assumptions about the kind of girl I am, but you have to look closer to see all the colors and different strokes that make up who I really am.

"Lennon, you better not be on that computer!" my mom barks, barging through my bedroom door.

"I have to be on the computer," I say with a smile. "School."

"You know what I mean," she says, heading over to my bed.

Quickly, I type: *Goodbye for now.* Then hit the send button before she has time to see what I'm doing.

She turns the computer to her, finding the school's homework page up on my screen. She's beyond mad that I stayed out all night with Duke. She loves Duke and his parents, but that doesn't mean my curfew goes out the window.

Thank God my senior year of classes started today, or the computer would be in permanent time-out. This way, I can sneak an email and check to see if he responds. I won't be so brazen to play a game or search anything, but I'm not going to miss communicating with my friend, and my phone is grounded along with me.

"I still can't believe what you did. I was worried sick," she says, rubbing her lower back. I'm not sure how much longer she'll be able to do garden work since her lower back is always hurting her.

"I texted that I was with Duke."

"Duke is still a teenage boy," she says, giving me that mom look that scares the crap out of me. "Nothing happened?"

"No, it didn't," I say, unable to hide the disappointment in my voice.

"Because you could tell me," she says.

I groan inside. Why do parents say things like that? It's so glaringly obvious that I can't tell her. If something did happen, she'd blow a gasket. Look at how she responded to my missing curfew. Still, there's nothing to tell.

My eyes start to fill. I cried most of the day yesterday, knowing Duke was gone. I know it's silly because he's only an hour and a half away. It's not like he's across the world, but those miles feel huge right now.

I hear my mom release a deep breath. "He'll be back, honey."

"I know," I say, sniffling a little.

"It will take a little while to get used to him being gone, but you'll see—it will be fine," my mom says, and I nod. "You have everything you need for your classes? Notebooks, binders?"

My computer dings with an email, and my heart misses a beat. "Yeah, I'm good," I say, giving my mom a smile, letting her know that I'm fine, and hoping that gives her the encouragement she needs to give me some privacy.

She kisses the top of my head, then heads for the door. As soon as it closes behind her, I click on my email, seeing Duke's response. One thing sticks out. His ending.

Goodbye never.

CHAPTER FIVE

LENNON

"Prom night!" my friend Brinley squeals. "You ready?"

I'm not going. Brinley's going, but she has a date. I don't, but I do have plans, and Brinley is my cover.

It's been eight months since I've seen Duke. We email or text every day. We've talked on the phone, but we didn't get to see each other over Christmas. His family traveled, and my mom and I did a couple of college tours, so we missed each other.

So we devised a plan. Being the sweetheart that he is, Duke offered to take me to my prom. Of course, I jumped at the chance, but Duke wasn't given permission to leave campus. Taking one's best friend to her senior prom doesn't permit missing any training. He was pissed. I was disappointed, so we decided to make our own rules.

That's why I need Brinley's help. She's my cover.

My mom thinks that since neither Brinley nor I had a date, we just decided to go together so we didn't miss our prom. The truth is, Brinley has a date. I even got asked by someone other than Duke, but I turned him down.

Instead, I'm taking my mom's car to Annapolis. Duke is sneaking out, and we are going to meet up. Since it's prom night, I was not given a strict curfew. I should be able to make the drive, spend a few hours with Duke, and get back without her ever knowing.

I don't want Duke to get into trouble, but he assures me he can sneak out for a few hours without getting caught. Honestly, I think he's sick of being told what to do. He should have thought about that before signing up for years of it.

I pull the car in front of Brinley's house to drop her off. Even though I'm not going to prom, I'm still wearing the dress. I'll stop and change on the way. But I had to look the part for my mom. She wanted to take pictures before I left, especially since I lied and said I didn't want to take pictures at the dance because solo pictures are just mortifying. She wanted to make me a dress, but my guilt got the better of me. I didn't want her slaving over something that no one would see but her and Brinley, so I borrowed a dress from Brinley instead to ease my conscience.

I hate lying to my mom, but I know she would never let me do this. I know because I've asked her several times if I could take the car and go see Duke, but the answer was always the same—no. My mom works a lot, even on weekends, so the last thing she wants to do when she's off is drive an hour and a half to take me to see Duke. She needs her car for errands and work, plus his schedule is jam-packed. But this time, nothing is getting in our way because I didn't ask for permission. I'm just going.

Brinley reaches for the car handle, then stops and turns to me. "You sure about this?"

"Yep."

"Call me if something happens," she says, playing with her long auburn hair. "Like the car breaks down."

I smile. She and I brainstormed every possible scenario of things that could go wrong. She reaches in her bag, then takes my hand, dropping the square wrapper in my palm.

"Just in case," she says.

My eyes bulge. A condom? We never brainstormed that happening. "Duke and I are just friends," I say, handing it back to her. I'm not one of those girls who talks about her crushes all the time, not even to Brinley. Because Duke and I are close and the opposite sex, people make assumptions, but in this case, she couldn't be more wrong.

"Lennon, don't be naïve. You're lying to your mom to drive to spend the night with Duke on your prom night. Trust me, he thinks he's taking your virginity tonight."

"No, he doesn't," I say, but my stomach jumps, doubt sneaking in. She raises her eyebrow at me. "Besides, why do you even have that?"

"Bought it for you," she says with a giggle. "I'm a good friend. Had to go to four convenience stores to find one with a dispenser in the bathroom. I wasn't about to buy it over the counter. With my luck, one of our teachers would be behind me in line."

"You're crazy!" I say, laughing. "It's probably expired."

"Old protection is better than no protection."

"Ah, no, it's not," I say. "Old protection is how you get pregnant."

She opens up my bag and tosses it inside. "Just in case."

Looking in the rearview mirror, I'm almost there. Duke told me to meet him right outside the entrance. Apparently, he now owes half the student population a favor for either covering for him, looking the other way, or unlocking a gate that should otherwise be off-limits.

I left Montclair a little after six, telling my mom we were going to dinner before the dance. It's almost eight now. I figure Duke and I can have until at least one in the morning, then that will put me back home around two thirty or three if everything goes smoothly. That's five hours. Five hours to catch up on eight months. I wonder if he's changed in that time. I know they cut his hair, but I wonder if anything else is different. Duke's not one to send selfies, so I've had to imagine how he looks now.

My hair is slightly longer, and my braces are off, but I'm pretty much the same. I hope it's not weird. I hope we are still the same together. When I check my hair in the mirror, it still has the loose curls I put in it for my fake prom. My makeup still looks fresh and natural, but I never stopped to change my dress, too excited to get here. It's black, form-fitting, and cut just above the knee. That should've tipped my mother off. Prom dress codes at my school are strict, and we can't have anything above the knee. Luckily, she didn't ask me about it.

I don't even make it to the school entrance when I see the outline of his body in the darkness. I'd know him anywhere. Suddenly, my heart thumps in my chest, and my legs feel weak, making it harder to press on the gas.

My mind flashes to what Brinley threw in my bag. Is Duke thinking this is more than two friends catching up? Would I let things go that far? I wouldn't. I've always said I'm waiting until I'm married. But there's a little part of me, and I know she could be tempted.

When I pull closer, the car door opens, and Duke hurriedly hops inside. I barely have time to register it's him before he has me wrapped in a big hug. "I've missed you so much," I cry, the joy of seeing him making me lose my filter.

"Me too," he says, pulling back slightly, his eyes lowering to the exposed flesh of my thighs.

"I didn't stop to change," I say, feeling the heat rise to my cheeks.

"I'm not complaining," he says with a little grin.

I take him in. Besides his hair being shorter and his muscles a little larger, he's exactly the same. Same cute dimple, same killer eyes, and being near him still turns my heart to mush.

"Now drive before my ass gets caught sneaking out."

Pulling away, I ask, "Where to?"

"Well, it is prom night," he says. "Dinner, dance, hotel."

Duke opens up the hotel room door. I thought you had to be twenty-one to get a hotel room, but apparently not. Wonder how much research Duke had to do to find a place? That took cash? He still had to put a credit card on hold when we checked in, but they assured him that nothing would be charged to it unless we ordered room service or used the minibar. He didn't say it, but I could tell he was nervous that his parents might see that charge. Then we'd have some serious explaining to do.

I look into his deep gray eyes, more than shocked that he rented us a room, but I still don't think Brinley is right. Duke's intentions have always been honorable with me, so there's no reason for me to think differently now.

He holds the door open for me to walk inside. The place is actually nice, but it's just a standard room—a bed and bathroom and not much else. It's not that I expected him to spring for a suite since we're only going to be here a few hours, but that bed seems to be mocking me.

"Did you go to a hotel on your senior prom night?" I ask quietly.

I can tell he's trying to hide it, but a smile sneaks out anyway. "Everyone does."

"Oh," I say, watching as he tosses my bag down on the bed along with our dinner from a local drive-through. Reaching for my bag that has my extra clothes, I say, "Think I'll change."

"Don't," Duke says, locking eyes with me. "We haven't danced yet. You should have the dress on when we dance."

I kick off my heels, and he chuckles, sitting down at a small table and taking out our dinner. "We're on the clock here. Tell me everything. How's senior year? Your mom? College decisions?"

I tell him I got accepted to several art schools, including one in England, but I don't think I can go overseas. He tells me about his daily routine and his decision to go into the Marine Corps after graduation and become a helicopter pilot, which will involve flight training in Florida after the Naval Academy. He tells me how sorry he is that he won't be home in time for my graduation, but he'll make it up to me.

As we talk, the only thing I can think of is that our lives are taking us away from each other, and I have to wonder if we will ever live in the same zip code again, will fate ever bring us back together, and if our friendship can go the distance.

Duke starts a song on his phone. He holds out his hand to me.

Guess this is the dance portion of our prom evening. Slipping my hand in his, he pulls me to my feet, wrapping his strong arms around me like a hug. At that moment, I'm glad I didn't change. My dress is so tight to my body it's almost like nothing is between us.

Resting my head on his chest, I hear his heart beating, strong and steady and sure. "Florida is far away," I whisper, peeking up at him.

"So is England," he says softly.

Warm tears roll off my cheeks, and he pulls me close, lowering us to the bed, my head buried in his neck. His arms are tight around me, and his nose is buried in my hair. There's nothing to say, so we don't. I just lie there in his arms and let my heart break.

"Lennon," Duke whispers softly in my ear, his fingers grazing my cheek as he pushes a few strands of hair off my face. "I let you sleep as long as I could."

"Huh," I say, nuzzling deeper into his chest.

"Lennon, it's three in the morning."

"What?" I cry, shooting up in the bed.

"You fell asleep."

"Why didn't you wake me?" I ask, attempting to find my shoes.

His gray eyes look away from me. "I knew you had a long drive ahead of you, and I wanted you rested."

"Well, I'm gonna be dead as soon as my mom finds out." Frantically, I grab my stuff, then motion to him. "Come on. Let's go."

He gets up, but he seems to be moving at a snail's pace as we leave the room and check out. I, however, drive like a bat out of hell to get him back to campus. I look over at him as we pull up, staring out the window.

"I can't believe I fell asleep," I say. "Wasted our time together."

"It wasn't a waste," he says, looking over at me, and the hurry I felt two minutes ago slips away. I want to stay. I want to make these final moments last.

His eyes on my mouth, he slowly leans toward me. My heart pounds, but I've been burned by him before. All those times I thought he was going to kiss me and never did. His hand cups my cheek as his lips land on mine. I can hardly believe this is real.

It's a soft sweet brush of our lips, nothing more. I don't know if I moved or kissed him back. He pulls back slightly, his certain eyes on mine, but I'm sure mine look shocked.

His lips turn up in the cutest little smile, and I smile back, giving him all the permission he needs to lean back in. This time, he parts my lips, his tongue slowly stroking mine. I feel it all the way to my toes and between my thighs, something I've never felt before. I might not have ever done this, but the aching need in my body tells me we are doing it right.

His hand goes to the back of my neck, deepening our kiss, and I know it's a good thing this is happening in a car in public because if we were at the hotel, he definitely would be on top of me, and that condom in my bag would be a temptation neither one of us needs.

We slow, kissing each other gently as our breathing returns to normal. Eyes closed, he rests his forehead on mine, and I whisper, "Goodbye for now."

Giving me his best smile, he says, "Goodbye never."

CHAPTER SIX

LENNON

A warm wind blows in off the lake. The sun has set, but summer's heat still swirls in the air. Every recent graduate and college kid home for the summer is at the lake for the Fourth of July.

"Hey, Lennon."

"Hey, Chase," I say to the teenage boy beside me, but I don't bother to look at him. No need. We've been in the same homeroom for three years straight. I know what he looks like—average height with brown hair and eyes. I continue to search the crowd, looking for Duke, who's coming here tonight.

Except I don't see him yet. After the semester's end, he did some additional special program that kept him away a few more weeks—until now. Tonight will be the first time we've seen each other since the kiss, a couple of months ago. The kiss we never talked about.

"You look great tonight," Chase says, stumbling for his words a little.

Glancing down at my sundress and cute sandals, I'm hoping Duke notices how I look. "Thanks," I say, searching the crowd, but it's getting dark out, the bonfire lighting up the beach.

"So I heard you're going to art school," Chase says.

"Yep."

"I decided on the University of Chicago," he says. "Hoping to study finance."

"Fun."

"So when you become a famous artist, I can help you invest."

"Illustration," I say, pulling out my phone to see if Duke messaged me. "That's what I want to do."

"Maybe we could grab a coffee or something one day, and you could show me some of your stuff."

I turn my eyes to him. Did he just ask me out? "Um."

"I probably should have gotten up the courage to ask you sooner, but I know you turned a couple of guys down for prom, and then you didn't even go," Chase says.

"One guy. I turned one guy down for prom."

"I heard three," he says.

"You heard wrong."

"So how about coffee?" Chase asks.

"We're both leaving for college soon," I say.

"So what? Duke's been at school a year now, and that hasn't stopped you from waiting around for him."

"No," I say firmly.

"No, what?"

"No coffee," I say.

"You have something against coffee?" he asks with a grin.

"I'm busy."

"Looks like Duke is, too," Chase says, his head nodding toward some trees.

My head whips around, and I see Duke emerge with his old high school girlfriend, her arms around his waist, both of them smiling. Her dress is wrinkled with the top few buttons undone. It's obvious what they've been doing tonight.

"Bye, Lennon," Chase says, leaving me in my tailspin.

Quickly, I turn my back, taking a few steps away as tears roll down my cheek. Her? It had to be her! Our kiss? The kiss that I waited years for. The kiss that meant so much to me meant nothing to him. Nothing.

How could I be so stupid? It's been three months since prom, and while we never talked about what happened, I just assumed he'd want it to happen again. I assumed we'd pick up where we left off.

Well, you know what they say about assuming. Makes an ASS out of U and ME. But I'm not the ass in this situation. He is. Duke is the ass. I'm just the stupid, hopeless romantic teenage girl who believed that kiss.

His kiss lied. His kiss is a liar.

His kiss told me he cared, that he wanted me, that he wanted to be with me, but it lied. And it hurts worse than any untrue words could.

"You okay?" Brinley asks, coming up beside me, her hand on my shoulder. "I saw."

"So I wasn't imagining it?" I ask, my voice breaking.

"Something definitely went down between the two of them. And I'm betting it was her." A cry escapes, and I cover my mouth, hating that image now in my head. "You want to go?" she asks. "Because I'll take you."

Do I want to go? It seems like a simple question, but it's not. Yes, I'm hurt and heartbroken, but Duke and I have been friends for practically my whole life. I don't want to lose that.

This is why you should never kiss your friend. Never cross the friends-to-more line because invariably, someone will get hurt, and the friendship will suffer. I don't want that to happen.

And I hate to admit it, but I'm jealous. I wanted it to be me who he snuck off with. I want to know what it feels like to be his.

"He's heading over here," Brinley says.

"With her?" I ask.

"No, he peeled her off pretty quick."

"Stall him for a second, will you?" I ask, wiping my face.

"You got it," Brinley says, walking away from me.

I have my back to them, but I can only imagine what Brinley is saying. I hope she's not giving him hell. I don't want him to know I'm upset. I don't want to turn this into a big thing, though it is.

He's my best friend, and no matter how bad I'm hurt, I don't want to lose that. I'll let him know in my own way, in my own time, that what he did wasn't okay with me. I learned a hard lesson here, but before I throw away our friendship over it, I'm going to crush the crush I have on him.

Knowing I've only got a few moments, I take a couple of deep breaths, hoping the oxygen will help mend the pieces of my heart, the pieces that thought that Duke and I belonged together, the pieces that thought he finally realized it, too.

From behind, his strong arms coil around me, and I yank away, my instincts taking over my plan to maintain my composure. "Don't come hug me after you've been in the woods with *her*."

He steps back like I've slapped him. "Sorry," he says. "Want me to go home, shower, then come back and hug you?"

My hands fly to my hips. "I want you to not act like a . . . a Lothario."

"Lothario?" he says with a chuckle.

"Yeah, it's like a man whore."

"I know what it is," he says, inching closer to me. "Clearly, all that ACT prep worked."

"Don't try to change the subject," I say, although we are both avoiding the real subject—our kiss.

"What do you want me to do?" he snaps. "She offered. It's kind of hard to turn down."

"Chase just asked me out for coffee," I snap. "I turned him down."

His jaw clenches. Does that make him mad? Jealous?

"Want to talk about what this is really about?" he asks. "Prom night."

"No," I say with more force in my voice than I've ever used with him. I know if we open this can of worms, things will never be the same between us again.

"Lennon."

"It doesn't matter now," I say quietly. "Think I'll just go home."

"Don't go," he says. "I've looked forward to seeing you for months."

"Yet you went to see her first," I snap.

"She was here when I got here. You weren't, and . . ." He mumbles a curse word under his breath, knowing that was a dick move. "Lennon, I think you're thinking more happened with her than actually did."

"Whatever it was, it was too much," I say.

He reaches out, but I step back. "You're my best friend."

"And tomorrow, I'll still be your best friend," I say. "But tonight, I'm the girl you hurt."

Crying all night is not good for one's looks, but it was what I needed. The only problem is I don't feel better. I told Duke I'd be his best friend today, but I'm not sure how to do that. Yes, I want to maintain our friendship, but I don't know how to turn off my feelings for him, and I hate what he did last night. Hate it. I'm not a person who hates much, even with my shitty start in life. I still think it's best to come at a situation with love and kindness or at least indifference.

That was what I always did in school when I was being bullied. I tried my hardest not to hate them back because hating hate never did a damn thing to end it. It takes more courage to be kind.

Running my fingers through my messy hair, I stumble out to the kitchen, my mom standing at the sink with her back to me. Crying one's self to sleep is also not good for the hair. "Morning," I say, but she doesn't respond. "Mom?"

"You see Duke?" she asks. "I thought I'd make him some chicken spaghetti while he's home. He used to love that when he was a little boy."

"Yeah, I saw him," I say, walking over to her and touching her elbow. "Mom?"

When she turns to me, her eyes are red. My mom isn't a big crier. She's tough. She's had to be, so this must be serious. "It's good he's back," she says.

"Mom, are you okay?" I ask.

She smiles at me. "Let's sit."

"I don't want to sit," I say. "Tell me."

"Lennon."

"Tell me, Mom. What's wrong?"

"You know how I've been getting those backaches?"

"Yeah, I've been telling you to see a doctor forever," I say.

"I went," she says. "It's important to remember I'm going to be fine."

"Okay."

"At first, the doctor thought I pulled a muscle. He prescribed some anti-inflammatories. But after taking them for a few weeks, nothing improved. So he recommended physical therapy."

"That could help," I say.

Her head shakes. "I didn't go because it's so expensive."

"Mom, what's the use in going to the doctor if you're not going to do what he says?"

She gives me a small, sad smile. "One day, I was really hurting. Worse than it's ever been. Connie drove me to the emergency room, and they did an MRI." Her once strong eyes look weak. "It's not my back. It's my kidney. It's cancer."

"No," I say. "They're wrong."

"No, baby."

"Doctors are wrong all the time. They always have those crazy stories online about doctors messing up and . . ."

"No," she says gently. "I have cancer."

She says it so surely, with so much certainty, like she's accepted it. Well, I don't accept it. No! She starts toting treatments to me, survival rates, but nothing is computing.

"Cancer," I whisper. My mom has cancer. "How serious is it?"

"The doctors think I'll be fine," she says, running her fingers through my hair.

Fine.

That's the word she keeps using.

Fine.

Everything is fine.

Fine.

That word—fine.

What the hell does that word even mean? Who wants to be fine? Fine is like okay. Nothing special. Blah. I don't want her to be fine. I want her to be over the moon fucking happier than she's ever been in her whole life. That's what I want for her. Happy and healthy.

"I wanted you to know before you left for school, and . . ."

"How long have you known?"

"A few months," she says.

"Months!" I cry. "You didn't tell me for months!"

A small knock on the front door causes us both to head to the den, Mrs. Connie poking her head in. With one look at her face, I know that she not only knows, but she knew my mom was telling me today. "Ready?"

I look at my mom. "I'm starting chemo today," she says.

"Is that why you finally told me?" I ask.

She nods. "The doctors want to be more aggressive."

I know what that means. It means that whatever they've been doing hasn't been working. "I'll come with you," I say, trying to push away my emotions.

My mom takes her hands in mine. "No, baby."

"You don't want me to come with you?" I say, tears rolling down my face.

"Oh, my sweet girl," she says. "Connie and I have it all worked out."

I look at Mrs. Connie, and it's obvious they've talked about this and so much more. More than I probably want to know right now. Just like Brinley and I had worst-case scenarios planned out for prom night, I know that my mom and Mrs. Connie have them planned out, too.

"You're busy today," Mrs. Connie says, giving me a small, sad smile.

"I am?"

"Outside," Mrs. Connie says, nodding toward the door.

Looking at my mom, she smiles. These two have plans for everything. She kisses the top of my head, then pushes me toward the door. "Go."

"But..."

"I promise we'll talk all night if you need to, but right now, you have plans."

And even though I'm still in my pajamas, I open the front door, seeing Duke leaning up against his truck, waiting for me. My hand flies over my mouth, and he opens up his arms. I run to him on bare feet, and he captures me, his arms wrapping around me.

"My mom... she..."

"I know," he says, and I hear his voice give way. "My mom told me this morning."

I collapse into tears, and he just holds me, right there in the street in front of my house.

"I've got you, Lennon," he says. "I'm here."

As I cling to his shirt, the tight hold he has on me never softens. Last night seems like a million years ago and so trivial right now. This is who Duke and I are. We are each other's rock, and I need that more than a boyfriend.

Pulling back slightly, he rubs his hand up and down my back, and I remember that I'm still in my pajamas, still without a bra, not that I've got much. Looking up at him, I don't know what to say. What do you say in times like this?

Lucky for me, Duke always knows how to make me feel better. His face breaking into a grin, he says, "In case you're wondering, I've showered since last night."

Laughing through my tears, I know that means we are all good. That what's happening right now trumps all of that. I wonder if this is the reason my mom waited to tell me. Duke? Was she waiting to break the news until he was home, knowing I'd need him?

"I can't go off to school," I say. "Not now."

"Lennon, your mom wouldn't want you to give up school. You've worked too hard."

"I know, but I can't leave her," I say. "I'm not saying I'll never go. Maybe just put it off until she's better." His gray eyes close. "Did your mom tell you something?"

"No," he says, wrapping his arm around me and leading me inside. My mom and Mrs. Connie are already gone. Not sure how I missed that. "But after my mom told me, I went to my dad."

"And?"

He sits me down on the sofa. "And he made me swear not to tell you. Miracles happen all the time."

"Does my mom need one?" I ask.

"If I had one to give to her, I would," he says. "It's bad, Lennon."

"Maybe I can give her my kidney," I say.

"Not sure it works that way with cancer," Duke says.

I get up, heading to get my phone. "I need to research. To figure out the best treatments, maybe a clinical trial."

"She has doctors for that," Duke says, taking my phone from me. "My dad helped her find the best ones in DC."

"Thank him for me," I say.

"What if you went to school in DC? It's only like an hour away. Not the easiest commute, but doable." he says. "I'm sure there are some schools with great art programs."

"It's July," I say. "Admissions are done. Scholarships are already given out. It's too late."

"Get dressed," he says.

"Why?"

"We're going to DC. I don't care if we have to go to every school and knock on every door. There has to be a school with one opening. One kid who changed their mind. I'm going to find it."

"Lennon, we're home," Duke says, putting his pickup truck in park. I open my eyes, staring up into his handsome face. My head rests in his lap, where I fell asleep on the drive back.

He did it. He said he'd find me a spot, and he did. I'd been accepted at a couple of DC schools earlier but turned them down, so I was surprised when one offered me another spot. No scholarships were available, but they said I could apply next year. And since I'll be commuting back and forth, that will save on room and board. I filled out all the paperwork while I was there. They already had all my records, so that made things a little easier.

Once Duke explained the situation, I guess it was too hard for them to say no. Although three other schools didn't have that problem.

Sitting up, I look around. We aren't at my house, but his. "My mom brought your mom back here after her treatment in case she got sick."

I nod, and he gets out, coming around to get my door. I'm exhausted. Crying will do that to a person, and I've cried off and on all day. Heading inside, his dad greets us at the door, pulling me into a hug. "You can't go wrong at a DC college."

I look back over my shoulder at Duke, giving him a smile. "Where's my mom? I want to see her."

"She's sleeping upstairs," Mr. Charlie says. "Connie's with her. Let her rest. It's late, so we figured you could both stay the night here."

"It's been a long time since I stayed the night here," I say, remembering how we always spent the night at each other's houses when we were younger.

"You two must be starving. Come into the kitchen," his dad says.

"It hasn't been that long since we had a sleepover," Duke whispers with a grin, and I'm sure he's thinking about prom.

Rolling my eyes, I motion toward the bathroom. "I'll be there in a minute."

Flicking on the light in the small guest bathroom, I look in the mirror. Somehow, I look older. Tears fill my eyes again. I can't even think about what my mom is facing. What could possibly happen? I have to be strong for her because she's always been strong for me. I know it couldn't have been easy for her to raise me alone after having me in jail, no less. But she did it.

I've been her whole world. She never dated that I know of. She worked and took care of me. Now I will do the same for her.

I splash some water on my face and wash my hands, then flick off the light and head toward the kitchen. As I make my way, I hear Duke and his dad talking. I stop and listen.

"That was quite a thing you did for Lennon today," his dad says.

"I'm just glad it worked out," Duke says. "I couldn't let her give up her dream and not go to school. It took me forever to convince her to study art."

His dad chuckles. "Couldn't let all your hard work go to waste."

"Dad, I need you to do something for me," Duke says, his voice serious. "I need you to contact *my* school." Duke clears his throat. "I need you to get me weekends home. You know how strict they are, but I need to be able to come home. Maybe not every weekend, but a couple of times a month."

"Son?"

"You are a doctor. You know people, a lot of people. Please, could you just try?"

"Your mother and I will be here for Iva and Lennon. We will take care of them. You have my word."

They are good people. The best. Everyone should have a Charlie and Connie in their lives.

"I need to be with Lennon," Duke says.

"I understand she's your best friend, but your education, your future, is important."

"She's more than that," Duke says, and my eyes grow wide, my heart starting to pound in my chest, so much that I wonder if they can hear me eavesdropping.

"How much more?" his father asks. "Do I need to be worried about her staying here?"

"No," Duke says so softly I can barely make it out.

"She's important to you," his dad says, and I imagine his hand landing on his son's shoulder.

"The most important," Duke whispers.

CHAPTER SEVEN
FIVE YEARS LATER

DUKE

"Nothing more than a catch and release."

That's what my captain had said with a smack on my back.

Still the new kid on the block, I get ragged on quite a bit by my brothers-in-arms. It doesn't matter how many flight hours I've logged or how much training I've gotten, the newbie is still the newbie, which warrants some ribbing. But today should be simple enough. Fly to some outpost to pick up some bigwig and deliver him back to base. In and out, no big deal. I could do it with my eyes closed.

Since we are in peacetime, most of my flights have been transport missions, getting cargo or troops from one place to another. Of course, we can provide ground support to troops in the field. But much of what I do revolves around the safety of others. It's my job to get my fellow soldiers where they need to be and keep them out of harm's way in the process or medevac them out if they are injured. Of course, I've received the same combat training they have. I can shoot a weapon, do close combat—all that shit, but very few of us are trained to fly helicopters.

It's been a long-standing tradition in all branches of the military to pen a "just in case I don't make it back" letter. Something that your fellow soldiers promise to get to your loved ones if the worst happens. Last words to those who mean the most. I'm not writing that shit. It's like planning for the worst, like a prenup. Why put that kind of shit in my head and out into the universe?

I'm making it back. This is a simple mission, and we are at peace, not war. Besides, this is what I've been working toward for so long, to serve my country, to wear the proud uniform of the Marine Corps. I've trained hard to fulfill this dream—workouts you can't imagine, drills, tactical assessments—and I'm not about to tarnish that by thinking about everything that could go wrong.

Besides myself, the chopper is carrying my co-pilot, a crew chief, and a gunner. The blades of the helicopter still whirling overhead, our passenger lowers his head as he hurries toward the bird. I can tell from his uniform he's at least a general.

"Thanks for the ride, boys," he yells, taking his seat.

Within a matter of minutes, we're back in the air. "Should be at the base in half hour," the crew chief informs our passenger. "Right before chow time."

The land gets smaller below us. I love flying, but takeoff is my favorite. Going from a stagnate position on the ground to rising above it makes you feel like a fucking god—like you can control anything and everything around you. You don't need to get a running start like on an airplane. You simply levitate off the ground like some sort of magician.

There's nothing routine about it even though this mission is pretty typical. And I love every fucking second of it.

"Shit," the gunner yells before I even register the bullet whizzing in front of the cockpit. "Get us the fuck out of here."

A rainstorm of bullets surrounds us. My gunner is yelling directions at me, but the fire is coming from the ground in every direction. Briefly, I look down and see men with guns blasting us. They don't know us, and we don't know them, but we are enemies just the same.

A rocket explodes on each side of us, shaking the whole helicopter. Struggling to maintain control, we start to spin, the ground twirling around me. I've trained for this, how to get out of this exact situation, but on instinct, my eyes close. My head is spinning, everyone is yelling, and the noise is unbelievable. It's hard to concentrate. My eyes squeeze shut, and I see her. I see Lennon's sweet smile. She's back home.

When I open my eyes, her image is gone, but she's still with me. Gripping the stick, I whip the bird around, giving my gunner time to take out the enemy below.

The pen shakes in my hand. I take a deep breath, thankful it's only now that my hand is trembling and not while I was flying us out of there, not while my crew shook my hand or my superiors debriefed me. It's only now, hours later in the privacy of my apartment on base, that the reality of what happened hits me. It was my first time under enemy fire. It wasn't a drill. No amount of training can prepare you for someone trying to kill you.

I worked out hard, showered, then tried to eat, but the reality that I could've died today won't leave me. I grab the pen with my other hand, trying to steady it. I swore I'd never write one of these fucking letters. But there are things undone. Words that need to be shared.

Lennon.

The pen wobbles again, and I look up from my desk. Base housing is pretty standard with no real frills. I don't spend a lot of money and haven't bought a car or a house, so I'm developing a nice bit of savings. I could move off base to something nice, but this is fine. A bathroom, bedroom, living area, and kitchen—what else does a single Marine need?

A drink. Right now, I could use a drink—a double.

"That was some of the best flying I've seen in a long time, young man," General Hale says as he knocks on my door, then walks right inside.

I wasn't expecting company and leap to my feet, saluting the man I picked up today, the one who almost got me killed. He's a slightly older practical-looking man, not one of those hard-ass military types who always look like they want to kick your ass. His eyes are kind and friendly.

"At ease," he says, glancing down at my desk and the paper and pen resting there. "Hope you don't mind me stopping in like this."

"Not at all, sir," I say, although I'd prefer to be alone.

"My wife insisted I thank you for her," he says.

"You told her about today?" I ask, surprised he shared the day's events with his wife. I adopted a policy that the less my loved ones know about what I do, the better.

"No, but she can always tell these things," he says with a grin. "My mother, God rest her soul, had the same ability."

"Mine, too," I say.

"I won't keep you," he says, glancing down at the paper and pen again. "But I'm going to keep my eye on you. I expect great things. And if you ever need anything, you call me."

"Thank you, sir," I say.

He heads toward the door, then turns back, motioning to the paper. "Whoever she is, thank her for me."

"Sir?"

His eyes smile. "The one you did that fancy flying for," he says. "The one you want to make it home for. Thank her for me. You loving her probably saved my life."

He walks out, and I pick up the pen, my hand now solid and steady and sure.

CHAPTER EIGHT
ONE YEAR LATER

LENNON

Placing my water bottle and chocolate chocolate chip muffin down on a table, I take a seat in a local coffee shop. I'm not a coffee drinker, but have you noticed that coffee shops have incredible baked goods? Unwrapping the muffin, I tear off a small bite. "This is for you, Mom." She loved anything chocolate.

In fact, the last few things I can remember her eating were chocolate. She died two years ago today. The treatment extended her life, but she never beat her cancer. She fought a long, hard battle. It seems a lot of her life was the same way, struggling. She smiled through the pain, but she suffered. I watched her die. Connie and Charlie were with us through the whole ordeal.

Death did not come quickly. In part, I'm thankful for that. We had time to say everything we needed to. But because her death was slow, her suffering was immense. I commuted to school, took care of my mom, and worked. Nothing about my college years was typical. Frat parties were replaced by doctors visits. Binge drinking gave way to chemo sessions. I dated here and there, but nothing serious or long term. My college years won't be the best of my life. They just might be the worst. Yet I don't regret a single second of it. I'd do it all over again. The one regret I do have is that I didn't push her for more information about my father. It would be nice to know who he is. His name at least. It would be nice to have the option to try to find him. But I don't. I just couldn't bring myself to ask her about him when she was suffering so much.

In the end, I lost her.

I'm convinced she held on just to watch me get my college diploma. She passed away with a chocolate candy bar next to her hospital bed, and her final words to me were ones she'd drilled into my head my whole life. *Never love a man more than he loves you.* She made me promise I wouldn't ever do that. At that moment, more than ever, she needed to know that I'd be loved.

Taking another bite of the muffin, I pull out my phone, finding an email from Duke. I know he remembers what day it is. As much as he could be, he was there with me through her illness. When he wasn't able to be physically close, he stayed in touch constantly. Some nights, I only slept because I knew he was on the other end of the phone. And he got leave and came home when I buried my mom. He was by my side as I said goodbye and listened to me cry over the phone for more nights than I can count.

We still write every day. He's still my best friend, and I miss him. I don't think I would've made it through my mom's illness without his emails, texts, calls, visits. But now he's over five thousand miles away at a Marine base in Japan. After the Naval Academy, he went on to become a Marine Corp helicopter pilot. It took almost two years to complete the training, and since then, he's been stationed overseas. We stay in touch. I can't imagine there being a day when we aren't best friends. But life has taken us in different directions. He's across the world, and I'm still in the same town we grew up in.

```
FROM: DUKE
TO: LENNON
RE: RAINY AS FUCK
```

It's fucking rainy again.

I'm thinking of you. I ate some chocolate in honor of your mom today. Wish I could be there with you, and I hope that . . .

"Lennon? Lennon Barlow?" a slightly familiar male voice interrupts my reading.

I look up into dark brown eyes. His face is familiar, but I can't remember who he is or where we know each other from. Dammit, I hate it when this happens. Time to fake it.

"Oh, hey! How are you?" I say, plastering a big smile on my face.

He laughs. "You have no clue who I am."

No point in lying. "Sorry."

"High school," he says, narrowing the field for me.

I spent those years trying not to make eye contact. "Um."

He takes a seat opposite me, putting his coffee cup down like we're old friends. "I wasn't one of the three guys that asked you to prom."

"Only one guy asked me . . ." A smile crosses my face. "Chase Arden."

"Guess we can finally have that coffee date," he says, flashing me a smile.

Holding up my water bottle, I say, "Don't drink coffee."

His grin growing, he says, "So that's why you turned me down. Here I thought it had something to do with that other guy."

"Duke," I say.

"He still in the picture?" Chase asks, holding my eyes. Was he this cute in high school?

"Friends," I say. "Always just friends."

"Sorry about your mom," he says. "I heard she passed away."

"Thank you. Two years ago today, actually."

"Shit," he says. "The last thing you probably want is to be hit on."

"Is that what's happening right now? You hitting on me?" I flirt, wondering if this is my mom's doing. If somewhere in the afterlife, she's orchestrating this, hand-delivering me a man to meet her standards.

"Trying," he says, and I feel the heat rise to my cheeks. "Did you become an illustrator?"

"You remember that?" I ask, and he just smiles at me. "Yeah, children's books. One of my books just won the Caldecott Award."

"Then you won a Caldecott," he says, and I smile.

I've been very lucky in my career, working with many publishing houses that specialize in children's books. Work has never been scarce. A bonus—I love what I do. Chase asks me a few questions about the book and my design. I tell him how the book is about a rainbow that's lost one of its colors. How it's a metaphor for our world, and how each culture makes our world brighter. It's one of those simple messages that you see in children's literature, but we often forget as adults.

"Finance isn't nearly as exciting."

"That's right," I say. "I seem to remember you promising to invest my money."

He chuckles, and I can tell he's happy I recalled that tidbit. "You still live in Montclair?" he asks.

"Yep. Same house even."

For years, my mom rented from Duke's family, but before she died, she bought the house and left it to me. I never asked what she bought it for, but something tells me they sold it to her cheap. She wanted to have something to leave me. She worked hard her whole life and, in the end, left me a house and a small life insurance policy. I know she was proud to be able to do that.

I've totally renovated the house since my mom died and even added on an office. As an illustrator, I work freelance. My old bedroom is the guest room, and I use the master for myself now. Something about being in my mom's old room gives me peace and centers me. Maybe it's because I kept a lot of her things in there.

"I live in Alexandria now. Just in town today seeing some friends," he says, then telling me how he's been in Chicago the past few years but missed Virginia, so he moved back.

"Bet your family is happy you're so close," I say.

His brow furrows, and I wonder what I said wrong. That seemed like a safe enough thing to say. He shakes his head. "I shouldn't expect you to remember. My parents died when I was two. My grandparents raised me. They passed several years ago."

"I don't think I knew that," I say.

"We had a lot in common in high school," he says. "We were both different from the other kids."

"I guess we were."

He gets up, and disappointment lands on my shoulders. I wasn't expecting that. But then he holds his hand out. "Dinner?"

I wasn't expecting that either.

There are two kinds of nervousness. One where you can't even think about food one bit and the other where all you do is eat to try to calm your nerves. But my stomach isn't jumpy at all. I should be nervous. Everyone is always a little nervous for a first date, but I'm completely relaxed for some reason. Maybe it's because I went to high school with Chase. He saw me in my awkward teenage years.

Or maybe it's because this date was spur of the moment, so there hasn't been time to stress. We were only at the coffee shop a few hours ago. I just barely had time to come home and change.

I slip on a pair of black kitten heels that go perfectly with the navy wrap dress I'm wearing. My hair is pulled up in a high ponytail, but the ribbons I used to wear are long gone. I'm ready.

When I woke up this morning on the anniversary of my mother's death, I expected a solemn day, but instead, it's been the opposite. I think most people go on a first date feeling hopeful, like they could be on the verge of a great love. I won't go that far, but bumping into Chase has been a welcome distraction. It will be a bonus if it turns out to be something more than that.

My doorbell rings, and a smile immediately comes to my face. I take a deep breath, check my reflection one more time, then hurry to answer the door. Chase is waiting with a similar smile on his face. He's dressed in a sport coat and holding a bouquet of bright yellow sunflowers. It's not until now that my stomach jumps in my belly, but it's not nerves. It's excitement.

"They're beautiful," I say as he hands them to me.

"You look incredible," Chase says.

That time, my heart is the organ jumping.

"Back in high school, you were always pretty, but now . . . Wow!"

My skin warms, and I'm sure my cheeks are turning pink. I step out my front door, checking it's locked behind me. "You were probably the only boy in high school who thought that."

He places his hand on the small of my back, leading me over to his car. "Not true," he says. "Your mom always made you the coolest clothes."

I freeze, and Chase does too. "You remember that?" I ask. It was fairly common knowledge that my mom made my clothes back then, but I'm shocked he'd remember.

A crooked little grin crosses his lips. "That pink sweater you used to wear to math class is etched in my brain."

Suddenly, I realize I just might be on the verge of something great. Maybe I'm standing on the edge of love. Then Chase takes my hand.

Used to be girls didn't kiss on first dates, but these days, I think it's more we won't have sex with a guy on a first date. And even that isn't a hard and fast rule. Well, unless you're me and have no plans to have sex until a ring is on your finger. Chase doesn't need to know that yet. That is not appropriate first-date conversation.

And as far as first dates go, this one is going well.

I know he has a job. We haven't struggled with conversation. By all standards, this is a good first date. He took me to a fancy place for dinner, which I didn't expect. I'm more of a simple girl. Give me a sandwich, some soup, and I'm good. Still, it's nice he wanted to spoil me. But I'm starving. The portions were tiny. A piece of chicken that small should not cost fifty bucks. I could get a whole box for less than half of that.

I place my hand on my stomach, willing it not to growl, but it rumbles so loud Chase looks over at me from the driver's seat and bursts out in a huge laugh. "I'm sorry," I say, an embarrassed smile on my face. "I swear dinner was delicious. I loved it."

Just then, his stomach growls, and he says, "I'm still hungry, too."

"Thank God," I say.

He glances over at me. "Double dinner?"

"Double dinner?" I laugh.

"Can't take you home hungry," he says. "And that tiny cake we had for dessert was literally gone in two bites."

He makes a good point. My eyes land on a flashing neon sign in a convenience store window, and it seems like divine intervention. "Fried chicken!" I cry out, pointing at the sign.

Without missing a beat, he swerves lanes and pulls into the parking lot. I reach for my purse. "Second dinner is on me," I say, but he places his hand over mine. He's leaned over slightly, his eyes studying my face. It's clear he doesn't want me to pay. "Next time's on me then," I say softly.

"Next time," he says, inching closer.

Smiling, I nod, leaning in. His lips land on mine. It's soft and sweet, and when he pulls back, he's smiling, too.

Lying in bed wearing a smile, I hold my phone up. Should I text Chase to thank him again for tonight? To make sure he got home okay?

I don't want to come off crazy, but it was a great first date. It was the best first date I've ever been on. He's sweet, polite, and easy to talk to. Duke is the only other guy I'm this comfortable with. I shouldn't text. I should go to sleep. It's after two in the morning, but who can sleep after meeting and going out with a great new guy.

My phone dings in my hand. My heart skips a beat expecting to see Chase's name, but it's Duke. The time change means it's late afternoon there already. He knows I should be asleep right now. He doesn't know it's impossible to sleep. I move to open Duke's text when my phone dings again.

Chase.

Their names are right there, together. Chase's name is on top, so I open his message.

Is it too late to call you?

Quickly, I type that it isn't, and within a matter of moments, my phone rings.

"Do you get paid any royalties when a book you illustrated gets bought?" Chase asks.

I laugh. "Why?"

"I might have just ordered every book you've ever worked on," he says.

My heart soars. It literally feels like it's floating above my body right now. "They're children's books."

"They're the books illustrated by the woman I consider the one who got away," he says. "So I had to have them. You know, in case she gets away again."

My smile spreads, and I wonder if I'm his Duke. Duke was always my unrequited crush. I wonder if that's what I am to Chase. It's funny to think that I could be that for him. "I guess you better hurry up and ask her on another date then."

"Lennon, would you like to go out again? Maybe day after tomorrow? And then a couple of days after that? And a couple of days after that?"

I giggle like a silly schoolgirl. "What about on the other days?"

"Telephone dates," he says.

"What do you propose we do on these telephone dates?" I ask.

"Hmm," he says, a hint of mischief in his voice. "Watch TV."

I laugh out loud. "You pass the test."

"What test?" he asks.

"The test where the guy says phone sex and sends a dick pic."

"Seriously, you've had that happen?"

"Every woman over the age of fifteen has had that happen."

"I was more thinking we could talk, maybe watch the same television show," he says.

"What's your favorite show?" I ask. "Mine's *The Amazing Race*. I used to dream about going on that show when I was younger." Duke and I spent hours talking about our strategy.

"Really?" he asks. "I'd rather have a plan. Take my time to see the sights. Know where I'm sleeping from night to night."

It's clear he's not a risk-taker. I guess most finance guys probably aren't, or the risk is calculated. He's Duke's opposite. Duke takes risks every day as a Marine. Risk versus safety? One was the love of a teenage girl, the other is the crush of a grown woman. "That sounds nice too," I say.

"So how about our next real date," Chase says. "What would you like to do?"

I stretch my legs out in my bed, thinking. "I've always wanted to try one of those places where you drink wine and paint a canvas."

He chuckles. "You literally could open a bottle of wine while you work."

"I guess so," I say.

"Do they have paint by numbers?" he asks.

"No, but they can sketch it out for you," I say.

"And it's not a nude model?"

Laughing, I say, "No, no dick portraits."

He chuckles. "You won't judge my stick figures?"

"Promise."

"Then it sounds to me like you've got yourself a date."

CHAPTER NINE

LENNON

"Another bouquet, huh?" Brinley says, raising an eyebrow at me as she plops down on my sofa. As a nurse, she works long hours, but she was off today, so we took the time to catch up.

There's nothing like fresh flowers in your house. Chase brought me sunflowers on our first date and has brought me fresh ones every week since. Twelve bouquets of the bright yellow flowers, three months of dating, and he hasn't forgotten once. I never asked him why he chose sunflowers for our first date. It's not a typical date flower. One usually thinks of a man bringing red roses, but then I looked up the meaning of sunflowers—unconditional love.

That might be more romantic than red roses, the symbol for romantic love. Both flowers might represent love, but romantic love is fleeting, and unconditional love isn't. So I'll take a sunflower over a rose any day of the week. Although love isn't something either one of us has said, and I doubt Chase studies the meanings of flowers. He's in finance, for goodness' sake. Still, the sunflowers always make me smile. I wonder if he'll bring me new ones tonight. He's coming over later.

"Does this mean you're going to let him deflower you?" Brinley teases. Brinley has informed me that most twentysomethings have sex somewhere between date one and ten. Chase and I have more than doubled that number of dates, and I've managed to avoid the subject altogether.

"Change of subject," I say, rolling my eyes.

"Have you told Duke about Chase yet?" she asks.

I'd rather talk about my "flower" than answer that.

"No, I haven't written to him in a few days," I say, knowing that's not like me.

"I bet Duke doesn't like that very much," Brinley says.

"He keeps asking if everything is all right or if he said something to piss me off," I say.

If the roles were reversed, I'd be worried sick about him. There have been times when he's been on a mission or out of contact for a few days, and I've made worrying look like an Olympic sport.

I haven't told him about Chase. And Chase is becoming a big part of my life. He's taking up a huge part of my time, and I'm leaving that out of my calls and emails with Duke. I'm not sure why. Duke and I never really talked about our relationships with other people or who we were dating. I guess neither one of us has ever been serious enough with anyone that we felt the need to tell the other.

"You should mention Chase to him," Brinley says. "It could be casual, like, 'Hey do you remember so and so?'"

"Let's talk about you," I say to Brinley. "How's the hospital?"

Brinley went to nursing school. Most people would think that's because she wants to help people, but Brinley says it's because working as a nurse is the easiest and most efficient way to meet a rich doctor. She's crazy like that and such a liar. She has a heart of gold, even if she tries to hide it.

"There's a new ER doctor," she says with a mischievous smile.

"Married?"

"Nope."

"Gay?"

"Nope."

"Born this century?"

She laughs. "Yes, but a woman! They hired a woman. I mean, I'm all for feminism, but I'm trying to find a man here. The singles scene in Montclair is sorely lacking."

She's right about that. Chase lives in Alexandria, which is a good forty-five-minute drive away. Still, he makes it several times a week to see me. I go to see him too, but usually, he insists on being the one to make the drive.

"Whoever said 'Virginia is for Lovers' was a liar." Brinley laughs. "I'm not getting any love."

"I could ask Chase if . . ."

"No blind dates," she objects. "You know how I feel about blind dates."

"Not all blind dates end in one of the parties being arrested." I laugh.

"Don't remind me," she says. "That's the last time I let my mother set me up. Seriously, he gets pulled over for running a stop sign, and when they run his license, they find he's wanted for credit card fraud!"

"Well, at least he was a gentleman and didn't try to outrun them."

"A high-speed chase would have been more action than I've gotten lately." She laughs.

The lights are dim in my living room, the only light coming in from the kitchen area. It's dark outside, but Chase shows no signs of being tired as his lips land on mine. Gone are the days of saying good night on my doorstep. He always comes inside now. Our goodbyes are getting longer and longer, but he does eventually always leave.

He leans closer until we're horizontal on my sofa, his dress shirt coming untucked slightly. Chase's mouth slowly kisses my collarbone, soft and sweet. I always knew waiting until I was married put me in the minority, but as I've gotten older, the minority now resembles something more like a dying species. And poor Chase has no idea.

His hand slides up the skin of my thigh, my dress rising with each stroke. "Can I stay?" he asks, his voice almost begging.

All it takes is me whispering his name for him to back down. He sits back on the sofa, looking like he's in physical agony. "I'm sorry,"

I say softly, sitting up and straightening my dress.

He looks over at me, giving me a small pained smile. "Don't apologize for being so sexy I can't help myself."

Rolling my eyes, I laugh, knowing it's time to get this out in the open. It's like ripping off a bandage. "Should I apologize for being a virgin then?" His mouth drops open, clearly unsure how to respond to that. "You know my history, how I came into the world. I promised myself that I'd wait for the right man, wait until I was married." He stares at me, blinking a few times. The man can compute complicated equations in his head, but a little virginity has him dumbstruck. The seconds tick by, and I swear I can hear the blood coursing through my veins. "I know I should've probably told you sooner. It's kind of a hard conversation to start."

His eyes study my face, his fingers combing through my hair. "I love you, Lennon Barlow. And I don't say that to try to get you into bed. I love you."

This time, it's me who's dumbstruck.

"Like batshit crazy love you. I think I have since high school when you didn't know I was alive."

"My mistake," I tease, planting a small kiss on his lips, remembering my own crush on Duke. I know how that feels, to crush on someone who has no idea. Everything feels so intense when you're young, a teenager. It's like every one of your feelings is on steroids. "You're really okay with this? You understand why I want to wait?"

He nods, flashing me the biggest grin. "I guess we'll have to get married real quick then."

CHAPTER TEN

LENNON

"Happy Birthday, Mr. Twenty-six!" I scream as Duke's face appears on my computer screen. It's not the best connection, but it's still good to see him. He's dressed in fatigues and slightly sweaty from his workout but smiling ear to ear.

"Happy twenty-fifth Birthday," he says back, eyeing my pajamas with birthday cakes on them.

The feed from Japan comes through with a lag, but it doesn't matter. Nothing would stop us from spending our birthdays together. No matter where we are in the world, we always see each other on our shared birthday. It doesn't matter that it's six in the morning here and eight at night there. Our day is our day.

"Did you get my gift?" he asks.

I hold it up, still wrapped. "You have mine?" He does the same, holding it up. "Just like when we were kids," I say.

"Lennon," he groans.

"You think you're too old now?" I ask.

"Yeah," he says with a grin.

"For me!" I beg.

He rolls his eyes, and I know I've got him. We start to count together. "One, two, . . ." There's a pause before we both scream *three* and tear off the paper.

My eyes immediately well up in happy tears. I can't believe he thought to do this. He framed the cover of the book I illustrated that won the award. Whoever said men aren't thoughtful never met Duke. "I thought for your office," he said.

"I absolutely love it," I say. "I'm really struggling on a book right now, and this is a great reminder that I can do this."

He grins, holding up my gift to him. "Peanut butter?"

I laugh. I'm the worst gift giver in the world, especially when it comes to Duke. I never know what to get for him. My graduation gift to him was the beginning of the end—a red hair ribbon. "I read that's hard to find in Japan, and their version is different."

He laughs. "I love it."

"Liar," I say. "Any word on when you'll be moved somewhere else?"

Usually Marine helicopter assignments are about six months, but can be longer depending on what's going on in the world. They've been longer these days because of a lack of qualified pilots. I'm hoping his next station will be Stateside. Florida's not exactly close, but that would be better than another continent. Of course, at only twenty minutes away, Quantico would be the most ideal.

"Nope," he says, sticking a spoon into his new jar of peanut butter.

"Duke, you motherfucker, where'd you get that?" I hear a couple of different male voices yell.

"Duke?" I ask as some other faces appear in front of the screen.

"Don't worry, Lennon," one of the guys says. "We'll make sure he has a good birthday."

I watch Duke trying to shove them away and can't help but laugh. "Big birthday plans?" I ask.

Another face appears on the screen. "Just so you know, the Marine Corps frowns on cyber strip teases."

Rolling his eyes, Duke pushes him out of the way. "Sorry, Lennon, I'm surrounded by idiots."

"It's okay. They're funny," I say.

"Love you too, Lennon," his fellow military brothers yell.

I watch Duke shoo them away, then blow out a deep breath. "They're gone."

"So you're going out for your birthday?" I ask.

"Guess so," he says, but his heart doesn't sound in it. "How about you? It's early there, huh? Still have the whole day."

I figure now is as good a time as any to spill the beans, and he gave me the perfect opening. "Brinley and I are going to the spa together today, then tonight I'm going to dinner with Chase."

His eyes lock on the screen, and even though he's thousands of miles away, I swear he's looking right through me. "Chase who?"

"Chase Arden. We went to high school with him. He was in my grade. But he was on the baseball team with you."

"Rode the bench," Duke says, his voice sounding cold.

"He probably could do all the stats for the team," I say, knowing that's true. Every time we've ever watched a game together, Chase always knows all the important stats of each player. "He works in finance up in Alexandria."

"So you know what he does, where he lives, and he's taking you out on *our* birthday," Duke says. "Sounds serious."

"We've been seeing each other for a few months," I say.

His eyes look away, nothing but dead air between us. I'm not sure what kind of reaction I expected, but not this. This is just weird. I thought he'd go all overprotective, not mute.

"He's a good guy," I say, just to fill the silence.

"Is this why you haven't been writing as much?" Duke asks. "He jealous or something?"

"No, Chase knows you and I are friends."

"Just seems odd to me that as soon as you start seeing him, you stop writing," Duke says.

"I haven't stopped. I've just been busy."

"With him."

"That's not fair," I say. "You could at least be happy for me. I found a nice guy who treats me well."

"I look forward to your emails each day," he says.

"They're so boring."

"Not to me."

"I'll do better," I say. "Just because I'm seeing Chase, it doesn't change anything between you and me."

"Look, I've got to go. The guys are waiting. Have a Happy Birthday."

I touch my finger to the screen. "Goodbye for now," I say with a smile.

His finger reaches toward mine. "Goodbye never."

"Twenty-five looks good on you," Chase says, pulling me into his arms. He always dresses nice for our dates, but tonight, he's wearing a suit. I guess my birthday warrants a suit. Or maybe he's still hoping to get me in my birthday suit.

"Halfway to fifty," I tease as his hands slip down my body. He's taking me out to dinner for my birthday at some fancy place in DC. From our first date, he always insists on taking me to the nicest places. I don't know why. Those places always have the smallest portions, and, as always, we end up having to stop off somewhere else to get takeout. "Double dinners" has become a running joke between us now. Tonight's restaurant is closer to his place than mine. It's completely out of his way to come pick me up, but he insisted on it for my birthday.

I think it had more to do with the fact that I agreed to spend the whole weekend with him at his apartment in Alexandria than being chivalrous. We discussed the sex thing, and he knows things will not go that far, but it's ridiculous for either one of us to drive back and forth when we plan on being with each other all weekend.

"Trying to impress me with your math skills," he teases me back, but then his eyes leave mine. "What's that?"

I follow his gaze to my coffee table, Duke's birthday gift to me resting there. I haven't had a chance to hang it yet. "Duke sent it for our birthdays." His forehead crinkles up, and it occurs to me that he might not realize our birthdays are the same. "Duke and I share a birthday."

"Of course," Chase says, stepping away from me slightly.

"Maybe you could help me hang it in my office?" I say, taking his hand.

He gives me a small smile. Maybe I was wrong. Maybe my friendship with Duke does bother Chase. I mean, if Duke lived here, would Chase care if I spent time with him?

CHAPTER ELEVEN

DUKE

Is this regret sex or a sex hangover?

Reaching for my shirt, I look toward the bathroom, where my random hookup disappeared behind that door a few minutes ago. What started as a night out with my buddies resulted in a few hours of really bad decision-making, followed by some below-average sex in her hotel room.

I start buttoning my shirt because I've got to get out of here. Fuck, I hate being the guy who comes and goes, but I've dug my own hole here. I can't even say it was a good time. I thought about someone else the whole time. I wonder if my bed buddy could tell?

The thing is, she's not Lennon. She didn't make me smile or laugh like Lennon does. She doesn't look like Lennon or sound like her. She's a poor substitute.

Getting up, I find the rest of my clothes. I feel like complete shit. My head hurts. My body is sore, but not in a good way, and I'm about to pull the ultimate dickhead move and never see this girl again after I used her. And it didn't even work. I feel worse than I did before.

Lennon is seeing someone. So what?

But she told me. We've never told each other that stuff. We never needed to because it was never serious. She told me this time. It's serious.

And it fucking pisses me off.

Why didn't I ever take my shot with her? Why did I let distance get in the way? Why did I assume we had time? Why the fuck would I think that? Lennon is a catch. Of course other men are interested in her. What the hell was I thinking?

Why the hell didn't I act?

The water turns off in the bathroom, and I know I'm about to face this woman. I wouldn't be surprised if she slaps my face for being up and dressed and ready to get the hell out of here, but I'm ready to take it. I would never just walk out, leaving her to find an empty bed.

I zip my pants as the bathroom door opens. She's completely naked. Her body is killer, but there's not one ounce of me that wants to stay or even look a second longer.

Her eyes widen, and I can't tell the color from here, and I guess I wasn't interested enough before to find out. Her brow furrows, "You're still here? I took extra long in the bathroom to give you ample time to escape."

"Sorry," I say. "I have an early day . . ."

She laughs. "That's the worst single guy post-sex line ever. You can do better than that."

"This was fun," I say, raising an eyebrow.

"It was for me," she says. "But I'm pretty sure I was the worst lay you've ever had."

"No . . . you're great . . . I . . ." My stammering stops when she shakes her head at me.

"No hard feelings. I knew what I was getting with you," she says. "An available dick attached to an unavailable heart."

This woman should be a philosopher or a poet. She's absolutely right.

With a nod, I make my exit, the hotel room door closing behind me. I look up at the ceiling as I lean against the closed door.

Unavailable heart.

We have this motto in the Marines—Semper Fidelis. It's Latin for "Always Faithful."

For the first time, in this shitty hotel, I realize what it really means. And it doesn't have anything to do with sex, although I've failed in that department. It has more to do with the heart. And I haven't been faithful to my heart—to my feelings for Lennon. *Is it too late?*

CHAPTER TWELVE

LENNON

"Is that what I think it is?" I ask, laughing.

"Of course," Chase says, walking through my front door. "It's our six-month anniversary."

He kisses my cheek as he passes me. "Couples don't celebrate six months," I say.

"So you didn't get me anything?" he teases, sitting down on my sofa and tossing the takeout bag of fried chicken on my coffee table.

"Is that really chicken from the convenience store we went to on our first date?"

"Same one," he says, grinning.

Sitting down beside him, I wrap my arms around his neck. "You're very sweet."

"If only you'd have figured that out sooner," Chase says playfully, tickling me a little. "We could be having our tenth anniversary instead of six months."

"Aren't you supposed to be good with numbers?" I laugh. "You asked me out when I was seventeen, so technically, we could only be celebrating our . . ."

He tackles me down to the sofa. His brown eyes spark as he pulls me to his lips. It's obvious that if Chase had his way, we'd be naked by now, but he never pressures me. Not one time have I felt like he was pushing me beyond what I'm comfortable with. He's never made me feel guilty or like I'm disappointing him. In fact, he usually stops things before I do.

He's just that decent of a guy. And he doesn't want that burden to always fall on me. But this time, I'm the one who puts the brakes on. "The food is getting cold."

He draws a deep breath, sitting up. "Maybe I should give you your gift first," Chase says, reaching into the pocket of his suit jacket and pulling out a box. It has no wrapping or no ribbon, but I recognize the name embossed on the top—jewelry.

My eyes catch his, a huge smile on his face. "What did you do?" I ask, totally surprised. I didn't expect a gift. It's a six-month anniversary, not a year.

He places the box down in my hand, and the smile on my face spreads. Shaking my head in disbelief, I slowly lift the lid. When my eyes land on the necklace, a little giggle escapes. "You don't like it?" Chase asks.

I reach for his hand. "Of course, I do," I say, looking down at my gift. "It's so you."

Blowing out a breath, he takes the box from me, removing the necklace. Turning around, I lift my hair as he puts it around my neck. "It's the infinity symbol," he says.

Turning back around, I lightly touch the metal against my skin. "Thank you," I say, walking toward a mirror so I can look at my reflection. "Every time I look at it, I will definitely think of you."

"I'm glad you love it," he says, "because I got you a ring to match."

When I turn around, he's holding out a tiny ring box. Inside is a ring with the infinity symbol in diamonds. For a second, I wonder if I'm misreading the situation. He's not down on one knee or anything.

"Lennon, you know I lost my parents when I was young. I've got no family left. You and I have that in common. You know how that feels. For my whole life, I've wanted to find someone to have a bunch of kids with, to have a family. You're the person I want to do that with."

"I am?"

"Of course, you are," he says, taking my hand. "Marry me?"

My stomach feels like it's in my throat. My heart is pounding in my chest. It's as if I've just been turned inside out.

I stare down at the ring shining brightly at me, my mom's words ringing in my ear. This is what I promised my mother. This is what she wanted for me.

CHAPTER THIRTEEN

DUKE

I've been dreading this day for three months, ever since Lennon told me about the proposal. I knew it was coming, but that doesn't make it any easier. I'm usually excited to open Lennon's letters or emails. It's the best part of my day. Reading her words, I can clearly hear her voice in my head. But I can tell by the shape of this envelope, this is one correspondence I wish would have gotten lost in the mail. I rip it open, the words shredding my heart.

Lennon

&

Chase

Formally request your presence at the celebration of their union

on . . .

CHAPTER FOURTEEN

LENNON

Candles that lined the tables are being blown out. My rehearsal dinner is over. Tomorrow, I will be a married woman. The wedding is at a local Montclair church. It's huge. The aisle is downright scary, but Chase wanted the whole big wedding thing. I didn't need all that, but he insisted. The reception is at a local ballroom. I think he invited everyone he's ever met. Weddings can take over a year to plan, but we didn't want to wait that long. Chase was persistent and found an open date. The only compromise was the wedding would be a day wedding. That's fine with me.

Tonight was smaller. Just those closest to Chase and me and our wedding party were invited to the rehearsal dinner. Although most everyone is gone now. Chase and I have been saying goodbye to everyone for what seems like forever. The dinner was fabulous. It was at a local steakhouse. No need for a double dinner tonight. Although for some reason, I wasn't able to eat a thing. Nerves, I guess.

"Don't worry. Duke will be here," Brinley whispers in my ear as she leaves the private room we had the rehearsal dinner in. She's my maid of honor, but Duke is supposed to walk me down the aisle tomorrow. I can't get married without him. He was supposed to be here already, but he hasn't shown up. He missed the rehearsal and the dinner.

Of all the people coming to the wedding, Duke is the one who means the most. I know he left Japan, but a lot can happen between there and here.

"Have you heard from him?" I ask his mom and dad as they come to say good night.

They exchange a glance. "He's on his way."

"Did something happen?" I ask, wondering what's holding him up. I've texted him a couple of times, and he hasn't responded.

Mr. Charlie shakes his head. "Duke is . . ." Mrs. Connie lightly elbows him in the side, stopping him. "I'll take over and escort you down the aisle if need be."

I thank him, holding my finger up to Chase to give me a minute. I need to say good night. Next time I see him, I'll be walking down the aisle. I hope I don't trip. "It's times like this I wish Mom was here."

Mrs. Connie hugs me, then says with a laugh, "We know. We're poor substitutes."

"But I find myself mad at her," I say. "I'm not even sure why. It's not her fault she got cancer and died. I know that." I shake my head. "I wish I would've asked her about my dad before she died. I know she said he was a bad guy, but I wish he knew I was getting married. Maybe he would've . . . I know, I'm living in a fairy tale."

They exchange another glance. This one looks even more ominous than before.

"What?"

"Not tonight," Mr. Charlie says. "Tomorrow is your wedding day."

"Do you know something about my dad?" I ask. "Did my mom tell you something?"

"Nothing more than she told you," Mrs. Connie says.

"Then what is it?"

They look at each other, and Mrs. Connie gives him a worn-out nod. "Why don't you say goodbye to the last of your guests first. Then we'll talk."

I step away, watching them sit back down, whispering to each other with concerned looks. These people are like family to me, and I've never seen them like this. Suddenly, hands land on my shoulders, and I jump slightly.

Duke?

But it's not him.

"You okay?" Chase asks, his deep brown eyes looking down at me.

"Yeah, I just need to talk to Charlie and Connie a little more."

He looks back over my shoulder at them. "I'll wait."

Giving him a small smile, I say, "It's getting late. You should go."

"You sure you'll be all right?" he asks, and I nod. He kisses me softly on the lips. "This is the last night I have to go to sleep without you. The last morning I'll wake up without you in my arms."

It's also the last day of my virginity.

The nerves hit my stomach. Why am I so nervous? Everything from walking down the aisle without tripping to not messing up my vows has me anxious. But the wedding night is a whole different story. It's my first time. Not his. I can't help but wonder if I'll disappoint him. I wish I wasn't so damn nervous. It's only sex. How hard can it be? No pun intended.

"Don't stay out much longer," he says, a glint in his eye, thinking about the same thing I am. "I need you well rested for tomorrow night."

"I'll be fine," I say, and he kisses me one more time before leaving.

When the door closes behind him, I turn back to Connie and Charlie, feeling anything but fine. A few waiters are clearing the tables around us, but they're almost done. I doubt they are going to care about our conversation, so there's no need to wait.

I take a seat across from Duke's parents, who both give me worried smiles. That might be the worst kind of smile there is. A smile should be happy, light, fun. It shouldn't be full of anxiety or sadness. My mind is racing with what they could possibly tell me. It's like a crazy soap opera playing out in my head. Mrs. Connie looks over at her husband, giving him a little nod.

"Please don't tell me that you had some illicit affair with my mother and that you are actually my father, and Duke is my half brother."

They both chuckle. "No, it's not nearly as sordid as that."

"Then what?"

"I really think this should wait until after your wedding. Your honeymoon," Mr. Charlie says.

"How am I supposed to enjoy those things knowing something terrible is waiting for me?"

"It's not terrible," Mrs. Connie says.

"Then tell me."

Mr. Charlie clears his throat. "I know your father's name. I met him once."

My eyes fly to Mrs. Connie, who gives me a small nod. "When? Where is he? How did you meet him? Did Mom introduce you?"

He holds his hand up. "Before I tell you everything, I want you to know that Connie and I did what we thought was right for both you and your mom."

I feel myself inching away from them slowly. It's like my subconscious knows pain is coming. "I understand."

He takes a deep breath and then begins. "It was your third birthday and Duke's fourth. The party was at our house—cowboy and cowgirl theme. We had pony rides."

"I've seen the pictures," I say, forcing a smile.

He tries to smile back, but this time, the worry won't let him. "Your mom forgot your cowgirl hat at your house. She was so upset because she had this whole vision in her mind and worked so hard making your outfit. The hat had a yellow bandana on it to match the ribbons in your hair. When she realized she'd left it at home, I offered to run to your house and pick it up for her."

Mr. Charlie is always nice like that, but I get the feeling that I might not think that way about him for much longer.

"I had just reached the front door when a man called out to me from the sidewalk. I turned around, and he stepped closer, asking me if Iva Barlow lived here." He looks at his wife. "I can't explain it, but

I knew he was your dad. Same blue eyes, brown hair. I just knew."

"What did he want?"

"He told me he had done Iva wrong and was looking to make amends with her."

"Make amends? That sounds like someone in recovery," I say. "Did he look like he was using, or did he look clean?"

"He didn't look strung out or anything, if that's what you mean," Mr. Charlie says. "He said he found your mom's address online. At that moment, I had a decision to make. So I told him that your mom had lived there, but she'd moved somewhere else a while back."

"Why would you do that?" I ask, my heart beating harder.

"Because I didn't know if your mom would want him around, back in her life."

"I guess she didn't," I say.

He looks at his wife again. "I never told her he came by."

All the air leaves my chest, and I leap to my feet. The room starts to spin, and images of my childhood whiz past me—Christmas mornings, birthdays, first days of school—without ever having a dad in sight. What would it feel like to have my dad around? Mrs. Connie stands up, too. "Lennon, honey, please listen."

It takes me a second, but I finally turn my eyes to her, holding her gaze. Mrs. Connie's eyes are soft when she starts. "Charlie told me about his visit that night. We talked about it and decided not to tell your mother. We didn't know for sure if the man was really your father, and we certainly didn't want to invite trouble into your lives."

"But that wasn't your decision," I snap. "You said yourself that he looked perfectly fine."

They take each other's hands. "He didn't know about you, Lennon," Mrs. Connie says. "Your mom never told him she was pregnant. She only found out after she was arrested, and he'd left her to take the fall. She never saw him again. Never even attempted to look for him."

My heart sinks into the pit of my belly. "He never knew," I whisper.

"No," Mrs. Connie says. "Iva told me that in confidence. She thought if you knew that, you'd want to go looking for him."

"I would have."

"Your mom had turned her life around. She was happy. She had you. We made sure to get her an unlisted number, and he never came back," Mr. Charlie says, and I can hear in his voice that he believes he did the right thing.

"What's his name?" I ask.

"His name was Justin Monroe," Mr. Charlie says.

Justin Monroe. I imagined my father many times in my life. He was the subject of many of my early sketches. But he was like a ghost, a shadow, or a man who lived in the dreams of a young girl. Suddenly, I realize what Mr. Charlie said.

"Was?"

"He passed away several years ago," he says.

"What?"

Tears start down my face. I didn't even know the man. He didn't know about me, but I'm crying. Why am I crying? When my mom died, a part of me still felt like someone's child. I didn't know who he was, but I knew he was out there. Now I know I'm an orphan.

"I kept tabs on him right after his visit," Mr. Charlie says. "I thought maybe I'd tell your mom if he seemed on the straight and narrow, but he got arrested for burglary. Then when your mother died, I had a private investigator search for him. I was hoping he was alive and doing well. I wanted to be able to give you that. But he had died two years prior to your mom. Drug overdose."

My stomach knots, and my legs wobble. I'm about to be sick, but at the same time, I want to scream and yell and hit something hard. Everyone lied to me—Connie, Charlie, even my mom.

Mrs. Connie steps toward me, her arms out like she's about to hug me. I step away, my head shaking. "You liars."

She stops in her tracks, and Charlie takes her arm. "Lennon, remember the first thing I said to you. We did what we did to protect you and your mother."

Hurt and anger fill my body. "It was wrong."

"Iva could have looked for him anytime to tell him about you, but she never did. She didn't want him in her life or yours."

"You don't know that."

"Lennon, think about it," Mrs. Connie says.

I'm too hurt to think. All I can do is feel, and all my feelings come rushing out. "You robbed my mother of making her own choices, of being able to confront the man who ruined her life. You robbed me of my father! Of maybe having two parents. Maybe he would've loved me. Maybe he would've wanted me."

My face collapses in my hands, tears seeping through my fingers, mascara stains ruining my beautiful rehearsal dress.

Their arms go around me, and I push away. "No."

"We know you're upset right now, but once you think about things, you'll see that what we did was out of love," Mrs. Connie says.

I can't hear them try to defend themselves. I grab a leftover bottle of wine, and head for the door, feeling more alone than I ever have in my whole life.

CHAPTER FIFTEEN

LENNON

The moonlight reflects off the water in the lake. It's after midnight—officially, my wedding day. I don't know why I came here. Perhaps because it's filled with so many happy memories—memories of Duke and me laughing, memories of when my biggest problem was unrequited love and high school horrors.

I bring the now half-empty bottle of wine to my lips, taking a quick sip. I should be sleeping peacefully in my bed, dreaming of my future husband, not walking the shore of the lake, drinking and seething. At worst, I should be tossing and turning in excitement to walk down the aisle.

A million thoughts race through my head.

Why do people think they can do anything in the name of love? Like love gives you a pass to lie to someone and keep secrets. Yeah, they try to pass it off as noble. They're trying to protect you. It's still lying.

Love should protect.

But love shouldn't protect through lies. Love, by its very nature, is a protector—not from pain or hurt but from being alone. Love protects us from facing the worst of life alone. That's how love protects.

When something terrible happens, you have someone standing at the ready to face it with you. Not someone who lies to you about it.

Love protects.

"Lennon."

I know his voice before I turn around. "Duke," I say, soft and needy.

Even in the moonlight, his gray eyes find mine. He's wearing military fatigues, and his cute little dimple is on full display. Placing the wine bottle down, I cry out, "You're home."

He opens up his arms. "Come here." Smiling through my tears, I run into his arms, and he picks me up, burying his nose in my hair. "Now I'm home." He holds me tight, letting all the time apart and all the distance melt away.

"I was so afraid you wouldn't make it." He places me down on the ground but gently runs his fingers through my hair, his eyes slowly rolling over my face. "How'd you find me?"

"You weren't at home, and Mom and Dad told me what happened. It wasn't hard to figure out where you'd go."

"They lied to me. They all lied to me," I sob.

"I had no idea," he says. "I would've told you."

Wrapping my arms around his waist, I hug him again. "Let's not talk about it."

He motions toward the bottle. "So what are we drinking?"

I laugh. How Duke does that I'll never know. He's always the cure of what ails me. Placing his arm over my shoulder, we start to walk. He bends down and picks up the bottle on the way, taking a long drink, then offers it to me. I shake my head, no longer feeling like I need it.

We walk and talk, and fall right back into our friendship. Not that we ever fell out of it, but it's different over the computer when you can't touch the person, smell them, feel them.

I know I shouldn't stay out any later. I know I should attempt to get some sleep so I don't show up at the altar looking like hell, but I don't want to let go of this moment. "I've missed this," I say. "Missed you."

"It's been too long," Duke says.

"Had to get engaged to get you home," I tease, but he steps away, bending down and picking up a rock. He examines it for a second before rearing back and throwing it, making it skip across the top of the water.

He looks back over his shoulder at me, his eyes piercing through me. "Why didn't you and I ever . . ." He steps back to me, lightly touching my cheek. "Why didn't *we* ever happen?"

My mouth falls open, and my head shakes, unsure why he'd ask. "Two reasons. You are you, and I'm me. You were always popular, had it all, the dream guy. Girls like me don't get the dream."

"Lennon, you can't believe that," he says.

"I don't now, but it was completely that way back in high school."

"What's the second reason?" he asks.

"My mom's advice. I would've loved you more than you loved me."

"Not possible," he says, inching closer, his body towering over me.

My eyes meet his. I have to be reading this wrong. I'm tired, been crying, been drinking. Surely, I'm reading his signals wrong.

"Lennon, I'm not here to give you away. I could never do that," Duke says.

"What do you mean?"

He looks me right in the eye. "Don't marry him."

"Why?" I whisper, afraid of what he'll say.

"Because it was always you and me. It was always supposed to be you and me."

It's like his words go right through me. I step back, confused. He's about a half decade too late. "You can't do this, Duke. Not today. I'm supposed to get married in a few hours."

"Lennon, just hear me out," he says, taking my hand.

"No," I say, my voice almost begging. "Don't do this. Please don't do this."

"I have to," he says. "I convinced myself on the flight over here to keep my mouth shut, but seeing you, holding you. I have to."

"Why now?" I ask. "Why do this now when I have someone who loves me, really loves me?"

"Do you love him?" he shoots back.

I don't give myself a second to think. "Of course, I love him."

I stomp off, needing to get out of this situation. Duke was the first boy I ever loved, but it never went anywhere. How dare he do this now? He had to know how I felt about him all those years ago and never did a damn thing except make out with other girls. Anger builds in my body, and I turn around, my finger in his face.

"People think you are some kind of hero. Big Marine. Think you are so brave, but you're not. This isn't brave. Brave would've been telling me a long time ago. Not today. Not when I'm about to marry someone else. This is selfish!"

"Selfish!" he barks. "Let's just be honest for a minute. You don't love him. You love him *enough*, and there's a difference."

My chest rises and falls quickly. I try to think of something to say back. Why can I not think of something to say? What's wrong with me? I love Chase. Does he love me more than I love him? That's what my mom always said was best, safe, secure. Not this. Not what Duke is doing right now. Blowing up my life!

"He doesn't make you feel like I do," Duke says, taking ahold of my waist and pulling me to his body.

Before I know what's happening, he takes my cheek in his hand, and his mouth lands on mine softly. And even though we only kissed that one night, his lips are still familiar. His tongue meets mine, and like I've been struck by a bolt of lightning, I push away.

"No," I say, touching my lips. "I'm marrying Chase today. In a few hours. That can't have happened. No, no, no." I look at Duke. "I can't have your lips on mine the day I'm marrying another man."

Tears rush down my face, and I feel myself growing more hysterical. Duke keeps saying my name, but I'm only focused on what just happened. It was only a couple of seconds, and I pushed away, but it still happened. Did I encourage this? How am I going to walk down the aisle to Chase? I have to tell him. Oh, God, I have to tell him!

Duke's hands land on my hips, and I yank away. I'm not sure about what just happened, but I am sure of one thing. My mother was right. You should find a man who loves you more, and it's clear to me that Duke is not that man, or he wouldn't have done this.

I look straight into his gray eyes, knowing it's for the last time.

"Goodbye, Duke. And not for now, but forever."

"Goodbye never," he whispers as I walk away.

CHAPTER SIXTEEN

DUKE

FUBAR – known in the military as "fucked up beyond all recognition." That's the current state of things with Lennon.

Lying in my bed, I stare at the ceiling and the fan swirling above me. My workday is done. Being stationed in Japan is normally a good assignment. The nightlife is decent. The fishing is amazing. There are some beautiful beaches, and if you like sushi, you are in luck. But over the years, I've missed home. I missed my old bed, my parents, American food.

Peanut butter.

Lennon.

It's been ten days since I've seen Lennon. I left the States that same day, just a few hours after the lake, and came back to the base, to serve my country, to try to forget about how fucked up my relationship with Lennon is.

A Marine Corps helicopter pilot's training is intense, with various courses, levels, and exercises. It takes almost two years to complete, but it's never really over. Since I've been back on base, I've logged more flight time than I normally would. Being in the air usually helps me think and get a new perspective on things, but it's not been working. I've worked out like a maniac, but that hasn't helped either.

I have to be ready for my next mission at a moment's notice. And I have to be on my game. Lives depend on me. Even the simplest gig of flying soldiers from point A to point B can go wrong. Nothing can be taken for granted when you're flying in hostile territory. It doesn't matter if it's wartime or peacetime, flying under the American flag means flying with a target on your back. Focus is the name of the game.

Corps chopper pilots are not a dime a dozen. We are few and far between. So much so, the military has even been paying retired pilots to come back into rotation. But this job can and does take its toll. Some can't handle the stress, while others can't handle being away from family. For others, our loved ones are what gets us through.

Lennon was always that for me. I never told her that. But I could be under the worst kind of enemy fire, and she'd center me. I don't think about the bullets or the lives that could be lost. My mind always goes to her.

When we were teenagers, I knew she was gorgeous. I knew my feelings for her were beyond friendship, but you never know how you truly feel about someone until right before you think you're about to meet your maker—she was the only thought in my head that day.

It was one of my first assignments after I got to Japan. Some bad intel led us into a fucking war zone. It was supposed to be simple. Afterward, I should've told her. Unfortunately, I was several continents away from her. Writing it in a letter was the coward's way out. I thought we had time. Still, she's been my center ever since. I think she always has been.

I thought once I got home, once we had some real time together, not over the internet, that we'd finally stop tiptoeing around each other. I thought I'd finally take my shot with her. Even when her letters started to slow, when she started seeing Chase, I never imagined she'd agree to marry him. In my mind, she had always been mine.

When I think of all the times I could've said something—all the phone calls, all the times she smiled at me. Hell, I could've told her before the rehearsal dinner. I'm sure Lennon thinks my plane was delayed, but I was home in plenty of time. I was just too much of a chickenshit to show up.

Opening up my email, I hope to see a message from her, responding to one of the dozen I've sent her. Even if she's just telling me to go to hell, that would be better than this.

I know from my parents that the wedding didn't happen. It wasn't like Chase left her waiting at the altar or anything. Instead, Brinley sent a message to all the guests simply saying that Chase and Lennon would not be getting married that day, and all gifts would be returned.

I have to wonder why she told him about our kiss. If it really meant nothing, then why risk telling him. She had to know he'd be upset. She had to consider he might end things. Maybe deep down in a place she isn't even fully aware of, she wanted him to cancel the wedding. Maybe deep down, she knows he's not the man for her. Maybe I'm just wishful thinking.

But I'd be lying if I said I wasn't happy she didn't marry him, but I hate it went down the way it did. I hate that she got hurt because of me. I hate that she hasn't answered one of my calls or emails. We haven't ever gone this long without communicating. I suspect she's blocked me. My parents are getting a similar silent treatment.

I need some answers. There's only one other person I can think to call. Without thinking, I dial her number. She answers with a yawn. "Brinley?"

"Duke?" she says. "It's like four in the morning."

"Sorry," I say.

"I can't talk to you."

"Did Lennon tell you not to talk to me?" I ask.

"No," she says, "but it's girl code."

"Brinley, please," I beg.

"Your charms don't work on me," she says. "What you did? I swear I wish Lennon would've slapped your handsome face right off."

"She told you?"

"Everything." She releases a deep breath. "She's happy, Duke. Chase really loves her."

"I love her."

"That doesn't mean your love is better," Brinley says.

"But . . ."

"No," she says. "You called me, so you listen. You don't get to decide that your love is better for Lennon than Chase's love is. And Chase doesn't get to decide that he's better for Lennon than you are. Lennon gets to decide that. And right now, she's decided it's Chase."

In my heart, I know we belong together. She's the only woman for me. God knows I've tried to love other women, but Lennon has a firm grip on my heart whether she means to or not.

"So they're still together?" I ask.

Silence.

"I've tried calling her, emailing, texting. She won't talk to me."

"She's been in Hawaii," Brinley says.

I know they were supposed to honeymoon there. Why would they still go? Are they trying to work things out? Is she chasing him? Is he chasing her? Or did they . . .

"Did they get married?" I ask quietly, but there's nothing but more silence. "Brinley, you've got to put me out of my misery here."

"As God as my witness, Duke, you better not do anything to mess this up for her again."

My heart beats harder. "That's a no. They didn't get married?"

I hear her curse under her breath. "No, they didn't. But that's not a license for you to go after her."

"She didn't marry him. That means something."

"It doesn't mean what you want it to mean," Brinley says.

"So they're still together?"

"Yes."

I can tell from her voice that she's not telling me everything. "Have they rescheduled the wedding?"

"They're moving in together," Brinley says.

"No," I say with a certainty to my voice. "Lennon would never live with someone before marriage. She's the only person I know who insisted on waiting until marriage for sex. She . . ." Suddenly, my heart sinks, reality smacking me right in the face. "She slept with him?" I ask, but don't really expect an answer, which is good because Brinley doesn't say a word.

I have to wonder if that's why Chase forgave her for our kiss at the lake. Men have been known to forgive most sins for sex. And I know I kissed her, and I know she pulled back, but there was a moment. It was short, but it was there. A moment when she let her desire win. I felt it.

"The plan was always for him to move in with her after they were married. His lease was up, so he's moving in. As far as I know, they've tabled any discussion of marriage for a while."

"Is she okay?" I ask.

"Now you decide to be her friend," Brinley scolds.

"I know my timing sucked," I admit. That night at the lake was a classic case of what we Marines call, "good initiative, bad judgment." My intentions were good, but my timing was horrible.

"You think?"

"The thing is I thought we had time. Lennon and me."

"You should have told her that before her wedding day," Brinley says. "Because it just seems like a typical case of a man wanting what he can't have."

"I hope Lennon doesn't think that," I say. "It's not true. I want her. I've always wanted her."

"Then why not ever do something about it."

"I wasn't ready," I say. "I wasn't ready for her, for us. Because she's it for me. And once I let myself go there with her, that was going to be it. And I wasn't ready for that at sixteen, or eighteen, or twenty-two."

"So now you're ready?" she asks.

"I am."

"And she's gone," Brinley says.

CHAPTER SEVENTEEN

LENNON

Chase sits down on the side of the bed, kissing my forehead. I reluctantly open my eyes, noticing I've rolled to the middle of the bed again. Couples are supposed to have sides. On our first night back from Hawaii, Chase got in bed before me, taking the left side of the bed. That's how I became a right side of the bed woman. But it hasn't stuck. Every morning, I wake up in the center of the bed. I can't help it. Granted, it hasn't even been two weeks since our non-wedding, so maybe I just need time to adjust to my new sleeping arrangements.

Chase motions to a cup of coffee on the nightstand. "I'm going to make a coffee lover out of you yet."

I notice he's all dressed for work in a suit and tie. "You leaving already?" I ask, glancing at the clock. It's barely six in the morning. His commute into Alexandria is less than an hour, and he doesn't have to be at work until eight.

"Still getting used to the commute," he says.

I give him a small smile. We're both getting used to a lot. Neither one of us has ever lived with someone else. I'm not used to him being here every night and every morning. We used to talk about how nice it would be to wake up together every morning after we were married. We never talked about him worrying about the morning rush-hour traffic.

Would it be different if we were married?

I swore I'd never live with someone first. I swore I'd never have sex without a marriage license. Now I'm doing both.

Of course, I always thought Duke would be in my life, and that didn't happen either.

"You okay?" Chase asks. "You look very far away."

"I'm fine," I lie. I've never lied to Chase before, but I don't want a fight. Chase and I seldom argue, but Duke is the one topic that can make him raise his voice. I understand why. If I were Chase, I'd be pissed too. But no matter what Chase wants, my brain, my heart still wanders to Duke. He was a huge part of my life for so long, but not anymore. Still, I can't shut off over twenty years of friendship overnight.

I miss Duke. I don't want to miss him. What he did was terrible. I have no idea what he was thinking—kissing me on the day I was supposed to marry Chase. What did he think would happen? Did he expect me to leave Chase? Did he think at all about what he was doing to my life? But no matter how mad I am at him, I still miss what we had. But when those feelings bubble up, I do my best to push them back down.

I have a man who loves me standing right here, and he has to be my focus. Getting on my knees in bed, I kiss Chase sweetly. "Why don't you play hooky today? We can finish unpacking your stuff."

"I wish," he says. "But I just missed all that work for our . . ." He stops himself before he says the wedding or honeymoon words, knowing my heart is still hurting over what happened. Chase calling off our wedding is a sore spot for me. It hurts. I think it will for a long time. I don't think Chase knows how bad I'm hurt. In one day, I lost my best friend, Connie and Charlie, and my wedding. Chase and I spent time talking about his feelings, how hurt and angry he was, but I can't talk to him about how I'm feeling about Duke and his parents. It would only make him upset, and he's been hurt enough. I love him. I don't want him hurt. "I'll finish unpacking after work."

I smile. That makes total sense. Everything about Chase is sensible and sweet. He's exactly what my mom wanted for me. Exactly what I promised her I'd find.

Shaking off my sleep, I walk to the kitchen, seeing Chase's coffee pot on my kitchen counter. I'm still not used to seeing it there. It was the first thing he unpacked after he moved in.

My cell phone rings, and my heart stops. My mind immediately does the math in my head. It's late evening in Japan. This would be a good time for Duke to call. I reach for it, hoping it's not him. Brinley's name appears.

"Hey," I say. "Everything okay? It's early for you to call."

"I work the seven to seven today, but I've been up for a while because Duke called me."

My heart twists. It's been in a knot since the lake, since that kiss. I'm so angry with him. He should not have done what he did. But more than feeling mad, I'm sad. I haven't felt this horrible since my mom passed away. Mad and sad are not a good mix of emotions. Happy sad I can handle. I can love someone and still hate their behavior. That's my situation with Duke. But this feeling of being angry coupled with sadness and a huge sense of loss feels yucky, for lack of a better word.

"Brinley, I can't listen to this."

"I know," she says. "I didn't want to keep it from you, though. So I'm telling you he called me, and that's it."

I want to ask if he's okay. I want to know if he feels bad for totally screwing up my life. I want to know if he meant that kiss, but I don't ask. It does me no good to know any of those things. I made my choice. I have to put Charles Duke III out of my mind.

"Tell me about Hawaii."

"It was beautiful," I say.

"Not that," Brinley says. "Tell me about you and Chase. Come on, I've waited years for you to lose your v-card."

CHAPTER EIGHTEEN

DUKE

Day one hundred and eighty-one without Lennon.

Love spells have been around probably since the Garden of Eden. A tonic to help lovers admit their feelings—otherwise known as alcohol. A spell that causes a woman to fall in love with you—otherwise known as sweet-talking. A charm to woo the opposite sex—otherwise known as expensive jewelry.

All are designed to make your intended fall under a love spell. Spells by design are supposed to be helpful and achieve a desired outcome, but what if love isn't a spell? What if it's the opposite? What if . . .

Love is a curse. The most powerful curse there is. After all, curses are designed to inflict harm and cause pain, and admitting my love for Lennon has definitely done that. Love cursed our friendship.

It's been about six months since I told her how I felt. Six months without a word from her. Love cursed communication, too.

She won't respond to any of my emails, letters, or phone calls. I thought I'd run out of ways to say I was sorry, but I haven't. I'm not sorry for loving her or telling her, but I am sorry for waiting so long and stealing that moment from her.

But I just couldn't watch her marry someone else. It might have been selfish, like she said, but it was also true. Loving Lennon is my truth. It always has been. It didn't matter that it wasn't spoken. It didn't matter if some other girl was on my arm. It didn't matter if we were across the world from each other. I was still under her spell.

Loving Lennon is my curse.

Happy Birthday.

That's all her email said, and that was over a week ago. I called her and left a message, figuring she wouldn't respond. She never does, but I haven't given up. There has to be a way back from this.

We always talk on our birthdays, so I had to try to call her. But she didn't answer. I sent her a gift like always—the complete DVD collection of *The Amazing Race*. I thought that might help her remember all the good times, but it was returned to me. If I thought it would help, I'd go down into a dogeza, a Japanese apology gesture where you get on your knees and touch your head to the ground—it's like an extreme bow. But I doubt that would work either.

I wonder how much of this is Lennon and how much of this is Chase. If I was in his shoes, I wouldn't want my girlfriend talking to me, either. This cold freeze just doesn't feel like Lennon, though. She's too sweet, too tenderhearted for this. She has to know she's driving me nuts. Maybe Chase has demanded she end her friendship with me. Maybe he made her choose. After what I did, the choice was probably easy for her. Fuck!

So I was shocked as shit when I opened up my email and saw a message from her. It took me a few minutes to even open the damn thing for fear she was telling me to go to hell, stop bothering her, she hated me, but all she said was those two little words.

Happy Birthday.

At the time, I thought it was an opening, but now I'm not so sure. We are apparently back to the silent treatment. And frankly, silence is worse than yelling.

I'd rather she curse my name, scream at me, and rip me a new one. At least it would be something. Something to hold on to. Right now, it feels like I'm reaching for a ghost.

Plopping down on my sofa, I close my eyes, tired from my workout. The base has a gym with any piece of equipment you can think of. I use it quite a bit. It's convenient since I live on base. Military housing isn't fancy, but it does the trick. It just makes life easier to live close to work. If I ever had a family, maybe I'd reconsider and live off base, but for now, it's fine.

Some of my buddies live in the same complex I do. They used to barge in all the time when I was talking to Lennon and aggravate the shit out of me. Now they all know better than to mention her name.

My parents don't mention her much anymore either. It's too painful for all of us. She's frozen them out too, and even though she and Chase live only minutes away, my parents don't know what's going on with her. I think my mom has even knocked on her door a few times, but no one has ever answered. You'd think they'd run into each other at some point, but our town isn't that small, and fate hasn't brought them face-to-face.

My cell phone rings, and I reach into my pocket and grab it. It's home. My parents call a lot. They haven't eased up at all over the years. It doesn't matter how old I am. They still want to talk to me every day. My mom worries. I know that. I don't get to see them much, and I'm their only child, so I understand. And when they call, they both are usually on the line, neither one of them wanting to miss talking to me.

"Mom and Dad," I say, trying to sound upbeat. I never want them to hear me down and out. That will just make them worry more, and there's nothing they can do from the other side of the world.

"Duke," my dad's voice comes through first, and I immediately know something's not right.

I hear my mom sniffle. "What's wrong? You guys all right?"

"We're fine," my dad says.

"Mom," I say, "I can hear you crying."

"Sorry, baby," she says, and I can tell she's trying to pull herself together. "Something's happened. Lennon's . . ."

"Lennon!" I say, getting to my feet.

"She's fine, son," my dad says. "Physically, she's fine."

"We don't have all the details," my mom says. "Chase is dead."

CHAPTER NINETEEN

DUKE

From the bottom of a small grassy hill, I see Lennon standing in a black dress, her brown hair loose and flowing, hiding most of her face. People have gathered around, all dressed in black. She's surrounded by darkness, no light around her. The priest is about to begin the graveside service.

Taking long strides, I make my way toward her. I missed the church service. For being the military, they sure don't do a good job of getting their serviceman home in a hurry. That's not totally fair, though, since a storm delayed my flight.

The flight and delay were torture. I needed to get to her. Even though things are rough between us, she's still my best friend. I had to show up for her. Getting leave and getting home wasn't easy, and I have to go back right after the service. Basically, I'm flying all the way around the world just for this moment. This terrible moment.

Brinley is standing at Lennon's side. She's the one who called my parents and told them about Chase. I don't know if Lennon knows that, but I'm thankful she kept them in the loop. Otherwise, I may have found out too late to make the trip home.

A lot of people are here, but Lennon is the closest thing to family that Chase had. His parents and grandparents have long passed, and he had no siblings. He and Lennon had that in common, I guess—no family related by blood. And Lennon's not Chase's family either. Guess I only have myself to blame for that, ruining their wedding. This might be the only time I have the slightest regret about that. Chase is in that wood box surrounded by a lot of friends and coworkers but no family. Judging by the lack of bling on Lennon's finger, she wasn't even his fiancée. There's no one in this world to carry on his family name. As an only child, a son no less, I know how important that is to my parents, my dad especially.

It's not like they pressure me to get married and have kids, but I know they are hoping for grandchildren and at least one grandson to carry on the Duke name. Good Lord, my son would be number four in the line of Charles Dukes.

My parents both give me small smiles. They are standing across the gravesite from Lennon. It's hard to know what the right thing to do at this moment is. Not only is it tragic, but the strain on our relationship makes it hard to know what Lennon wants from us. Does she want us close? Does she want us to keep our distance?

Lennon's looking straight at his casket, her hands folded over her stomach. Even in grief, she's the most beautiful woman I've ever seen. I've never told her, but I can't tell her now.

As I draw near to her, I hear whispers from the crowd swirling.

Poor thing. Why'd they call off the wedding?

If I can hear them, then I suspect Lennon can, too.

Murder.

One glance from me, and the funeral guests shut their damn mouths. This is not the time or place. We all know Chase was murdered in Alexandria. Apparently, he was at some convenience store pretty late at night and got caught up in a robbery attempt. No one knows why he was in Alexandria that late at night when he lives in Montclair. The rumor mill is circulating with all kinds of shit from he was cheating on Lennon to he was laundering money for the cartel.

Stepping up behind Lennon, I take a deep breath, having not been this close to her in so long. The breeze blows, and I can smell her shampoo. The priest begins to talk, and I wonder if Lennon knows I'm here, that I'm behind her, that I've got her. It's not the first gravesite where I've stood beside her. I was beside her when she had to bury her mother. She's been through entirely too much for her young age.

I want to pull her into my arms, hold her close, and whisper that she's not alone—but I don't.

Gently, I lift my hand, placing it lightly on her shoulder. I feel her tremble. She doesn't look back at me. No words pass between us, just my hand rests there.

She leans her cheek down.

I feel her tears on my skin.

CHAPTER TWENTY
SIX MONTHS LATER

DUKE

Pulling my old truck in front of Lennon's house, I've never been more sure of anything. I spent the plane ride after Chase's funeral writing Lennon the longest email in the history of emails. I didn't apologize again. I didn't bring up the night I kissed her at the lake. I simply wrote a letter to my best friend. I wrote down how much her friendship has meant to me and how much it still means. I told her about all the boring shit that's happened since we last talked. I promised her my support. I wrote until my fingers hurt as much as my heart.

She wrote back.

We haven't missed a day since. It's like it used to be. She tells me about her days, how she feels just like she used to, minus the fact that both of us are ignoring my declaration of love for her. I don't know if she thinks I don't love her anymore—which isn't true—or if she's just choosing to ignore it. I do know she's not ready. She's still grieving. For the first few months after Chase was killed, Lennon hoped the police would find his killer, but after a while, they pretty much told her there was no hope. They had no leads, no witnesses, no one had come forward with information, and there were no cameras at the scene. They had nothing really to go on. I can't imagine how hard that is.

Other than my parents, I don't keep in touch with many people who live in Montclair anymore, but from what Lennon tells me, she seems to be laying low—even more than usual. I know Brinley checks on her a lot, so much so, Lennon gave her a key. She visits Chase's grave every week, but other than that, she doesn't go out much. She works from home, has her groceries delivered, and hasn't even considered dating. She's not ready for what I want, so I'm trying to give her what she needs—a friend.

We haven't talked on the phone. She's avoided that. I wanted to see her face, to look in her blue eyes, to see for myself that she's all right, but it hasn't happened. I'm not sure if she doesn't want me to see her cry or if she's worried she'll cry and won't be able to stop. We don't discuss what happened. She hasn't given me any details. Chase was shot, killed, and the police have no leads. That's all I know.

After landing back on US soil, my parents picked me up, and we had lunch while we caught up. I dropped my stuff at their house, jumped in my old truck, and came straight over here. I didn't tell Lennon I was coming home, and that I've got thirty days of leave. I wanted to surprise her, and I didn't want to tell her and then have it fall through for some reason.

Winter is over, but spring hasn't fully wrapped her arms around this area of the country yet, the air still crisp. Sticking my hands in my pockets, I stand on the sidewalk staring at her house. The house we spent so much time in as kids. If we weren't at my house, we were here. It was my second home.

While Lennon has started communicating with me again, she hasn't seen my parents or talked to them other than a polite "thank you for coming" at Chase's funeral. At some point, I'm hoping to mend that fence, but for now, I'm just happy she's not still giving me the silent treatment.

Making my way to the front door, I lightly knock. I can't wait to see the look on her face. Nothing. I don't hear any movement inside, like someone coming for the door or anything. I knock again and wait. Nothing happens, and I step to the front window and peer in. The lights are all out. There's no activity inside.

Shit! Do I just sit and wait? Maybe I should have told her I was coming.

Montclair isn't that big, but it's big enough that I don't want to chase her around town, especially since I have no idea where she is.

There is one thing that I do feel the need to do. Hopping back in my truck, I drive through my hometown. I haven't spent any real length of time here since I was eighteen and went to college. Summer break, a quick leave, a holiday, but none of those visits felt as important as this one. This one feels like the visit that will determine the rest of our relationship—where we go from here. Are we destined to always be just friends? Or destined for more?

I know this town like the back of my hand. It doesn't matter how long I've been away or how many new houses or stores come into the area—I know all the roads, all the shortcuts. I could probably drive through town blindfolded, but there's one place that I don't know that well, thankfully having only had to come here a couple of times in my life.

Slowing down, I pull into the cemetery. I didn't know Chase well—a casual acquaintance in high school. Mostly, I knew him as Lennon's boyfriend—the guy who was in my way. As much as I wanted him out of the picture, I would've never wished for this. I'm not sure what exactly I'm doing here. It's pointless to apologize to a headstone.

Closing the door to my truck, I place my hands in my pockets, keeping them warm. My steps are slow, and my eyes are down. It's weird how a place can do that to you, change your whole demeanor. Ten minutes ago, I was grinning like a fool thinking about surprising Lennon, but now everything feels somber and heavy. Glancing around, I'm trying to remember the way to his grave when I spot her in the distance.

Her back is to me, but I know it's her. From here, I can only see the outline of her body, a shadow, not the whole person. She's merely a silhouette of the woman I know.

Her brown hair blowing in the breeze, she's kneeled in front of his grave, placing a bouquet of sunflowers down. I freeze, not wanting to interrupt her moment. I know she comes here each week. I wonder what she says, and if she cries, or screams, or simply sits quietly. I wonder if she's been able to say goodbye. And if the goodbye is *for now* or *forever*.

CHAPTER TWENTY-ONE

LENNON

Some loves last a lifetime, but they all end the same way—with a goodbye.

Life is a series of goodbyes. Some are short. Some are long. Some hurt more than others. But there's no way around it. Life is one long goodbye.

It doesn't matter how long you live or how much you love. It doesn't matter if you're a good person or a terrible asshole. In the end, we all must say goodbye to everyone and everything we love.

Which is what I'm trying to do now—say goodbye to you.

Looking down at your headstone, I never dreamed I'd have to write an epitaph in my twenties. I also never dreamed that I'd be the reason you are in that ground.

I wipe my cheek. The weight of your death rests squarely on my shoulders, and my heart starts to ache.

No two heartbeats are exactly the same. It's true. Everyone's heart beats differently depending on its size and shape. All any of us can do is try to find the heart that beats in time with ours. But what do you do when that heart stops beating?

A cool Virginia breeze blows through the cemetery, and I bend down, placing fresh sunflowers on the ground in front of your grave. But getting back to my feet isn't as easy as it used to be, my six-month baby bump getting in the way.

This is wrong. A pregnant woman should not be standing at the foot of her baby's father's grave. It's not the natural order of things. It's not how things are supposed to be.

Rubbing my belly, I'm sad that our little bundle of joy will never know you. You will only ever be a ghost to her. You will only be a goodbye.

I sink back to the ground, lying on the grass and dirt, desperate to be closer to you, my hand resting on the cold stone of your headstone. Tears roll down my cheeks to the grass. Maybe they travel all the way through the dirt to your casket. I can only hope they reach you, so you'll know how sorry I am.

Did I not love you enough? Is that why this happened? I'm sorry. I'm sorry. The words echo through my heart over and over again. Please hear me. Please send me a sign that you hear me. That you forgive me.

Any minute I'm going to wake up from this nightmare. This can't be my life. This can't have happened. You can't be dead because of me. I can't do this. I can't do this alone.

"Lennon." The wind whispers my name faintly. Or maybe it's simply your ghost.

CHAPTER TWENTY-TWO

DUKE

Standing just a few feet behind her, softly, I say, "Lennon."

I see her stand, wobbling a little as she gets to her feet. She shakes her head a little like she's hearing voices in the wind. Grinning, I say a little louder this time, "Lennon."

She turns.

My mouth drops open. She's just as beautiful as ever, but my eyes can only focus on one spot.

She's pregnant.

It's most guys' nightmare to face a surprise pregnancy, but this is a whole other level. I love the woman, but the baby's not mine. It's not like I want to be an expectant father right now, but the thought that she's carrying another man's baby blows my mind. This wasn't my plan. I'm sure it wasn't hers either.

Lennon looks down at her belly, her hands softly landing there. Our eyes lock, and she starts laughing and crying at the same time.

We walk toward each other slowly. There's no rushing, no leaping into my arms. We're both in shock. Her from my presence and me from the presence of someone else in her belly.

"How are you here?" she asks.

"Month-long leave," I say, my voice short and to the point. "I wanted to surprise you."

"Surprise," she says, rubbing her belly bump.

"You're . . ." I can't complete the thought. I don't hug her. We just stand there.

"Yep. Seven months."

"Why didn't you tell me?" I ask.

She looks away. "I don't know."

"Did you know?" I ask. "At the funeral?"

She nods. "No one else did. I just couldn't tell anyone then. I was burying my baby's father. I was a mess."

"But we've been talking for months," I say. "Was the plan to just surprise me one day? Hey, by the way, I had a baby?"

"Of course not. It's hard to explain," she says, looking away like she's searching for a way to explain. "At first, I was so overwhelmed. I couldn't even focus on the pregnancy at all. I didn't even tell Brinley until I started to show. At that point, you and I had been talking for a few months, and it felt weird to tell you. I didn't want to do it by email or on the phone. I'm sorry."

"You don't have to apologize," I say. "I guess I just don't get it. Why wouldn't you tell me?"

"Would you still be here if I had?" she asks quietly.

Shaking my head, I pull her into my arms. "I'd have been here sooner."

"You keep looking at me like I've got three heads," she says, sitting down beside me on her sofa with a warm mug of tea. I followed her home from the cemetery—that short drive producing about a million questions in my mind.

"You're pregnant, Lennon."

"I'm aware," she says, smiling at my stunned stupidity.

I want to know how this happened. I know *how* this happened, but Lennon was supposed to wait until marriage. Once Chase moved in, it was obvious that notion was out the window, but pregnant!

"Did Chase know?" I ask quietly. She places her mug down on the table, looking out a window, and she gives me a little nod. I inch closer to her, placing my hand on top of hers. Her head whips around, and she moves her hand out from under mine. "Talk to me,

Lennon," I say. "Because I feel like you've been holding a lot in for the past six months."

"I can't," she says, a little sob escaping. Gently, I encourage her head to my shoulder. She turns, burying her head in my neck, and her hand grabs my shirt, clinging to me.

At that moment, I know the month of leave I have isn't enough. In combat, those closest to the action are said to be "on the front line." As a helicopter pilot, it's not a position I've ever been in before, but it's where I need to be right now with Lennon. She needs me.

I can't be overseas. But I still have about six months left to fulfill my five-year commitment to the Corps. After that, I assumed I'd continue serving my country because being a Marine Corps helicopter pilot is my career. My entire career has been spent overseas, but now I need these next few months to be Stateside, preferably in Quantico. I need to be close to Lennon.

"It's my fault," Lennon cries softly. "It's all my fault."

Running my fingers through her hair, I whisper one thing I'm certain of. "Nothing is your fault."

"It is," she says, holding on tighter to me.

Wrapping both my arms around her, I say, "I'm not going anywhere. Use me as a human snot rag as long as you want."

She bursts out laughing. God, how I've missed that sound. She leans her head on the sofa, smiling over at me. Everything I feel for her comes bubbling to the surface—the friendship, the love, the attraction, the admiration. It's all still there. It never leaves me. I can push it down, try to ignore it, tell myself it's bad timing, but it never surrenders.

I love her. Her being pregnant with Chase's child hasn't changed how I feel one bit. How is that possible? I'm so screwed here.

That night at the lake, I had it so wrong. The thought of another man having her propelled me to do what I did. But I was wrong.

Love is not the thing we aspire to have; it is the thing we aspire to give.

And I need to give her all my love and support now.

"You said you're here for a month?" she asks. I nod, and she rubs her stomach, and I know what she's thinking. I won't be here when the baby's born. God, I have to get a transfer. I can't miss the birth of her baby. I need to be here for her. The thought of her giving birth alone makes my chest ache. That can't happen.

"I'm putting in for a transfer," I say. "To Quantico."

Her posture straightens. "Why didn't you tell me?"

"Just decided," I say.

"Duke, don't do that for me," she says.

"If not for you, then who?" I ask.

She inches away again. Clearly, her heart has shut down. I place my hand on top of hers again, and this time she leaves hers.

Military men and women spend a good amount of time standing sentry, on guard. You better be patient if you want a career in the military. Waiting is part of the job.

Maybe all that waiting has prepared me to wait for Lennon.

The moonlight peeks through the curtains of Lennon's house. She's asleep on her sofa, her feet resting on my lap. I don't remember the last time I slept, probably on the plane on the flight home.

Lennon and I talked until late at night, mostly about nothing. She wanted to hear about my life and fell asleep midstory. I guess military stories seem like lullabies compared to what her life has been like the past few months. I spent the rest of the night watching over her while she slept.

Her house has changed some, but it still feels like home to me. I wonder if that has to do with the walls themselves, the memories, or the woman who lives here. I look down at her belly. She's not huge yet. I never asked if she knew if she was having a boy or a girl. That's just one of many things we need to talk about.

We never talked about what happened between us that night. That was over a year ago now, and neither one of us has ever dared to broach the subject. At some point, we'll have to.

Looking around her place, I wonder if she's not sleeping well when I see a folded-up blanket and pillow on a nearby chair. Is she scared to live here alone because of what happened to Chase? What the hell did happen? I know she's not telling me the whole story. What happened after she left me that night at the lake? How did she get from there to here? Where is her engagement ring? Her finger was empty even at his funeral. So many questions and no fucking answers.

I see a stack of mail on her kitchen counter. There must be a lot to take care of when a person dies, loose ends to tie up. Did Chase leave her anything? Did she pay for his funeral? Fuck, more questions.

Leaning my head back, I look over at her peaceful face, so beautiful. My mind drifts back to her prom night all those years ago when she fell asleep in the hotel. I didn't sleep that night, either. It never occurred to her to ask me why I was awake when she'd been sleeping for hours. I'm not sure what I would've said if she had asked. Maybe the same answer that I have for not sleeping tonight—who can sleep with a beautiful woman lying next to you?

Grinning, I remember kissing her on prom night. That kiss had been years in the making. It was worth it. I'd wanted to kiss her for a long time but never wanted to risk the friendship. I wasn't ready for what I knew would be an intense love. But that night, I couldn't help myself. I had to know if her lips were as soft as they looked.

I look down at her full pink lips. They were softer than I ever imagined. I'm sure they still are.

Of course, I had to be an ass and hook up with my ex the next time I was in town. I knew what I was doing. I knew it would hurt Lennon, but she was getting ready to leave for college. I didn't want her not to go because of me, and neither one of us was ready for that kind of long-distance relationship. We were kids.

Still, she forgave me.

Has she forgiven me for our last kiss? I've never asked her.

If I had to do it all over again, I wouldn't have kissed her then, on her wedding day. I would've kissed her years before and never stopped. That was my mistake. My mistake was ever stopping kissing her. I should have always been kissing her, only her. I shouldn't have let that we were young stop me. I shouldn't have let the distance stop me. I shouldn't have let my fear stop me. Nothing should stop love. I know that now.

She lets out a breathless moan, and my eyes turn back to her. Two kisses. A lifetime of friendship. That's what we share.

My eyes roam to her belly, and I let my fingers lightly touch her little bump, and I say softly, "I can be your friend, too."

CHAPTER TWENTY-THREE

DUKE

Yawning, I stand in Lennon's kitchen. I need to get back on Virginia time. The best way to avoid jet lag is to put yourself on the time of the place where you are. Which means I need to wake the hell up. Besides, what good will I be to Lennon if I'm a zombie, and if there's anything that I'm sure of in this situation, it's that I need to be there for her.

It's not that I think she needs me. I know she doesn't. She's fully capable of handling most anything on her own. I just want to show her that she doesn't have to.

My cell phone dings in my pocket, and I pull it out, seeing it's my mom. Love my mom. She's the best. Smiling, I look down at her text, asking me if I need anything at the grocery store. That's code for— you were out all night, I worried sick, and you better text me back so I know you're alive.

I type a quick response, then shove my phone back into my pocket. "Booty call?" Lennon asks from behind me.

Turning around, I see her standing in the doorway, her hair wet from the shower. Suddenly, my whole body comes alive, and I'm no longer tired. "What?"

Giving me a coy smile, she says, "Was it a long war, soldier?"

"We aren't at war," I say, my voice hard with annoyance.

Does she really think I could confess my feelings for her and then just fall into bed with someone else? I'm not a stupid teenage kid anymore. It's been a really long time since I've been with a woman, too long—before that kiss on the beach, before the wedding invitation. It was on our birthday, the one when she told me about Chase, so well over a year ago.

"It was my mom."

She looks away from me, walking over to the refrigerator. The subject of my parents is not one she cares to talk about. "Guess you need to get home," she says quietly.

I reach for her hand, stopping her before she grabs some fruit. "Not before I make you breakfast," I say.

She squeezes my hand before letting go. "You didn't need to stay last night," she says, taking a seat at a little table in the kitchen.

Looking back over my shoulder at her, I say, "I wanted to." She glances up at me, and in that one look, I know she's happy I stayed. "Now, anything I should avoid food-wise? Morning sickness?"

"Not one time," she says proudly, rubbing her stomach. "This little girl loves everything."

This time, I turn fully around. "Girl?" Lennon nods, a tiny smile playing on her lips. Damn, she's beautiful. I turn back toward the counter. "So what do the girls want for breakfast?"

I start to hunt around for something to make, my eyes landing on a kitchen appliance that shouldn't be there. Lennon would have no use for it. She doesn't drink coffee.

She must notice my gaze because she gets to her feet, her fingers lightly touching the pot. "Chase loved coffee. It was his."

And just like that, our little playful moment is over. Grief has a way of doing that, popping up when you least expect it. It's like a little tap on your shoulder reminding you to be sad.

"I've been packing some of his stuff up," Lennon says, motioning to a few bags by the door. "I make myself do at least one thing a day. The first thing was his toothbrush. I cried for four hours. It's gotten easier since then, but I can't seem to get rid of his coffee pot."

She looks so lost, so sad. I hate that she's sad. I hate that I hurt her.

"Want me to brew a pot?" I ask. Her eyes dart to mine. "I've lost guys in the Corps," I say. "And the thing I've learned is that when something like that happens, our instinct is to try to forget, to block it all out, but really we need to remember. Forgetting only makes us feel worse. Remembering is how you feel better."

I reach for the coffee pot, shaking it a little, like I'm asking her a question. She looks at me, her brow furrowed like she can't believe I'm encouraging her to think about Chase. Frankly, I'm surprised myself, but I'll do anything for Lennon, anything to help try to make her feel better. Even if that means I have to set my own feelings for her aside.

"Brew it," she says.

The smell of coffee fills the air. Neither one of us has a cup, but the aroma surrounds us, lingering like the memories of the man who loved it.

Lennon takes a deep breath, a little smile playing on her perfect lips. Chase is still very much with us. He always will be now—in memory and with that baby girl.

Lennon's going to have a daughter—be a mom. It's surreal.

"Duke?"

I look into her blue eyes, realizing I've been staring at my plate, lost in my own thoughts. "Sorry, I was just thinking about your mom. How you'll raise your daughter in the same house you were raised in."

"Want to see her nursery?" Lennon asks, already on her feet with the biggest smile on her face.

I follow her to her old room, although I know the way. Before she opens the door, she looks back at me, like my opinion means the world to her.

"No one's seen it yet. Not even Brinley," Lennon says.

My heart misses a beat. Then she opens the door. I'm not sure what I was expecting—an explosion of pink, but it's not. It's mostly soft whites with just the slightest touches of pale pink, but it's the walls that have my attention—all painted a soothing white except for one.

"The lake," I say, my voice quiet, my eyes roaming over the serene backdrop for the white crib. Pale blues and grays capture the spot of our youth so perfectly. There's even a ripple in the water like the ones created by the skipping of a rock. This is the spot of our childhood, the spot where I kissed her, where I told her how I felt, where things fell apart.

"I knew I wanted to paint something," she says, "but I didn't know what. I just started throwing some paint on the wall one night, and in the morning, this is what was there."

I feel her studying my face. It's clear to me that she has no idea what she's done. The lake was our place, not hers and Chase's. At least, I can't imagine it shared the same significance for them.

"Is it not whimsical enough for a baby's room?" she asks. "I could just paint over it."

"I actually can't imagine anything more perfect," I say.

Smiling, she touches the mobile hanging over the crib, the plush numbers looking like they're floating in the air. "For Chase," she says quietly.

"I'm sure he'd love that."

"He was excited," she says, "about the baby."

I don't say a word, hoping she'll open up some more. When she doesn't, I place my hand on top of hers, resting on the edge of the crib. It occurs to me that her finger is still empty. "Your engagement ring?" I ask, and she jerks her hand away. "I'm wondering . . ." Her blue eyes bore through me, and I shut my mouth.

"He took it back after you kissed me at the lake. The necklace he gave me that matched it, too," she snaps, walking out of the baby's room. I guess she doesn't want to tarnish it with any bad vibes.

"I didn't know," I say. "I thought maybe with the baby, you and Chase would've . . ."

She stops in her tracks. "Don't you dare."

"What?"

"Don't you dare judge him," she says.

"I'm not," I say, reaching for her hand. "We never talked about what happened after the lake that night. There are months of your life that I know nothing about. I'm curious how you got from there to here."

"Not now," she says, casting her eyes away from mine. "I need to try to get some work done. It's been hard to concentrate, and I'm behind."

Lennon's always been good at putting walls up. With her start in life and the way she was bullied because of it, she had to be, but never with me. She was never like that with me before. "I understand. I've got some things to do myself."

Stubborn as the day is long, she just gives me a nod. I turn to leave, pausing at the front door, seeing the bags of Chase's clothes she has waiting there. Turning around, I see her still in the same spot. "I'll take these with me and drop them at the donation place on my way home."

She wipes a tear from her cheek and then smiles slightly. "Goodbye for now."

"Goodbye never," I say with a wink.

CHAPTER TWENTY-FOUR

DUKE

Pulling into my parents' driveway, I see my mom on her knees in the garden. No one has touched her garden but her since Iva died. She has mulch and soil delivered, but she does all the gardening herself. She won't even let my dad or me help her.

The truth is, she uses the time to talk to Iva. My dad and I have both overheard her telling Iva stories, keeping her updated and asking for advice. Even though they were from totally different backgrounds, and several years apart in age, they were inseparable. No person could take Iva's place in my mom's life. She was her best friend, and that spot is reserved forever.

I know the feeling. Lennon is my best friend. Always will be.

I see my mom get to her feet, walking toward my truck. Quickly, I pull out my phone and text Lennon that I'll be picking her up for dinner later and to wear something warm. Perhaps I should have asked her, but I'm in the military, where we are used to giving and taking orders.

Hopping out of my truck, I see my mom looking at the bags of clothes that I forgot to drop off for Lennon. "Some of Chase's things Lennon wanted me to get rid of."

"Why don't you let me take care of that?" She wraps her arms around my waist. "How is Lennon?"

It occurs to me that my parents have no idea that Lennon is pregnant. If they did, they would have told me, and I would've been more prepared at the cemetery. "She's pregnant." My mom steps back slightly like I just announced the baby's mine. "I don't have all the details. I know Chase knew before he died, but not much else."

"Iva," my mom whispers. Then she turns around at warp speed. "I have to see Lennon. I need to go to her. For Iva. I have to be there."

"Mom," I say, leading her over to the front steps. "Give it a few days. Lennon will still be pregnant."

"But . . ."

"She's not ready, Mom," I say, both of us taking a seat on the steps.

She places her arm around my shoulders, and we sit for a few minutes, neither one of us saying a word. Finally, my mom asks, "How are you, baby?"

Shaking my head, I look up at the clouds, the sky a bright blue. "The same." A grin comes to my face. "I feel the same."

My mom turns my face to hers. "You still love her? Want to be with her?"

"Maybe more," I whisper.

My mom releases a deep breath. "You need to be careful."

"I know."

"Are you going to listen this time?" she asks. "Because I told you the same thing before you went and blew up Lennon's wedding."

"I remember," I say, the memory like it was yesterday. "You did a good job of that yourself that night."

She playfully smacks my head. "Bad timing must run in the family."

Clasping my hands together in front of my face, I say, "I've never seen Lennon like this. She seems so lost, so alone."

"She lost someone she loved."

That stings like a motherfucker, and my mom knows it, patting my arm. "It's more than that. I was there when she lost her mom, and this is something else."

"This was sudden. She had a chance to say goodbye to Iva."

"I thought the same thing, but something Lennon said made me think there's more to it. She said it's her fault."

"He was shot and killed," my mom says. "It couldn't have been Lennon's fault."

"I know," I say, shaking my head.

"You look tired, baby," she says. "Why don't you go inside and rest?"

"Can't," I say, getting to my feet. "Need to talk to someone at Quantico."

"Why?" she asks, standing. "You're on leave."

"And when my leave is over, I need to be transferred home."

"Duke?"

"Mom, please don't try to talk me out of this."

Gently, she pushes my shoulder. "Talk you out of this. This is the best thing you could've said to me!"

I type General Hale into the search bar on my phone. It's time to call in that favor. He's not a hard man to find, now a four-star general. He's moved up in the world since our fateful flight. That might turn out to be good news for me. When you're asking for a favor, the more power, the better.

Maybe the universe is on my side with this one. After checking a few websites, it's only a matter of minutes before I discover he's not only powerful but he's also stationed in Virginia, at Quantico. This couldn't be more perfect. My heart quickens. This has to work. Quickly, I find a phone number and dial, asking to make an appointment.

The lady on the other end of the phone doesn't sound happy to be at work at all, her voice short and to the point. "He doesn't have anything for a month."

Shit! I'll be back in Japan by then.

"Wait," she says. "He could squeeze you in tomorrow."

Things are lining up. Someone up above is watching out for us. I bet it's not Chase.

Now I just have to hope that General Hale remembers me. But I'll worry about that tomorrow. I've got better things on my mind. Tonight, I'm seeing Lennon.

When I pull in front of Lennon's house, she's already outside waiting, wearing black leggings and a long-sleeve shirt that hugs her belly. Her brown hair is no longer tied up in ribbons but hangs loosely around her shoulders, and I can't help but smile.

She hops in my truck before I even have a chance to get her door for her. Seeing her sitting in the passenger seat feels like we're in high school all over again. I can't remember how many times I drove her home, her sitting next to me, talking and laughing day after day about the latest gossip at school. Like the teacher we were convinced watched porn in class because he was always watching something on his phone and sweating slightly. That was always good for a chuckle.

Back then, I didn't realize at those moments that I was falling in love with her, and she'd be the love of my life.

Now I know. And now I can't do anything about it but wait.

Looking over at Lennon, I'm amazed that her belly seems bigger than it did this morning. Could I really raise another man's child? Do I want to? Should I be thinking about that now? Probably not, but this is Lennon I'm talking about. If it was any other woman, maybe I'd hesitate, but I've hesitated enough with her. I love her. How could I not want to help her raise that baby?

"Hey," she says. "Where are we going?"

I nod my head toward a basket at her feet. "Picnic at the lake."

A smile blossoms on her face. "I haven't been to the lake in forever."

"Why? You love it there."

She looks over at me like I'm an idiot. "Chase didn't love the lake before. He wasn't much for the outdoors, and after what happened with you there, he hated it."

"He hated me, huh?" I ask.

"Pretty much."

"If I were him, I'd hate me, too," I say. "Is he why you never responded to any of my calls or emails?"

She looks out the window, watching the charming houses of Montclair roll by. Each one more picturesque and larger than the next. The gardens of flower beds are just beginning to bloom with the spring flowers. "I responded to one."

I glance over at her, but she won't look at me. "So I'm right. Chase asked you not to communicate with me? Because the silent treatment never felt like you."

"I read every one," she says softly. Her eyes turn to me. "I listened to every message."

I really wish I wasn't driving right now, so I could keep staring into her blue eyes. "I had no idea."

"Chase didn't know," she whispers, the guilt thick in her voice. "I was mad at you. So mad. But you were my best friend, and after a while, I missed you."

"I missed you, too," I say, parking the car in front of the lake.

"Chase made me promise not to talk to you," she says, rubbing her belly.

She broke that promise to wish me a *Happy Birthday*, and I'm sure his intentions were for her not to read my messages either. Our friendship was stronger than he thought.

"Back at the scene of the crime," I say, grinning at her.

She laughs. "It seems like so long ago."

That makes my heart ache. To her, our kiss is in the past, something to be forgotten. To me, our kiss is the future, the future I want. I want a lifetime of kissing her.

Still, I know she's been through hell. She's still in it. I have to manage my expectations here and keep our friendship at the forefront of my heart.

Hopping out of my truck to get her door, I take the picnic basket and lead her down to our favorite spot by the lake. It has the best view of the water and the trees. There's a slight breeze creating soft ripples across the water, making the reflection of the trees look like an impressionistic painting. Lennon was the one who taught me what that even is.

No one else is around, and I spread a blanket out on the ground, then remember her condition. "Maybe we should find a table instead."

"Hey, I'm not that big." She smacks my shoulder, then sits down on the ground with ease. "So what did you do today?"

"Hung out with Mom and Dad," I say, knowing I should probably try to start making some inroads there, but I have enough of my own shit to work out with Lennon. "Scheduled a meeting at Quantico tomorrow."

She opens up the picnic basket, pulling out a bag of chips. "Duke, I'm so happy you're home, but I can't help but feel like you're doing that for me."

"I am," I say. She looks up at me, her eyes shocked at my honesty, but I know she's not ready for the full truth. "Did you get some work done today?"

She releases a deep breath before tossing her bag of chips aside. "I'm blocked."

"What's the book about?" I ask.

She lies down on her side, her head resting in her hand. "It doesn't matter. I illustrate children's books. They are supposed to feel happy, bright, glass half full, but I can't seem to capture those feelings anymore. But if I don't come up with something soon, I'm going to lose this job, and I . . ."

Her mouth clamps shut like she was just about to expose trade secrets. "Lennon," I say, sitting up straighter. "Everything okay? Money-wise?"

"Funerals are expensive," she whispers so quietly I can barely hear her above the light breeze off the water.

"Didn't Chase leave you anything?"

"We weren't married," she says, cutting me off.

"You're carrying his child!" I bark louder than I should.

She leaps to her feet—impressively, I might add, for her current state. "He . . . I only just . . . We hadn't known that long when he died. I'm sure if given the chance, he would've made arrangements."

"He was a finance guy," I say. "I would've thought that would have been the first thing he did."

"When the baby is born, I can get a DNA test to show he's the father, and some of his assets can then go to the baby. It's not a huge amount. His retirement fund listed a charity as a benefactor, so there's nothing I can do about that. I sent his car back to the dealership." She looks over at me. "It's been a mess trying to figure it all out."

"Life insurance?" I ask.

"He didn't have any," she says. "So I paid for the funeral out of my own pocket. Like I said, any money I do eventually get will be put away for the baby, not me. I thought maybe I would start a college fund. It would be okay if I could just concentrate and get some work done, but it's been hard, and now I have more doctor's appointments and ultrasounds."

"How bad is it?" I ask.

"It will be fine," she says, starting to walk along the shore of the lake.

"Lennon," I say, grabbing her hand. "How bad?"

"I just need to finish this book," she says.

"Promise me you'll come to me if you need help," I say.

"Duke, I can't."

"Yes, you can," I say.

"You sure do like to save people," she teases.

"Trying to distract me isn't going to work," I say.

"Really, Duke, I'll be okay."

Bending down, I pick up a rock. "How about this? If you can skip this rock, then I'll drop the subject, but if it sinks, you promise me?"

Smiling and narrowing her eyes, she takes the rock from me. She examines it, putting it just so between her fingers, then she turns to the side, rears her arm back, and tosses it. It glides over the water, skipping not once, not twice, but three times before falling to the bottom of the lake.

"Holy hell," I say. "After twenty years, you chose now to finally do it."

She bursts out laughing. "How did I do that?"

"Fuck if I know," I laugh out.

"Oh," she says, grabbing her belly. "Baby girl must be laughing, too."

Grinning, she takes my hand, guiding it over to her stomach. I feel all these little movements like she's doing somersaults in there. "That's crazy."

A hard kick hits my hand, and I pull away. "Don't think she likes me."

Lennon smiles, placing my hand back. "She'll love you."

Our eyes meet, and for a fraction of a second, I wonder if she's talking about herself. I wonder if she's telling me she just needs time—that one day she'll love me.

"I hope so," I whisper.

CHAPTER TWENTY-FIVE

DUKE

"Thanks for the picnic," Lennon says, reaching for the door handle on my truck. We talked and ate, and I could have stayed that way all night, but we were forced to leave when the air got chilly.

She doesn't open the door, staring at her house as if ghosts await her. Her shoulders suddenly slumped with the weight of the reality of her life.

"What are you doing tomorrow?" I ask. "Want to take a drive to Quantico with me? You can't go on base with me, but there's a museum."

"Sure," she says, then draws a deep breath and asks, "Would you stay here tonight?"

I know she's not asking me to stay for any sexual reasons, and I also know how hard that was for her to ask. She's not one to ask for much. Even when she was being bullied in school, she never told me or asked me to intervene. She's strong like that.

Nodding, I wipe a tear from her cheek, wondering how many of those she's shed over the past few months, wishing I could've been there to wipe all those away, too. We walk to her front door, and my dick pulses against my jeans. I know she didn't ask me to stay for that reason, but it's been forever. She's so fucking beautiful, and being so close to her makes my mind drift to things it shouldn't.

I have to get control of myself. She's pregnant, for fuck's sake. She shouldn't render my dick hard as a rock. She's grieving, but that just makes me want to hold her.

Unlocking the door, we step inside, and she turns on a lamp, leaving the room mostly dim. She disappears into the bathroom for a minute, and I plop down on the sofa, willing my dick to stand down. My cock wants to take her to bed. My heart wants to tell her I love her. My head wants them both to shut the hell up.

"You okay?" Lennon asks, coming back into the den.

"Yeah."

She sits down, angling herself to me. "You want to talk about it, don't you? That night at the lake?"

I can't help it when my eyes go to her lips. "I'd like to know what happened after you left. Why did you call off the wedding? Surely, you told Chase it was my fault."

She rubs her lips together. "I went straight to see him and told him what happened."

Her eyes catch mine, both of us avoiding using the word "kiss" like saying it will make it happen.

"He was furious. He didn't understand why I'd be at the lake with you in the dark, so late, hours before I was supposed to marry him. He never came out and said it, but he thought I invited your attention."

"So he's the one who called off the wedding?"

She nods. "I was sure it was over. I spent what should have been our wedding day in tears, and he spent it at the jewelry store returning my ring and the necklace. But the next day, he called me and asked me to come to the airport. He wanted us to go on the honeymoon we had planned. I didn't know if he wanted to get married there or just wanted to try to work things out. Either way, I went."

"Did he suggest you elope?"

"No," she says, looking away. "The opposite. He admitted he rushed to marry me because of . . . because I wanted to wait until I was married."

My neck tenses. What a bastard! But I know I can't let my disgust show if I want Lennon to keep talking. When someone dies, there's this thing that happens where you turn that person into some sort of hero, only thinking of them in a positive way. Eventually, that fades, but right now, Lennon is very much in the hero worship phase of grief.

"He suggested that we take marriage off the table for a while, a year at least."

"Was it your idea or his that you live together?" I ask.

"His," she says.

"Did you feel like you could say no?" I ask. "Or did you think you'd lose him if you did?" Her eyes dart to mine, and I know I'm dangerously close to crossing a line. "I only ask because you were always so sure about not wanting to live with anyone until you married."

Tears start to roll down her face. "Chase would have respected my decision on those matters. I made my own choices."

"You were happy with him?" I ask, the very words burning my throat.

"I know you don't want to hear this, but he loved me, really loved me." She's sobbing so hard her chest heaves like all the air has left her body. We reach for each other at the same time, and she collapses into my chest. "He loved me more. My mom always said to find a man who loved you more, but all I can think about is how good he was to me and how much I did wrong."

"No," I whisper. "Chase didn't strike me as the type to settle. And any man would be happy, thrilled to call you his."

"But I lied to him," she says. "I read your messages. I sent that one email. The one thing he asked me to do was to stop contact with you, and I didn't even do that."

Obviously, Chase was jealous of what Lennon and I shared. That's why he did that. He was threatened by our friendship, and maybe he was right to be. Pulling back, I cup her face in my hands. "I'm sure you made him happy. I'm sure he felt loved."

"Loved enough?" she asks, my words from that night at the lake cutting through the bullshit like an arrow.

As I look into her eyes, there's so much I want to say, but I start with, "I'm sorry."

The corner of her mouth turns up just slightly. "I know. I listened to your messages, remember?"

My fists clench as frustration builds in every inch of my body. She has no idea what that night was about for me or how I felt.

She places her hands on top of mine, settling me. "I forgave you a long time ago," she says.

Intertwining our fingers, I lower my head to hers. "I wish I could make this all better for you."

"You make it so much better," she says softly.

I can feel her breath on my lips and smell her sweet scent. It would only take a second for my lips to be on hers. But I know in that same second, I'd ruin everything, and that breaks my heart.

"Will you stay the night?" she asks. "I slept so well with you here last night."

"How about I stay the next twenty-nine days?"

To my surprise, she doesn't resist. "I'd love that."

Lennon's house is two bedrooms—her bedroom and the nursery. She added on a home office a few years ago, but there's not even a sleeper sofa in there, so I'm stuck on the sofa in her den. Not sure why that didn't occur to me when I offered to stay here for the rest of my leave, but it didn't.

Throwing my arm over my head, I try to stretch out, but her sofa isn't that big. At this point, I'm sure I'm overtired. I haven't adjusted back to Virginia time, and this tiny contraption isn't helping matters.

My brain won't shut off. But I keep circling back to one thought.

If only I'd told her how I felt earlier.

If I would have told her how I felt the minute I realized how serious my feelings for her were, none of this would have happened. If I would've picked up the phone after that fateful flight with General Hale and told her I loved her instead of writing a stupid letter that I never intended to send, then she wouldn't be hurting right now.

She would have never gone out with Chase. She wouldn't be pregnant and alone. She wouldn't be in pain.

We'd be in love. I could make her happy. We'd probably be engaged or married by now. We'd spend countless hours making love. I'd have been her first. That's the way it should've been.

I don't regret my career choice or that it took me around the world, away from her. I do regret using it as an excuse. We could've been long distance. She maybe would've moved with me. Who knows? Either way, none of this would have happened.

The floor creaks slightly. I haven't stayed the night in this house since I was a kid, but that noise gets my attention. Maybe I've been a Marine too long. Our ears are trained to suspect the slightest noise as a threat.

I sit up, finding Lennon tiptoeing into the kitchen. She covers her mouth. "Sorry, I didn't mean to wake you."

"Wasn't sleeping," I say. "Why are you up? Everything okay?"

"Can't sleep," she says, grabbing a bottle of water. "Maybe you weren't the cure I thought you were."

"Or maybe you need to be closer," I say, putting a pillow on my lap and patting it. She hesitates for a second, but then I cock my head at her, and she walks over, placing her water bottle on the side table.

I expect her to place her feet in my lap like she did last night, but instead, she rests her head there. Her eyes close, and a little yawn escapes. Usually, I prefer to rev a woman up, but this is nice, too. Grabbing a blanket, I toss it over her, grinning at the fact that I'm once again her human pillow.

"Um," she moans. "You're always so warm."

I let my arm rest gently around her. "Try to sleep."

She turns her head slightly, looking up at me. "You can't be comfortable."

Moving her hair to the side, I encourage her back into position to relax. "I'm good."

"The nights are the hardest," she whispers. "At first, I thought it was because you get used to sharing a bed with someone, so I started trying to sleep out here, but that didn't work either. I just lie awake, replaying things. So many things have happened. Things I haven't said out loud to anyone. I know it's keeping me tied to this grief. And the grief keeps me tied to him. But I can't let him go."

A lump forms in my throat. "You can tell me anything."

"Maybe," she whispers. "Someday."

God, that sounds so far away, and I know she has to let him go if she's ever going to be happy, and I'm not just thinking about her happy with me. I mean for her to be happy ever again. I want that for her. When I think about that night on the lake, I remember how I wanted her more than anything to love me, to choose me.

If I had one wish now, it wouldn't be for her to love me. It would be for her to always be happy, even if that happiness didn't include me.

"We do this thing in the Corps," I say, "where we write letters to our loved ones, in case we don't make it back."

"I hate thinking about you in any kind of danger," she says.

"It's called a *goodbye letter*. Essentially, you write down all the things you need to say to the person. All the words that you hope will sustain them and see them through life without you. Maybe you should try writing Chase a goodbye letter? In the beginning, it can feel overwhelming to try to capture everything you feel on a sheet of paper, but somehow, writing it all down helps. Gets things out of your head, your heart, and out in the world."

"Even if no one is there to read it?" she asks in a whisper.

"No one's ever read my *goodbye letters*. Thankfully."

"Don't joke about something like that," she says, her body tensing in my arms.

"Don't worry. I'm not going anywhere."

CHAPTER TWENTY-SIX

DUKE

"Look at this," Lennon says, shaking me awake. "I woke up this morning, and this little guy was suddenly so clear to me. I mean, look at him!" Rubbing my eyes, I try to focus on the sketchpad she's holding. "He's cute, right? I've got the whole book outlined. This is just one page. I always draw them out on paper first, then work on the computer. What do you think?"

I'm sure I've only heard about half of what she said, but I focus my eyes. "An emu?"

"That's right!" she says. "I'm glad you didn't think he was an ostrich. Emus have three toes, see? Ostriches only have two."

"This is for the new book you're illustrating?"

"Yes," she says, her voice so excited. "You see why I've been stuck. What child's book has an emu as the main character? Anyway, I woke up this morning, and his little face was just in my head."

"That's great, Lennon," I say, taking a closer look.

"I have you to thank for it."

"Me?"

She holds it out again. "Anything look familiar? I gave him your eyes."

"You made me an emu!"

"Just the eyes. The same steel gray-blue color," she says. "You don't have bird legs." She cracks up laughing, and I reach for her, tickling her a little.

She squirms, giggling. "That's for making me a soft, fluffy bird."

"What did you want me to make you?" she asks, laughing loudly, still wriggling around in my arms. "A stud?"

"Uh-hum." Someone clears their throat loudly. I stop tickling Lennon, looking up, and find Brinley standing by the front door. "I rang the doorbell."

"We didn't hear it," Lennon says, straightening her hair and giving her friend a hug, but Brinley's eyes go to me, and I suspect I'm in trouble with her.

"I heard you squeal and got worried, so I used the key you gave me," Brinley says.

"Oh, I was just laughing at Duke the Emu," Lennon says, holding up her work to show Brinley.

Brinley laughs so loud she snorts. "It does look like him."

"The eyes only," I say, rolling mine.

Lennon places her sketchpad aside. "Everything okay? I didn't forget about some plans we had, did I?"

"No," Brinley says, eyeing me again, then reaching in her purse. "Just wanted to check on you before work and drop off the information on the Lamaze classes at the hospital."

Lennon waves her off. "I told you I'm having an epidural. That's not necessary."

"Hey, I'm all for the drugs," Brinley says. "But this could help you until you get to the hospital or . . ."

"I said no," Lennon says, her voice firm.

Brinley turns to me, shoving the Lamaze class information in my face. "Talk to her, please."

"Um . . ." I look at both women, both of them with their hands on their hips, standing their ground. Frankly, I think I'd prefer to be facing a national threat than these two. "Brinley has a point," I say to Lennon. "Remember how fast your mom delivered you." I don't toss in any more details. We all know that Lennon was born on the floor of a jail cell because she came so quick.

"No," Lennon says. "I'm going to get ready so we can get to Quantico."

She promptly leaves the room, and Brinley turns to me. "Quantico?"

"I'm trying to get transferred," I say. "What the hell was all that about? Who knew Lamaze was such a hot button topic?"

"It's not about Lamaze," Brinley says. "It's about not having a partner for Lamaze. I offered, but Lennon doesn't want to deal with it."

Exhaling, I look down at the information recommending that pregnant women start at around the sixth or seventh month. Lennon is there.

"Welcome home, by the way," Brinley says, giving me a small hug.

"Thanks."

"And congratulations."

"On what?"

"On getting Lennon to laugh," she says. "I haven't heard her laugh in so long."

I can't help but grin. "The way you looked at me, I thought you wanted to kick my ass."

"Just shock," she says. "But I will kick your ass if you ever hurt her again."

"Trying my best not to," I say, thinking that grief is similar to land mines. You try your best to tiptoe around them, but it's impossible to know where the triggers are. Eventually, you step on one, and it explodes, like this Lamaze thing.

"I've got to get to work," she says, then calls out, "Lennon, I'm leaving."

Lennon comes walking out, brush in hand. "Sorry if I was being bitchy, Brinley."

"You're my bitch," Brinley says, making Lennon smile. "Besides, I left it in Duke's hands now." She motions to the paperwork, raises an eyebrow, then saunters out the door, leaving me with a clear mission.

Before I can even open my mouth, Lennon holds her hands up. "Don't you start. I'm getting the epidural. I don't need to go to classes for that."

"What if I want to go to the classes?" I ask.

"What?" she asks quietly.

"Well, I plan on being here when she's born. Maybe I need the classes so I will know how to help you."

"That's really very sweet," she says.

"Then it's settled. We'll sign up today. We can start while I'm home on leave, then finish once I get transferred."

"We don't know if you'll get transferred," she says.

"Then we'll wait to sign up until we know for sure," I say with confidence.

"Duke?" She takes a deep breath, then sits down on the sofa. I take a seat beside her. "Those classes are for moms and dads. I don't want to explain to people that you aren't the father. That you're only there because her father is dead."

"I'm there because it's *you* having a baby."

"You are the last person Chase would want me doing this with," she says.

"I think you're wrong about that," I say. "He may have hated me when he was alive, but he wouldn't want you alone. He'd want you to have someone with you to hold your hand and cheer you on. He'd want that for you because he loved you."

"How do you know?"

"Because that's what I'd want if I were him," I whisper.

Our eyes meet, and it's the first time since I've been home that I think she realizes that my feelings for her go beyond friendship. Quickly, she breaks the contact, and just like that, it's over.

CHAPTER TWENTY-SEVEN

DUKE

Sitting outside General Hale's office is similar to when I sat outside the principal's office in high school after I bloodied that asshole's nose for flipping Lennon's skirt up in front of everyone. I knew I did the right thing but wasn't sure the principal would see it that way. It turns out, he didn't. I hope this time is different. I know I'm doing the right thing again, but I'm not sure General Hale will see it that way.

I glance at his name on the door. General Greggory Hale. Please remember the favor you owe me.

Military offices are similar to school offices in appearance as well as personnel. There's not much to look at. The décor is pretty bland. Everything is brown, even the one poor houseplant that's last brown leaves are hanging on by a thread. The secretary gives me a once-over with her eyes. I'm not sure if she wants to hurt me or fuck me, or hurt me while she's fucking me—not that I'm into that.

I've never dated anyone in the military, never screwed one of them either. I decided when I was still at Annapolis that was a bad idea. It's sort of like an office romance, but with a much bigger office. I didn't need or want those complications. My relationships with the opposite sex tend to be easy, short, and free from drama. But the current state of my heart is anything but uncomplicated.

The door flies open, and I stand, saluting the man before me. He looks older than I remember, but his kind eyes are just the same. "General Hale, sir."

"Lieutenant," he says with a hint of a grin. "Walk with me."

The secretary gives me another glance as we walk out the door, through the building, and out into the fresh Virginia air. The grass is spotted with green, trying to come back to life after the winter months. It's cut short. Most of the buildings are a plain brown brick, and some soldiers march in formation in an open grassy field, a common sight in most bases around the world. A base is designed to be its own community. It houses its own post office, doctors, dentists, schools, and most have housing for soldiers and their families. The commissary is our grocery store. A military base is a busy place even without all the men and women serving there.

General Hale takes a deep breath. "Been all over the world, and no air is better than home. Am I right?" he asks, looking at me. "You've been home a few days now, right?"

"Yes, sir, on both fronts," I say, keeping step with him while being careful not to pull ahead or look like I'm leading.

"Saved any more generals lately?" he asks with a smirk.

I joke, "That's classified."

"Guess I'll have to read about it."

"Actually, I'm relieved you remember me, sir."

"I don't owe my life to many lieutenants or owe them favors either," he says, glancing at me. "I'm assuming you're here because you need something."

"Yes, sir."

He turns to me slightly. "Speak freely, son."

"I want to be transferred here. I'd like to be assigned to the Marine Helicopter Squadron One. Immediately."

Marine Helicopter Squadron One, HMX-1 for short, is the name of the chopper pilots assigned to Quantico.

Marine chopper pilots are in high demand, but being assigned to the HMX-1 squadron takes extra steps. You have to have so many flight hours, apply, fill out more paperwork. Security is paramount because this is the squadron assigned to fly the president of the United States, among other high-ranking officials, including the vice president. So this is a big ask.

The military loves its traditions and its regulations. We start each workday with a bugle call. We end the workday with much the same and the playing of the national anthem. Taps is played in the late evening to signify the day's end. We have rules for eating, dress, for literally everything. And I'm breaking one.

Transfers are not handled like this.

Things like hardship assignments allow a soldier to be transferred because of family illness, but Lennon isn't technically my family. Accommodations are made for soldiers who are married to other soldiers. Hell, there's even an option for a switch assignment where if you find a soldier who holds the same position as you who wants to switch locations, you can do that. There isn't, however, a clause for a Marine Corps chopper pilot in love with his best friend, who is grieving and pregnant.

"I figure if anyone can make this happen, it's you, sir," I say.

He doesn't look at me. Instead, his head turns up to the American flag flying in the wind. "What does that mean?"

Shit, I don't think this is a good sign. I feel a lecture about duty coming on. "The stars are for the fifty states. The stripes represent..."

"No," he says, still admiring it. "To you. What does the flag mean to you, personally?"

I look up at Old Glory. It's been a long time since I thought about what it means to me and why I went to Annapolis in the first place. Our flag is one of the most recognizable symbols in the world. It means a lot of different things to a lot of people. Not all of them good, by the way.

I have a distinct feeling that I better get this right. "Hope," I say.

His eyes turn to me. "Most people say freedom."

"Certainly, freedom as well," I quickly say. "But hope implies a trust. Trust that when I'm under that flag, I am free, and we will get through whatever we face together. Trust that even when we fall short of liberty and justice, we still strive for that. Hope that tomorrow will be better than today. Above all else, to me, the flag represents hope."

"Hope that an old general will pull a few strings for you?" he asks, his face completely unreadable.

"Sir, I believe I can be an asset to HMX-1," I say.

"I'm not interested in the bullshit, soldier. I want the real reason."

Hopping out of the military Jeep, General Hale and I look up at the National Museum of the Marine Corps. It's clear he has no idea why I asked him here. He wanted the real reason for my transfer request, so I figured it was best to show him. The museum is a bizarre-looking silver building that looks like it's wearing a triangle hat, but the inside is amazing. I'm hoping Lennon enjoyed it.

As we walk toward the front, I see her standing outside. From a distance, she sees me, waves, and walks over.

"That's the reason," he says with disbelief.

"Look again," I say.

He strains his eyes a little bit. "Pregnant?"

"Yes, sir."

His posture softens. "I sympathize, son. I do. Missed the birth of two of mine."

I glance at Lennon getting close. "The baby's not mine." I can feel the questions before he even has time to ask them. "The baby's father is dead."

"In combat?"

"No, he wasn't in the military."

"A friend of yours, then?" he asks.

"No, pretty sure he hated me."

"I'm not following," he says.

"She's my best friend since we were little," I say. "She's pregnant and alone. Scared and grieving. She has no family. I can't let her do this alone, sir. I can't."

He takes one more look at me as Lennon joins us. I place my

hand on the small of her back, encouraging her to join me. Smiling, she extends her hand and bows at the same time, then she laughs. "I'm sorry. Am I supposed to bow or salute or . . .?"

General Hale's eyes light up. He's charmed by her already. Instead, he takes her hand, raising it slightly, and bows his head. "Single mothers are the ones who should be saluted." Lennon's hand goes to her belly, and she glances at me, surprised I shared her situation. "I'm sorry for your loss."

"Thank you," she says softly.

He glances back and forth between Lennon and me. "The letter?" he asks, and I immediately know which letter he's referring to—the first goodbye letter I ever wrote after saving his life. "Her?"

"Yes, sir."

He nods. "Seems I owe you a thanks," he says to Lennon.

Lennon looks at both of us. Her eyes are confused, but she's wearing a small smile on her face. "Why do I feel like the only one left out of some inside joke?" He simply winks at her, then takes his leave. "What was that all about?" Lennon asks.

"The day I saved his life, I wrote a letter to you," I say, leaving everything else out.

"You saved his life?" she asks. "You never told me that."

"It's not important," I say. "Unless it helps get me transferred."

"Oh, Lieutenant," General Hale calls back to me. "Consider the favor repaid. You'll be hearing from my office."

CHAPTER TWENTY-EIGHT

LENNON

I glance over at Duke from the passenger seat of his truck. I still can't believe he's here. After everything that happened, I never thought we'd be like this again—be friends again.

When he showed up at Chase's funeral, I can't even say I was surprised. He's always been there for me since we were little. He was my playmate, my partner in crime, the one I turned to, the one who always showed up for me. My heart knew he'd be there. That's the type of man he is.

He's transferring here, calling in favors, changing his career plans to be my friend, to be by my side while I give birth to Chase's baby. I know not many men would do that—best friend or not. I'm blessed to have him in my life—to have him back in my life. His absence was something I never stopped feeling, no matter how hard I tried.

He looks over at me, grinning. "Guess you need to sign up for Lamaze class now," he says.

My baby girl somersaults in my belly. Is she happy about that?

No matter what Duke says, I'm not convinced that Chase would be happy with my choice of birthing partner. Perhaps this is just one more thing I'll need to ask his forgiveness for. That list is getting pretty long.

But I don't want to do this alone. My mom did that. I know firsthand how hard that was for her. I think that's one reason I didn't tell Duke about the pregnancy. I didn't want to face the fact that I'd have to give birth alone, parent alone. I was so sad over Chase, and I just didn't have the strength to face one more thing. But Duke being here makes me feel stronger.

"I need to swing by my parents' house," Duke says.

"Why?"

"If I'm going to stay at your place, I need to pick up the rest of my stuff," he says, turning onto their street.

I've avoided driving anywhere near their house since the night of my rehearsal dinner. They tried to reach out to me, but between what they did and what Duke did, I couldn't hear it. Then Chase insisted I cut off all contact with Duke, and that included his parents as well. When Duke started writing to me after the funeral, I considered reaching out to them, but I didn't have the energy to deal with anything but my own guilt and grief. Grief is an energy thief. It zaps you from the ability to do the simplest things. Even showering feels like running a marathon when grief consumes you.

"Maybe you should take me home first," I say.

"I'll just be a minute," Duke says.

"Nothing with your mother is a minute," I say with a small smile.

"True," he says, pulling into the driveway. "But I'll be quick."

Duke hops out of his truck, and my eyes go to the garden. This may be Duke's home, but that's my mom's garden. I open the door, slowly stepping out. "The garden," I say. "So many memories of my mom out here."

I close my eyes, picturing my mom on her knees, hands in the dirt with a huge smile on her face. That's how I want to remember her, not the way she was at the end—frail and weak—but like how she was here—alive and happy. I want to remember how Duke and I used to play in the yard while she worked, and Mrs. Connie would watch us as she and my mom chatted. We spent so many hours of our childhood like that.

I locked so much of that away for Chase. I couldn't share those things with him. Every birthday was with Duke, so those memories were off-limits, along with countless others. I chose Chase, but I lost a part of myself doing that. But it all comes floating back—easy—like it never left me.

I hear the front door open and open my eyes. I know that Mrs. Connie sees her son, but it's me she's looking at. She hasn't seen me since Chase's funeral, and now she's seeing the little girl who used to wear ribbons in her hair and play in her yard—pregnant.

My hand finds my belly. Duke steps in front of me, breaking my connection to his mother. He's fully prepared to side with me, to protect me if I'm not ready, and to take the heat from his parents.

"You can wait in my truck if you want," he says.

I take a deep breath, reaching for his hand and giving it a little squeeze.

"I have your stuff ready, baby," his mom says, her voice sounding more unsure than I've ever heard it.

It's funny when you're a kid, you think grown-ups all have their act together, always know the right thing to do, then you grow up and realize everyone is just doing their best to figure life out. No one has the answers, not even moms.

"Thanks, Mom," Duke says, walking up to the porch. I follow him. Seeing Mrs. Connie is like having a piece of my mom right in front of me. It's hard not to grab it, but I don't, keeping a good distance back.

His mom opens the door, reaching inside and rolling out Duke's suitcase. He takes it from her, but then she reaches back inside and pulls out a simple white box. She steps around Duke, toward me, holding the box out to me. "For the baby."

I hesitate for a moment before taking it. "Thank you," I say softly, but then we both just stand there in silence. The hurt I felt at my rehearsal dinner has been replaced by a new pain—the pain of Chase's death, but I can't just forget what their lie cost me.

Duke joins us, gently taking the box from me and holding it out in front of me. "Why don't you open it?"

I glance at him, his eyes as strong as their steel color, then lift the lid from the box. Immediately, my eyes fill with tears, my hand softly caressing the fabric. Speechless! There are no words. I look at Mrs. Connie. This isn't just a gift. It's giving my baby a piece of her father.

"Duke came home the other day with all these old clothes that belonged to Chase. I remembered this lady who made quilts in town, mostly for graduation gifts, from old shirts. I called her, and she made this baby blanket."

I remove it from the box, holding it up. It's a patchwork of different colors and fabrics. As I hug it to my chest, my eyes well up even more.

"I told the lady not to wash the shirts. Maybe it will still smell like Chase," Mrs. Connie looks directly into my eyes, tears rolling off her face. "A child should have the right to know their father."

We all know she's not just referring to this baby but to me.

"When Duke told me you were pregnant, I just kept thinking about how sad and awful it is that your child will not know their father, and then I realized that I took that away from you. We made a mistake, Lennon. I swear to you in my heart we thought we were doing the right thing, but it wasn't right."

I drop the blanket back in the box, and Mrs. Connie takes me in her arms. My baby bump gets in the way, and we both laugh through our tears. "More of me to hug these days," I say.

Duke's mom strokes my hair. "I'm sorry. Charlie and I both are."

"Me, too," I say, wiping my face. "I should've remembered all the wonderful things you both did for my mom and me, instead of just focusing on that one thing. But then Duke pissed me off," I say, tossing him a look. "And I didn't know how to fix things."

"Maybe I can finally get your mother to stop haunting me," Mrs. Connie says. "I swear I haven't slept through the night since all that happened. I think Iva is messing with me from above."

"The garden looks nice," I say, clutching her hand. "It's like she's here."

She smiles, wrapping her arm around me. "Before she died, your mom and I had a lot of conversations. Talked about a lot of things."

"You mean you had your marching orders," I tease.

"Exactly. One of those conversations was about this moment," she says, tossing her son a look and lightly touching my belly. "I promised her Charlie and I would look after you and her grandbabies. I hope that's okay."

"Actually, I'd love it if you'd be this baby's grandparents," I say, hugging her again. "I never had grandparents, and since Chase didn't have any family either, I want my baby girl to have . . ."

"Girl?" She screams so loud I think we all now have some hearing loss. Then she smacks Duke on the shoulder. "You didn't tell me Lennon was having a girl. We must go shopping."

My smile is so huge my cheeks hurt. I think my smile and laugh muscles have atrophied over the past few months. Maybe it's time to get them back in shape.

"Lennon has the nursery done already," Duke says.

"Clothes then," his mom says, almost jumping up and down. "Where's my purse?"

"Now?" I ask.

"Unless you're tired?" his mom says, turning to Duke. "Quantico! Sorry. How was that?"

I can't help but laugh. Duke is now second fiddle to my unborn baby, and I'm sure that's totally fine with him. "You and Lennon go shopping. We'll talk later," he says.

"Okay, baby," his mom says, scurrying back into the house. "A baby girl."

I giggle. "Still crazy as ever."

Duke nods, placing his hands on my waist. "You're not too tired to go?"

I shake my head. "I feel so much lighter. Energy to spare."

Mrs. Connie emerges with her purse. "CeCe," she says. "That's what the baby should call me."

"CeCe?" Duke asks.

"Iva and I talked about it. We didn't want to be grandmothers. That sounds so old-fashioned. So we came up with names. Iva made me swear when the time came that I wouldn't let you name the baby after her. She hated her name almost as much as she hated the idea of being called Grandma. So I'm CeCe, and Iva wanted to be called Queenie."

CHAPTER TWENTY-NINE

DUKE

I hung around my parents' house after Lennon and my mom left to go shopping. I haven't seen my dad much and thought it would be a good time to catch up, but it's been hours now. How late do baby clothing stores stay open?

My mind is going a million miles an hour. Will I hear back from General Hale? How long will the transfer take? Today, I uprooted my entire life, my career. Usually, you have advanced notice before a base transfer—time to plan, to make arrangements, to say goodbye—but I'm bucking the system big time.

As far as assignments go, Japan has been a good one. I've met some great people there. It's beautiful. There are far worse places to be stationed. I have no idea how this transfer will affect my career or future promotions. Then I think of Lennon, and I really don't care about any of that.

"How much damage do you think your mother is doing on my card?" my dad asks, pulling me from my thoughts.

"Best not to look," I say.

My parents' house never seems to change. It's weird. It doesn't matter if they get new furniture, paint the walls, or get new flooring. It still feels the same. And my dad's chair is one thing that never changes. He's had it since I can remember. Apparently, it was the chair he used to hold me in and let me sleep on his shoulder. He still sits in it each night. It's an old brown recliner that also rocks. The leather is worn and aged, but it still sits proudly in their den.

He flicks off the television, turning to me. It must be serious because we usually talk with the game on, distracting from emotion, I guess. "Lennon forgive me, too?" he asks.

"I think you and mom are a pair. Joint forgiveness."

"But it was me who met him and turned him away."

"She's moved past it," I say. He nods. "Mom already crowned herself grandmother, gave herself a name. The whole bit."

He laughs. "She and Iva."

"You knew."

"Oh, yes." He laughs, a glint in his eye. "I, however, want to be Grandpa."

But I don't join in his laughter. It occurs to me that Lennon is Mommy. Chase is Daddy. My parents are CeCe and Grandpa. Even Lennon's mom has a special name. Who am I? Where do I fit into this baby's life? Lennon's life. Best friend. What is your best friend to your child?

"Son," my dad says, worry coming over his face, "everything all right?"

"Just wondering what my name will be."

"What do you want it to be?" he asks.

"I don't think I get to decide that," I say.

"You know, the moment your mother found out Lennon was pregnant, she felt attached to that baby." I look up at my father's wise eyes. "I did, too."

"Me, too."

"We all love her mother." I just nod, wanting more than anything to be able to say those words to Lennon. "So let me ask you again, who do you want to be to that baby?"

"Daddy," I whisper.

My old man smiles at me like he's known that all along, like he's known that longer than I have. "I have to tell you when Iva and your mom were having those conversations all those years ago, that's what they always thought. That you and Lennon would end up together."

"But we didn't."

"Not yet," my dad says.

"That one looks kind of big for a baby?" I say.

Lennon stands in front of the closet in the nursery, a sea of pink and white hanging inside. We've been hanging up her haul from her shopping trip with my mom for an hour. "That's because it's twenty-four months," Lennon says, placing it toward the end, hanging the outfits up according to size. "But it was on sale. So your mom said we had to get it."

With a small smile on my face, I nod. She holds up another outfit. This one is white with tiny pink flowers on it. Her head tilts, and I realize I've missed something. "Hmm?"

She lays it aside. "This is boring you, isn't it?"

"No," I say, glancing at the baby blanket my mom had made, now folded over the edge of the crib. "Just got some stuff on my mind."

"Like what?" she asks. "The transfer?"

"That's part of it."

"What's the other part?" she asks.

"Nothing," I say, getting to my feet and heading toward the door.

She grabs my hand, and my heart misses a beat or two. "You've been a good friend to me, Duke. The best," she says, and my heart sinks.

How is it that one little word can hurt so much? Friend is supposed to be a happy word, but in this case, it hurts like a bitch.

"But you seem to forget that I'm your friend, too." She motions between us. "I'm here for you, too, you know? Whatever you need."

"Whatever I need?" I inch closer, a tension filling the space. You can feel it in the air all around us, a heat, a desire, an aching want.

The skin on her cheeks turns pink, and she steps back. "Well, within reason."

Reason has nothing to do with it. There is absolutely nothing reasonable about me wanting her so badly. In fact, it's the opposite of reasonable. It's downright foolish. I thought by the time one was in their mid-twenties, they'd be done being a fool in love, but apparently not. Apparently, I saved all my stupidity for this situation.

"So what do you need?" she asks, a cute smile on her face.

"A bed," I say, raising an eyebrow at her.

"Whatever for?" she says back, her voice a little flirtier than before.

"Let's just say your couch isn't doing it for me."

"Hmm," she says. "I would've thought you were more of an anytime, anyplace, anywhere kind of man."

"Is that a challenge?" I ask, taking hold of her waist.

She playfully smacks my arm. "I was referring to sleeping."

Smirking, I say, "So was I."

Shaking her head, she glances around the room. "I don't think there's room for a bed in here, and I know there isn't in my office."

"It's fine, Lennon," I say. "I'm fine on the couch."

"No, it's not. If you're going to be here at least a month, then you can't be on the sofa that long. And once you get transferred, you'll definitely need . . ."

"Transferred. You want me to stay here when I'm transferred?" I ask. We hadn't discussed what we'd do at that point. I'm more than surprised that she's thought about it.

Her cheeks blush again. "I'm . . . I didn't . . . I mean, if you want to."

"Do you want me to?"

"Duke, that just came out. I'm sure you'll be ready to have your own space, privacy."

I tilt her chin up to look into her eyes. "Do you want me to live here once I get transferred back?"

"There's not even a bed for you," she says, turning her eyes away from mine.

"Do you want me here?" I ask again.

"I can't ask you to stay here."

"Lennon, do you want me to stay?"

"Don't you want to go out? Watch a game at the bar?" she asks, her voice growing quiet. "Or date?"

"You didn't answer my question," I say.

"You didn't answer mine," she says.

I bend down to look right into her blue eyes. "I'm happy here with you. I don't need anything else. Not a game or a bar or a date."

"Not even a bed?" she asks, a hint of a smile on her lips.

"Not even a bed," I say.

I've been reduced to jacking off in her shower. Flirting with Lennon is a bad game to play. The only thing I get out of it is a serious case of blue balls. And I'm not even sure she's flirting back.

I'm not going to feel bad that I used her shampoo to lube myself up either. The sweet smell of her surrounding me is a sad substitution for being buried in any other part of her. What the fuck am I doing?

Women have always been easy for me. Correction, every woman but Lennon has always been easy for me. My friendship with her is easy. My sexual attraction to her? Not so easy. The fact that I'm madly in love with her damn near drives me insane.

Stepping out of her shower, I run my fingers through my hair. It's only been a few days, but it already feels longer than the standard high and tight Marine Corps cut, which requires my hair be no more than three inches long anywhere on my head. The fact that I'm on leave doesn't mean I can ignore the rules. A Marine is a Marine no matter where he is, but as long as I'm not hanging around base or looking like something the cat dragged in, I can let it go a little bit.

Quickly, I dry off, slipping on a pair of sweatpants and throwing on a T-shirt, tucking my dog tags underneath. Between taking care of business in the shower and the past few days, I'm beat. Opening the door, I head toward the den but stop when I see Lennon's bedroom door open, her curled up on top of the covers in the middle of the bed. It seems like a good sign that she uses the full bed and doesn't regulate herself to one side, saving the other for a man who's not there.

Quietly, I step inside, taking care not to wake her. Christ, she's beautiful. And she's the type of woman who has no idea. She never has. Even in high school, she was a complete knockout. That's why the popular girls were always so mean to her. They were threatened. They just used the jail baby shit as their weapon. Most of the guys would've tripped over themselves to ask her out, but Lennon was quiet, shy, and that often comes off as unapproachable if you don't know better. Plus, I think they knew I'd kick their asses.

I reach for a blanket at the bottom of her bed, lightly covering her. Turning to leave, I spot something in her closet—my clothes. She's hung up my clothes in her closet. And they look like they belong there, like that's always been their home—next to hers.

I glance back over my shoulder at her sleeping and wonder if it was hard for her to place my clothes where Chase's used to hang. I turn back to the closet, wondering if I'm looking for meaning where there isn't any. If she simply didn't want me living out of a suitcase, and this was the only available spot.

I hear her whimper and turn around to see she's still asleep. Stepping closer, I see tears running down her cheeks, crying in her sleep. God, she can't even seem to find peace while she rests.

A famous Marine Corps quote is, "pain is weakness leaving the body." Of course, they like to use this when we are in physical pain from running long distances or doing a massive number of push-ups. But they're wrong. Pain isn't weakness. It is strength. Only strong people allow themselves to feel their pain. It's strong to work through it. Lennon has that strength. I know she does.

Leaning down, I wipe her cheek with my fingers. "Shh."

The tears only come faster.

"I'm here, Lennon. I'm here."

Her body jolts awake, her eyes flashing wide open. When her eyes find mine in the darkness, she starts crying harder, and I wonder if she was hoping to find someone else. Someone who won't ever be here again.

She looks around at the room, the blanket covering her, my face, like she's trying to make sense of her surroundings, her reality. "You were crying in your sleep," I say.

That makes the sobbing worse, and she reaches for me, pulling me beside her, clinging to my shirt. Wrapping my arms around her, I hold her as tight as I can. "Were you dreaming about him?" I ask in a whisper.

She answers by moving even closer to me. I feel her hand on my neck, the chain that holds my dog tags. Placing my hand over hers, I pull them out to show her. In the darkness, I watch her fingers run over them.

Most people probably don't know that dog tags are made with exactly three hundred and sixty-five beads. This is so if a soldier is taken prisoner, he or she can keep track of the days. It's also not common knowledge that a soldier also has a shorter tag with twenty-four beads to track hours. This shorter one is used as a toe tag in case of death. Scary, but fucking true.

If anything happened to me, this is how I would be identified, how they'd get my blood type and my name. This little tag is the difference in my body making it back or possibly getting the right medical treatment.

She clings to them, pulling them to her body like they are not just my lifeline but also hers.

CHAPTER THIRTY

DUKE

You know that feeling you get when you sleep in a new place for the first time? The confusion? The restlessness?

This is not that.

I slept so soundly that it was like I was home for the first time in a long time. Only this isn't my parents' house, and I'm not in my own bed. I'm in Lennon's.

I slept in this house many times as a child, so I assume part of my comfort is because of that, but I also know it's more, so much more. Stretching out my arms, I realize I'm alone. That's not a good sign. It had to make her uncomfortable to wake up next to me. I didn't mean to fall asleep here. She was crying. I was holding her, and the next thing I know, I'm waking up.

Awkward mornings-after are a real thing, and I'm sure I'm in for one this morning. And I don't even have the sex hangover to get me through. It's best to get this over with quickly, so I get up ready to face the music.

When I step into the hallway, the house is quiet, but the smell of coffee is unmistakable. She's thinking about Chase again. I wonder if there's a time when she's not thinking about him. Perhaps the better question is—is there a time when she's thinking about him, and it doesn't hurt like hell? I suppose that's the real goal.

Walking into the kitchen, I find her at the table, head down with crumpled-up pieces of paper all around her. Judging by the tension in her shoulders, she's not making her grocery list. More likely, she's taking my advice and trying to write a goodbye letter to Chase. And from the look of things, she's not having much luck.

She balls the paper up, gets up from her chair, and throws it in the trash can with as much force as one can throw a piece of paper. When she turns around, her eyes land on mine, but she simply attacks the rest of the balled-up papers on the table, gathering them up and giving them the same fate as the first, ending with a frustrated little grunt. Has she reached the angry stage of grief?

"I can't do it. I was never any good at writing," she says.

"You wrote to me for years," I say. "I always loved getting your letters and emails."

"Well, I can't write to Chase. I've never written him a letter before."

"Then maybe that was bad advice I gave you," I say. "Maybe you should draw your goodbye instead."

"Maybe," she says, trying to move past me, but I take her hand.

"What do you want to do today?"

Quickly, she releases my hand. "I need to work and go to the cemetery to see Chase."

"Want me to drive you?"

"No."

"Anything I can do around here to help you out?"

"No."

"Lennon, what's wrong?"

"Chase is dead!" she yells, throwing her hands up. "He's dead. What else is there? Does there need to be something else? Because I think that's enough."

"So this sudden anger doesn't have anything to do with the fact that you woke up with me in your bed this morning?"

She steps back from me, and I know I'm right. The guilt is written all over her face. "That can't happen again, Duke."

"Lennon, you were crying in your sleep."

"Then let me cry," she says. "Alone. When I suggested you needed a bed, I didn't mean mine."

"You reached for me, though."

"I know that!" she cries. "Don't you think I know that? How terrible am I? Chase is dead, and I'm . . . I'm . . ."

"Not dead," I say, trying to reach for her again, but she won't let me touch her. "You were sad and needed a friend. You didn't do anything wrong last night, Lennon."

"That's the problem," she says, glancing up at me from under her lashes. "It didn't feel wrong."

I will myself not to smile even though hearing her say that makes me so damn happy. "Chase has been gone for over six months. It's okay for you to let yourself feel better."

"I know that. I know Chase would want that."

"It's time," I say, gently rubbing her belly. "There's a lot to be happy about."

"I am."

"There's no timeframe on these things, but it has been several months. No one would think bad of you for having some fun or putting yourself back out there. Hell, other people would probably be dating again."

Her eyes flash to mine, like that's a totally foreign concept to her. "I'm pregnant."

"So."

"No man wants to date a pregnant woman."

"I wouldn't be so sure about that," I say, staring into her blue eyes.

She doesn't break the connection, but says, "I'm not ready."

"I know that," I whisper.

"It might be a while before I'm ready," she says.

Time to take a risk. "I'm not going anywhere."

She doesn't give me anything but a nod, then walks away.

My regular life on base is pretty much filled with testosterone. Yes, some women serve, but it's still mostly men. Back in Montclair, my life on leave is the total opposite. I've lost contact with most of my old buddies from high school. Aside from my dad, my life is filled with females—Lennon, her unborn baby girl, my mom, even Brinley.

If I compared the two, life in a male-dominated population is a hell of a lot easier than what I'm currently maneuvering. But if I'm being honest, I wouldn't trade Lennon's estrogen-filled house for the world. Which doesn't make what I have to tell her any easier.

The call from General Hale's office came in. It's not the news we were expecting.

To make matters worse, she's been avoiding me all day, visiting the cemetery and then locking herself away in her office. On the upside, it's given me some time to think.

Lightly, I knock on her office door, then poke my head in. She's sitting at her computer, hair up in a bun, pencil between her perfect lips. The passion and concentration on her face get my heart's attention, wanting her to be so focused on me, on us.

She glances at me, immediately removing the pencil from her mouth and sticking it in her hair. God, she's adorable. "It's getting kind of late. Dinner?" I ask. She reaches for a protein bar on her desk, holding it up. "That's a snack. Not dinner."

"Some people eat them for breakfast, and breakfast for dinner is a thing," she says.

Her logic makes sense in a Lennon sort of way. "You've got to be craving something."

"I don't get cravings," she says, her voice quiet.

"All pregnant women get cravings," I tease.

"Not me," she says firmer this time.

Stepping closer to her, I ask, "Chinese food?" I swear I can see her little girl jump in her belly. "Mandarin chicken?"

She smiles. "Spring rolls."

I grin. "You got it. I'll go pick it up."

"No," she cries, leaping off her chair. "Have it delivered."

"It will be faster if I go."

"Delivery," she says.

"I'm starving," I say. "I'll only be gone twenty minutes."

"Duke?"

"Twenty minutes," I say with a smile.

Pulling up to Lennon's house, I see her pacing back and forth on her sidewalk. She must really be starving. Grabbing the takeout sacks, I get out of my truck. "What are you doing out here?" I ask as she rushes to me. The look on her face is priceless. "Hungry?"

A relieved smile comes over her face, and she takes one of the bags from me, wrapping her other arm around my waist. "Guess so," she says. "Seemed like you were gone forever."

I pull out my phone to check. "Eighteen minutes," I say.

"Seemed longer," she says, placing her bag down on the coffee table in the den.

I laugh. "My bed not only is a sofa but now is the dining room chairs."

"About that," she says.

"Don't worry about it, Lennon."

"What if we get a sleeper sofa? We could go shopping for one together tomorrow."

She's really not ready. This is long term. I won't be back in her bed for a long while. I knew that, but hearing her say it out loud sucks. "I'm fine on this, really."

"But . . ."

"It won't be much longer," I say, thinking it's best to get this over with quick.

"You're not even a week into your leave," she says.

"General Hale's office called today," I say. "The transfer is going through."

"That's great," she says.

"There's a catch," I say, taking a deep breath. "I need to cut my leave short."

"How short?"

"Two weeks."

"That means you have to go back at the end of next week," she says, her whole body deflating.

"I'm sorry. I know this isn't what we had planned." She just shakes her head, the disappointment obvious, but she knows there's nothing I can do. "The positive side is I will have two weeks left when the baby comes, and I've been assured that I can have that time."

She moves closer to me. "Really?"

"Wouldn't want to be anywhere else," I say. "There's one more thing." Her gaze meets mine. "I'll have to go back to Japan first. Do some paperwork. Pack up the rest of my things."

"How long?" she asks.

"I'm hoping not more than two weeks."

She draws a deep breath, placing her hand on my knee. "Okay."

Resting my hand on top of hers, I say, "I hate having to leave."

She squeezes my hand, then pats her belly with her other hand. "We'll be okay."

"I've already talked to my parents. They will be here if you need anything. My mom will stay with you, or you can stay there. Whatever you need."

"Duke," she says with a small smile. "Try not to worry."

Impossible. Love comes with worry. To love someone is to worry about them. When someone tells you they worry about you, they might as well be saying I love you. Worry is code for love. Maybe I should try that on Lennon. Instead of telling her I love you, I should say I worry you. That would surely confuse the hell out of her.

"I was born to worry about you," I say with a grin.

"My OB says my pregnancy has been a doctor's dream. Textbook. No reason to think she'll tell me differently at my appointment next week," Lennon says.

"You'll see her before I leave then," I say. "I'm due to fly out Saturday."

"My appointment is Friday," Lennon says.

"Do you want me to go with you?" I ask, my voice with a cautious tone, knowing I'm stepping on Chase's territory whether or not he's here. She looks over at me, her blue eyes with a look that I don't recognize. I've known her my whole life, but this look is a first. "I mean, I don't have to be in the room when they do the exam or whatever. If that's weird." She cracks a smile. "Fuck, I swear I'm not some creepy pervert."

Playfully, she pretends to wipe my brow. "Breaking a sweat there, soldier. You can defend our nation's liberty, but a little old gyno has you sweating bullets."

Laughing, I say, "I just don't want you to be alone."

"I know you've seen me cry a lot, but that doesn't mean I'm going to break when you leave," she says.

"Let's not talk about me leaving," I say.

CHAPTER THIRTY-ONE

DUKE

The next few days pass without much fanfare. Unless you call falling deeper in love with each passing day fanfare. We are essentially living together. She's the first person I see in the morning and the last at night. We spend as much time together as life allows, knowing that life will soon force us apart again.

We don't talk about it. We both know it's coming, so there's no reason to linger on it. My goal is to see her happy, and talking about my departure will only bring more sadness.

I haven't slept in her bed again. If I hear her crying, I go in her room, sit on the floor, whisper that I'm there, and pat her hand until she settles. She's fallen asleep on the sofa with me more than once, and on those nights, she sleeps peacefully.

Most mornings, I wake up to find her surrounded by crumpled-up paper as she tries to write or draw her goodbye to Chase. The smell of coffee fills the house every morning. Brinley's been over several times. My parents have, too. We are going to do a crash course in Lamaze when I get back. Things are good, at least as good as can be expected. She seems more settled, stronger.

Lennon works. I try to make myself useful by doing things around her house, plus I work out and see my parents. I make sure she eats. She's on a deadline to get her current project done by the time she's thirty-six weeks pregnant. She's worried she'll deliver early and wants to be able to focus strictly on the baby for a month or two after birth.

Yawning, I sit up on the sofa. Maybe it's the military background, but sleeping on this sofa is actually not so bad. I've slept on worse, and knowing Lennon is not far away helps. Stumbling into the kitchen, I find Lennon in her usual spot, papers surrounding her, and the smell of coffee from Chase's old coffee pot in the air. I set the automatic timer on the pot and fill it every night, so it starts every morning when she's up. It seems to bring Lennon some comfort, so it's the least I can do.

"Any luck with the letter?"

"Not really. Goodbyes were always our thing." She looks up at me. "Goodbye for now."

"Goodbye never," I say with a grin. She forces a smile back, pushing her papers aside. "It might not feel like it, but you're making progress."

"How can you tell?" she asks.

"For one, you didn't cry yesterday," I say. "Never even saw your eyes tear up. Not once."

A swift breath leaves her chest like she's been kicked in the stomach, and her eyes find mine. Fuck, maybe I shouldn't have pointed that out. I might have just opened the floodgates. I sit down next to her, placing my hand on hers. "You're not forgetting him. You won't ever forget him," I say.

"But it hurts less to remember him," she says, her perfect pink lips turning up slightly. Her cell phone dings, and she looks down. "Don't be mad."

"What?"

"I might have suggested to your mom that she and your dad come over Friday night as a little farewell dinner for you." She gives me the cheesiest smile.

"I won't be gone that long. No need for a dinner."

"I also invited Brinley," she says.

"So this suggestion is more of a sure thing?" I ask.

"Pretty much carved in stone."

Groaning, I'd much rather spend my last night with just Lennon, but it looks like I've been outvoted. "I don't want you going to all that trouble," I say.

"It's just three people," she says. I'm not sure when she last had people over who weren't there to look in on her.

What's a man to do when an adorable woman is smiling at him. "Okay, but no cooking or cleaning. I'll pick up takeout."

"Delivery. You shouldn't have to do anything," she says with a certain determination in her voice.

"I'm not going to get out of this, am I?"

"Not a chance," she says.

"Okay, but today you have to do whatever I want."

She almost jumps out of her chair, reaching into a cabinet and pulling out a disposable cup. "We will, but first, I need you to come with me," she says, pouring some coffee in and placing the lid on top.

Grinning, I wonder what she's doing. Neither one of us has ever poured any coffee from that pot into a cup. It's understood that's Chase's coffee. "Where?"

"To see Chase."

She places the cup of coffee down on top of his headstone. It's the first time I've ever really looked at it. It's simple—his name, birth and death dates, and the infinity symbol.

Lennon catches me staring. "I couldn't figure out what to put as his epitaph, so I just put the symbol to say he'll live on." She places her hand on her belly. "Always be with me."

"That's beautiful."

"No one knew I was pregnant," she says, "so I couldn't put loving father. We weren't married, so loving husband wouldn't work. I still don't know if it's right."

I watch her stare down at it, the pain bubbling under the surface. She may not have shed a tear yesterday, but that doesn't mean they're all gone. They will never be gone. I hate that. I hate that she will always carry this pain, no matter how much time passes or how much the pain fades. She will never be rid of it. And surely, some of it will be passed to her daughter. I fucking hate that. Hate that I can't fix it, take it away, or carry it for her, for her child.

"You've never brought me here before," I say quietly. "Why today?"

"I need to ask you something," she says. "And I wanted to do it here, close to Chase. Because it concerns him. His child."

That little pronoun stings. It's hard to let go of the dream. The dream I had for Lennon and me. The one where she's not sad, and we're happy together. The child in her belly is mine.

"Let's hear it," I say.

She places her hand on his gravestone. "I told you how Chase didn't have his affairs in order. I don't blame him. Like I said, he didn't have time, or I know he would've taken care of our baby and me."

"Okay," I say, unsure where this is going.

"I don't want to make the same mistake," she says. "So I spoke to an attorney. The one who's helped me sort out all of Chase's affairs." Her blue eyes find mine, and I couldn't look away if I wanted to. It's like I'm held hostage in their color. "If anything happens to me, I want you to have custody of this baby. So the reason we are here, and what I need to know from you, is if you'll be her guardian."

My head shakes without me realizing it. I don't like what she's saying. Nothing can happen to her. I can't even think about it, but Chase's headstone is staring me right in the face. Things do happen. No, not to Lennon. Not before we've had our chance. Not now. Not ever.

"I have to know she'll be okay," Lennon says. "And I know you'd love her and make her a happy little girl."

"With you," I say. "I'll do that with you."

Her face softens, and she reaches for my hand. "I understand if you don't want to. I know I'm asking a lot. You can think about it."

"I don't need to think about it," I say. "I wouldn't have it any other way."

She throws her arms around my neck. "Thank you, Duke."

Lightly, I kiss the top of her head. "Nothing can happen to you."

She pulls back slightly, but we keep our arms around each other. "I'm leaving everything to you and her," she says. "The house, life insurance. Anything I have."

I nod and force a smile, knowing she needs me to hear this no matter how much I hate it.

"Brinley has my living will," she says.

"What?"

"She's a nurse. It makes sense."

"Lennon, I know you want to be prepared, but this is some morbid shit."

"That's the one thing I know you wouldn't be able to do."

"Damn right," I bark. "And I wouldn't let Brinley pull the plug on you, either."

"At ease, soldier," she says, resting her head on my chest, and just like that, my heart settles.

CHAPTER THIRTY-TWO

DUKE

This is a first. I've never been to an OB/GYN's office before. All the magazines suck. They are all about lactating and childcare. There are several guys here, so you'd think they'd have at least one sports magazine. And there's a television on that keeps replaying the same videos about newborn care, something about cradle cap, whatever that is.

I assume every other guy here is the biological father, not the best friend. Some of the women are here alone. Their babies' fathers are probably working, not dead. Lennon must feel like she's alone. Her circumstances are so different. This should be one of the happiest times in her life. Instead, her baby's father is dead, and she's planning for her baby's future without him.

It's been several days since she asked me to be the guardian of her baby. There wasn't a second that I thought about saying no. I'm not sure why she chose me exactly. Brinley would know more about raising a baby, a girl no less. Still, Lennon wants me involved in her daughter's life. That means something. She knows I'll love that little girl. I guess everything else can be figured out.

"Lennon Barlow," a nurse calls her name.

Lennon gets up, heading toward the exam rooms, and I follow her. She said she wanted me to come back with her. She wanted me to meet her doctor so that when she delivers, her doctor will be familiar with me.

We stop in the hallway by a scale outside the exam rooms. "Don't look." Lennon laughs, putting her hands on my shoulders and turning me around. "Some things are sacred."

The nurse smiles at me as Lennon steps up on the scale, having already removed her shoes and dropped her bag to the floor. I turn my head slightly, feigning a peek, but I know better than to actually look. Women take their weight very seriously. I'm not sure why. It's just a number. Sexy is sexy no matter what the scale says.

"No peeking," Lennon playfully scolds me, then tells the nurse. "Just hold up how many pounds I've gained on your fingers."

"What if it takes more than two hands?" I tease.

"Oh, my God," Lennon says, stepping down off the scale. "You did not just say that."

I bend down, holding out her shoes, and help her slip them on then grab her bag for her. We both fall in line behind the nurse leading us toward the exam room. "You know I think you look great," I whisper to Lennon.

"You do?" she asks.

"You've always been beautiful," I say. "Being pregnant only adds to that."

She smiles, but her eyes narrow like she can't make sense of something. "I don't think you've ever said that to me before."

"Sure I have."

"I don't think so," she says.

"Well, I've thought it many times," I say.

Why me thinking she's beautiful has her so confused, I'll never know. I think most men would agree with me on this, so I'm not sure why it's sparked a debate. Before she has time to respond, the nurse has her up on the table, checking her blood pressure and asking her questions. She already pissed in a cup, which was news to me. I had no idea that pregnant women have to pee in a cup for every doctor's appointment. That's a lot of piss.

The nurse excuses herself, leaving Lennon sitting up on the exam table and me sitting in a nearby chair. The room is small with no window. I hope the doctor's medical abilities are better than her interior design because the only decoration on the wall is a diagram of a woman's reproductive system. If that's what passes as "artwork" these days, then Lennon needs to give them a lesson or two.

"Just let me know if you want me to step outside," I say.

Lennon smiles. "They won't check me or anything today." I must look confused because she clarifies. "Won't check to see if I'm dilated. They won't do that for a few more weeks. And if you're going to coach me through this delivery, you better get used to it."

"Right," I say. I've never seen Lennon naked. Not even on accident. To think, the first time will be when she's giving birth. I know I won't be exactly seeing her naked then, but it still seems weird as fuck.

"You can change your mind," Lennon says.

"Why would you say that?"

"I just want you to know you can," she says with a shrug. "People change their minds all the time."

"Maybe their minds," I say, getting up and taking her hand. "But not their hearts. And my heart is with you. Always."

Her eyes fall to my lips, and we both start to lean toward each other. I've only kissed her twice in my life, but I know her signs and her body language. An OB/GYN's office might be the oddest place to have our next kiss, but I don't give a damn. I feel her breath lightly on my lips, drawing me closer.

The jingling of the doorknob forces us apart, and a young female doctor walks in. "Lennon," she says with a bright smile, but her eyes go to me. She's probably curious who in the hell I am since Lennon's never had a man at her appointments before. Lennon told me her doctor knows about Chase and has been great with her, but I wonder if she prepped her about me.

"Dr. Ashley," Lennon says, motioning to me. "This is Duke. He's agreed to be my . . ." She looks over at me. "Well, my birthing friend," she says with a giggle. "We've been best friends since we were kids, so best birth friend sounds about right."

What the hell? Two seconds ago, her lips were almost on mine. Now she's given me some silly friend nickname.

"Well, best birth friend," Dr. Ashley says to me with a smile, "it's nice to meet you."

"You, too," I say.

"Duke's got to travel back to Japan tomorrow," Lennon says. "So he wanted to come today."

"Japan?" the doctor asks.

"Marines," I say.

The good doctor's eyes turn to me, and she smiles. "Thank you for your service."

I give a little nod of my head. It's always nice to be thanked for my service to my country, but it's not something I expect from people. Honestly, other professions deserve just as much thanks—like teachers.

Lennon clears her throat. "He wanted to make sure the baby and me are good before he leaves."

"That's very sweet," the doctor says, her skin turning a little pink. "You must have a very understanding wife? Girlfriend?"

I shake my head, placing my hand on top of Lennon's. "Nope, just a best birthing friend." It comes out more annoyed than I mean it to, but I hope Lennon gets the message.

Lennon's blue eyes lock on mine, and we stare at each other in some unknown contest, but if she's waiting for me to blink, to change my mind about her, then she's going to lose. I meant what I said. There's no changing my heart. It belongs to her.

"Let's have a listen to the heartbeat," Dr. Ashley says, breaking the tension.

Lennon leans back, and the doctor lifts up her shirt, exposing the smooth skin of her belly, her belly button now nonexistent because it's flush with the rest of her skin. I've seen her pregnant belly under her clothes, but not like this. It doesn't look like she's got any more room in there, but she still has almost two months to go.

The doctor places some slimy stuff on her stomach, then holds a wand-looking thing to her skin. A loud airy sound fills the room.

Swoosh.

Swoosh.

I look down at Lennon. "That's your baby girl?" I ask, and she nods with a huge grin on her face. "Wow."

The doctor listens for a minute or so, telling us everything sounds perfect. Then the doctor removes the wand, the heartbeat suddenly gone, but I continue to stare down at Lennon as they talk. It's not like I have much to offer to the conversation, tuning out once the talk turns to episiotomies. In no universe do I want to think about someone with a knife near that area.

And honestly, I'm too amazed to say much, anyway. Yeah, I know there's a baby in there, but to hear her heartbeat coming from Lennon's body is mind-blowing. Maybe if I'd known about the pregnancy from the beginning, I wouldn't be so shocked, but right now, I'm at a loss for words. For the first time, it really hits me. There's a little life in there.

Without any thought, my hand goes to Lennon's belly, her shirt now back in place. Gently, my fingers glide over her bump. I wonder if the baby can feel that, if she knows I'm here. Does she know my voice? Suddenly, I want to go back to Japan even less than I did before. It's not just Lennon who's going to miss me. That little baby isn't going to understand where I've gone and why my voice has disappeared.

Dr. Ashley shakes Lennon's hand, then reaches into her pocket, handing me her business card. "Lennon already has my number, but here it is again, just in case. The best birth friend should have it, too."

With a small smile, she tells me to have safe travels back to Japan, then heads out the door. I reach to grab Lennon's bag for her when she not so playfully smacks my shoulder. "Flirting with my OB/GYN, seriously?"

"What?" I ask, rubbing my arm.

"You were totally flirting with her."

I look at the door, replaying the last few minutes. "No, I wasn't," I say. I was flirting with Lennon. Was my aim off?

"Come on," she says. "Telling her that you're single. Getting her number."

"Umm, she asked about a wife or girlfriend. She gave me her card. I didn't ask or volunteer any of that." Lennon's perfect little nose wrinkles up, making me wonder. "Jealous?" I ask, opening up the door for her, but before she can come back with some sassy little comment, I grin at her and say, "Because you don't need to be."

CHAPTER THIRTY-THREE

DUKE

"Everything set?" I whisper to Brinley as she walks by me after finishing up dinner. She smiles and nods, and my mother gives me the same.

We've planned a little something for when I'm back overseas. Something that I hope will make Lennon happy and make the time pass quickly. The best part is that Lennon has no idea. I wish I could be here to see her face when she finds out, but I'm sure I'll hear all about it and be blamed for it.

We got food delivered for tonight's farewell dinner, so there wasn't much to do to clean up, and now everyone is getting ready to leave. It was a good night. Lennon's smile and laughter filled the house. She seems more like her old self with each passing day. I'm not sure what she was like those months she didn't talk to my parents or me, but I can't imagine it was like this. This part of her was missing. I wonder if she felt that.

Brinley and Lennon hug goodbye. Then both my parents hug Lennon and me. My mom steps outside, but my dad's eyes catch mine, and I know he wants a second. "I'm going to walk them out," I say to Lennon before stepping out into the night. My dad takes out the car remote and pushes the button for the door to unlock, then he motions to my mom that he'll be there in a minute.

With my mom out of earshot, he says, "You and Lennon both look happy."

"She seems to be feeling better," I say.

He places his hand on my shoulder, his eyes catching mine, a certain pride beaming from them. "Not every man would take on a single pregnant mom-to-be," he says. "I'm proud of you."

No matter how old I get, it still feels good to hear that from my dad. "Thanks."

"I know it can't be easy," he says.

He's right. It's not easy to put aside what I want, what I feel, but Lennon comes before all that. I know that now. I was selfish with her once before, at the lake, and I won't do that again.

"I imagine it's going to be very difficult for you to get on that plane tomorrow," he says.

I don't want to think that in less than a day, he and my mom will be picking me up and dropping me off for my flight. We'll be over six thousand miles apart again.

"Before you go, make sure she knows how much you'll miss her," he says.

I nod, swallowing around the lump in my throat, unsure how to actually go about that. "Watch out for her while I'm gone," I say.

"We will," he says, giving me one more pat on the shoulder before leaving.

I stay outside, watching them drive away before I turn back for the house. When I open the front door, I find Lennon with her shoes on and a light jacket in her hand. "Going somewhere?" I ask.

"Remember what we did the first time we had to say goodbye?" she asks. "Before you went off to school?"

"We stayed out all night, and your mom grounded you."

"Too old to be grounded," she says. "Let's go to the lake. Just like we did that night. Watch the sun come up."

"As nice as that sounds," I say. "You are very pregnant, and I doubt staying up all night and sitting on the hard ground is what the doctor ordered."

She looks down at her current state. "Good point. How about we stay up all night, sitting on the sofa, and watch the sunrise from the yard?"

"Perfect," I say.

She tosses down her jacket, flips off her shoes, and we collapse down on the sofa. I place my arm on the back, and she leans into me, snuggling closer. Leaning my head down, I take in her sweet smell. Her hair had the same scent that night when I leaned over to steal her hair ribbon. In some ways, that night at the lake seems like a lifetime ago. But I still remember it so vividly.

"Thanks for tonight."

"Sure," she says, turning her head a little like she's adjusting her pillow, only it's my shoulder.

"I'm gonna miss this," I say softly.

"Me, too," she whispers, pulling my arm around her like a blanket.

Smiling down at her, I place my other hand on her belly. "I wasn't expecting you when I came back home a few weeks ago," I say. "But I'm gonna miss you, too." I swear I feel a little kick, but Lennon doesn't move, so maybe I'm wrong. I let my hand gently rub her stomach. "Lennon?"

"Hmm," she moans quietly.

All the things I need to say run through my head. I want to make sure she doesn't sink back into a dark place while I'm gone. I want to make sure she eats, takes care of herself, and doesn't overdo it. I want her to know she has people who will help her and support her.

But mostly, I want her to know how I feel. Not even that. I want her to know how much I feel for her. I want her to not only know that I love her but also how much I love her.

How much?

So much.

I glance down at her, half asleep in my arms, and release a deep breath.

"My heart will wait," I whisper, gently kissing the top of her head.

My parents honk the horn for the second time. We need to go. My stuff is already in their car. It's not much. Something inside me figures the less I take, the quicker I'll be back. Lennon and I are standing inside her house, behind the closed front door, both knowing the world waits on the other side.

"Got everything?" she asks.

Not even close. I'm leaving the most important things behind. She and her baby.

Love doesn't know how to say goodbye.

Our eyes meet, neither one of us ready for this moment. "I have something for you," she says, reaching into a drawer. "I think it's better than the hair ribbon," she teases with a smile, then hands me the little square piece of paper. I look down at the black and white photo. "That's her last ultrasound picture."

Looking down at it, I feel my throat closing up. This means something. Something important. I wonder if Lennon realizes that.

"We'll both be waiting for you," Lennon says softly.

I take hold of her waist. "Don't have that baby until I get back."

"I won't," she says, reminding me she still has weeks to go.

All I want to do is kiss her—slow and deep. Kiss her like she's never been kissed. Kiss her so thoroughly it makes up for all the kissing we've missed.

But I don't want to kiss her and run out the door. Instead, I bend over, planting a little kiss on her belly before turning to leave.

CHAPTER THIRTY-FOUR

DUKE

The life of a bachelor, especially a military bachelor, is comparable to that of a nomad. I don't have much stuff. And the stuff I do have isn't worth shipping all the way back over to the United States, especially considering it's on my dime to ship it. Normally, the Corps would take care of those expenses, but since this transfer was at my request, I'm not getting those perks.

I'm not sure if it's because I didn't follow proper channels or if perhaps I've pissed off someone somewhere along the way, but this transfer is not easy. There seems to be piles of paperwork, endless amounts of grunt work, and nonstop red tape to cut through.

When I glance at the clock, it's nearly eleven at night here, which puts it about nine in the morning for Lennon, but this is how we have to talk, so I'm happy to lose a little sleep. My phone rests next to me in bed. I look over at the ultrasound picture on my nightstand. I might not be able to see Lennon first thing in the morning or last at night, but I can look at that little black and white picture, and something about that brings me so much joy. It doesn't make sense, but I guess love often doesn't.

My cell phone rings right on time. "I can't believe you did this!" Lennon cries.

I organized a little surprise for her before I left, and last night she was let in on it. "You like it? It's nice? I only saw pictures online."

"It's amazing," she says, describing the spa to me. I arranged for her, Brinley, and my mom to go away for a long weekend to a spa that has all these special massages and treatments for pregnant women. Obviously, they have stuff for Brinley and my mom, too. "Thank you so much. This must have cost a fortune."

"Don't worry about it," I say. "I wanted to do something nice for you while I was away, and Brinley didn't think you'd want a baby shower. You have everything anyway, so I came up with this instead."

"You are an amazing man, Charles Duke III." She giggles.

"And you are going to be an amazing mom," I say.

"When are you coming home?" she asks, her voice so excited and happy at the thought.

"Should be next week. I'm counting the days," I say, stretching out on my bed. Most of my place has already been cleared out or packed up. Only the everyday essentials are still here—the things I'll pack at the last minute.

"Wish I could talk longer," she says. "But there's this whole spa day planned with lunch and everything."

"We'll have plenty of time to talk when I get back."

"Good," she says, but her voice doesn't sound confident.

"Everything okay?"

"I've been doing a lot of thinking since you left, and there's some stuff we need to talk about."

"Like?"

"Like you living here permanently," she says softly.

"I thought that was settled?" I ask, sitting up.

"Look, I have to go. Let's talk when you get back."

And just like that, she's gone.

CHAPTER THIRTY-FIVE

LENNON

"Do you want a mirror when you give birth?" Brinley asks. "The hospital provides them on request."

"I don't plan on doing my hair and makeup to greet my child," I say.

"You'd be surprised how many women do that," Brinley says. "They want to look good in the pictures. But I wasn't talking about a mirror for that. I'm talking about a mirror for the end of the bed so you can watch the baby come out."

"Hard pass," I say. Brinley was nice enough to give me a little tour of the maternity ward at the hospital. She walked me through all the preregistration paperwork. That way, when I go into labor, I just have to show up and give them my name. Which seems like a good idea because asking for a copy of my insurance card mid-contraction probably isn't the most opportune time.

Hospitals aren't anyone's favorite place. Especially if you've had a loved one battle a terrible disease like I have, but this floor of the hospital is a happy one for the most part. The nurses are smiling, wearing their pink scrubs as they go from room to room. I don't hear any women screaming, so that's a good sign. The hallways are wide and painted in a soothing cream.

"You will labor in one room," Brinley says, opening a door. "Then be moved to another after you give birth."

The labor room is nice looking. All the equipment is hidden away in wooden cabinets. There's a nice big window and a television. Lightly, I place my hands on my ever-growing belly. This might be the room where I meet my baby for the first time.

"Since you're getting an epidural, you'll be in bed. Won't be able to walk around or anything."

I nod. The reality of motherhood is staring me right in the face. That's the way this pregnancy has been. There are these moments when it sort of smacks you in the face. I'm a mom. I'm going to do this. There's no turning back.

"You okay?" Brinley asks. I nod. "What time does Duke get back? Today? Tomorrow?"

"Mmm, his flight is delayed. So I'm not sure. Soon."

"Good," Brinley says. "How are things there?"

I sit down on the bed for a moment. "What do you mean?"

"I mean, he's living with you. Plans to help you with the baby."

"He's my friend," I say.

"I'm your friend too," she says. "And I haven't moved in. I mean, I will if you want." I smile. "You sure he's only your friend?" Brinley asks.

"Yes. Duke wants to help me."

Brinley holds up her hand. "I'm sure he does. But is that all he wants?"

My mouth opens slightly, but no words come out.

"He's offering to help raise another man's baby. A lot of men wouldn't do that. Unless . . ."

"Unless what?" I ask.

"Unless they love the baby's mother."

My head shakes. "Duke doesn't think about me like that."

"Sorry," she says. "I'm supposed to be giving you a tour of the hospital, not playing matchmaker." She ushers me out of the labor and delivery room. "Let me show you where you'll spend most of your time." We walk down a hallway, through some double doors, and Brinley waves at a nurse behind a desk. She nods her approval, and Brinley leads me into a different room.

This room has a lot less equipment. It's basically a bed and a small sofa. There's a bathroom, a television, and one lone chair.

"Make sure you bring your own pillow," Brinley says. "Hospital pillows suck."

Waving at Brinley over my shoulder, I open the front door to my house. After dropping my purse by the door, I collapse on the sofa, rubbing my stomach.

Hospital pillows. I can't forget to pack my own pillows. That's just one more thing to remember. As if I don't have enough on my plate. I need to finish the book I'm currently working on. Remember to pack pillows, push this baby out, then provide for her and raise her without her father.

Chase.

He would've loved today. He loved having a plan. If he were here, he probably would have alternate routes to the hospital planned out. I look down at my belly. Sometimes, I don't recognize myself. My boobs alone sometimes send me into a double-take. I'm not flat-chested anymore. Not only is my body completely different but my life is nothing like I planned.

Never in a million years did I think I'd end up pregnant and unmarried. If Chase were alive, would we be married? I think he would've asked me again. I believe he would've wanted us married when our baby was born.

He took my ring back. I wonder if he would've bought me the same one—the one with the infinity symbol or if he would've thought that bad luck. Maybe I'm wrong. Maybe he wouldn't have asked me again. I won't ever know for sure.

How did my life get turned so upside down?

Guilt settles into my body, and my stomach tightens. I've made so many mistakes. There are so many things I'd do differently. I hope Chase knows that. I hope he understands what I'm doing now.

Duke.

Brinley suggested today that there's more to my relationship with

Duke. That's nothing new. I feel like people always make assumptions when your best friend is the opposite sex. No one understands the friendship that Duke and I share or how deep it goes.

Sure, there was a time I thought we'd be together. Those were the dreams of a love-sick teenage girl. When my mom got sick, I realized Duke was more to me than my crush. He became my rock. He probably always was. That was more important than my crush. And now, he's my rock again.

It's not about sex.

But it is about love. A love between friends. A love that only Duke and I understand. At least, I think we understand.

CHAPTER THIRTY-SIX

DUKE

A couple of bags in hand, I sit in the back of the taxi. My flight from Japan was delayed, then delayed again. I spent the night in an airport when another flight was canceled.

It was a fucking nightmare, so rather than bother anyone to give me a ride, I decided to take a cab to Lennon's house, texting everyone to let them know I'd be arriving soon.

Honestly, my mood is shit. It's been shit since she told me she wanted to have a conversation about me living with her.

Since then, we've talked every day, but both of us have avoided anything heavy, not wanting to do that over the phone. I used that same excuse for years. I'd tell Lennon how I felt when I was home, when I got transferred back, when we could actually be together, and not over the phone or video chat.

Looking back, that was a big-ass mistake. I hope it's not this time.

We turn onto Lennon's street, and I see my dad parked in front of her house. He's leaned up against his car, and even from a distance, I can see he's in dad mode. Something's wrong. I can feel it. I hand the cabbie a wad of bills, grab my bags, and hop out.

My dad turns to me, looking exhausted. Neither one of us bothers with the usual hugs, welcome homes, or any of that. "What happened?" I ask, my heart beating faster and harder than normal.

"Lennon's fine," he says. "She's inside resting. Your mother is with her."

I don't wait for any more explanation before I bolt inside the house, my dad following me. Lennon's on the sofa, her feet up, with a huge glass of water in her hand. My mom is seated in a chair beside the sofa but gets up when she sees me. "Kept my promise. I didn't have the baby," Lennon says with a big smile, placing her water on the table.

Dropping my bags to the floor, I rush to her, taking her hand. "What happened?"

"I'm stupid," Lennon says. "Scared your parents half to death."

"Lennon called us early this morning," my dad says.

"She thought she was going into early labor," my mom says.

"Jesus Christ," I say, looking down at her.

"I waited for you," Lennon says, smiling up at me.

My dad laughs. "That's all she kept saying. The whole way to the hospital. 'I promised Duke I wouldn't have the baby without him. He's going to kill me.'"

"But you're fine?" I ask.

"Braxton Hicks," my mom says.

"What the hell is that?" I ask.

My mom says, "I got them all the time with you. They're sort of like practice contractions for the real thing."

"I feel so silly," Lennon says. "I woke up. My stomach was so tight, like a hard knot, and I freaked out."

"But this is normal?"

"Completely," my mom says. "The doctor thought maybe Lennon has been overdoing it. She was a little dehydrated, but she and the baby are perfectly healthy."

"Your mom and dad stayed just to be sure," Lennon says. "But I feel totally fine now."

"Thank you," I say to my parents, getting up and hugging them both, my heart rate starting to normalize.

My mom runs her hands through my hair. "You must be exhausted. We can stay if you want to rest or take a shower."

"We should let him and Lennon catch up," my dad says, winking at me.

"I'm due at Quantico the day after tomorrow," I say. "But I

promise to see you guys before I start."

They both kiss Lennon goodbye, then hug me again and head out. I return to Lennon, kneeling beside her. "Must you shock the shit out of me every time I come back home?" I ask.

Smiling, she shrugs. "I think it's my right as a woman."

"I don't know what I'd do if anything happened to you."

"Hey," she says, taking my hands and placing them on her belly. "We're both fine."

"Sorry," I say, shaking my head. "It's been a long few days. I saw my dad outside and thought the worst."

"Your mom is right," Lennon says. "You're probably exhausted."

"I'm okay," I say. She raises an eyebrow at me. "Honestly, I'm pretty tired."

She sits straight up. Well, as straight as she can get these days. "I have a great idea. Dr. Ashley told me to take it easy today. Why don't you shower, then we'll spend the day doing nothing but watching trash TV and catching up. We won't leave bed all day except to go to the door to get any delivery food we order."

Normally, if I spend all day in bed with a woman, I'd want to be doing something else, but right now, that sounds absolutely perfect.

My hair still damp from the shower, I throw on a T-shirt and sweatpants. I'm half asleep when I emerge from the bathroom. And while Lennon said we were going to spend all day in bed, I didn't think she actually meant in her bed, but that's where I find her.

She greets me with a smile, patting the space beside her. She's wearing an oversized shirt and sweatpants, and she's the most beautiful thing I've seen in weeks. "I've got drinks and snacks, blankets. We're all set." I look around at the nightstands filled with stuff. "What do you want to do first? TV? Talk? Nap?"

Is kissing her until she's breathless an option?

"Talk," I say.

"A man who wants to talk," she says. "You are a rare breed."

"Chase didn't like to talk?" I ask, sitting down on the bed beside her.

"No, he did," she says.

"How are you doing?" I ask. "Got the goodbye letter done?"

She shakes her head. "No, but I'm feeling better. I still get sad. It's mostly the guilt that's . . ."

"Guilt?" I ask. "You've mentioned that before."

"That's something I'm not ready to talk about," she says, looking away.

Too tired to argue, I say, "Then let's talk about me living here."

Her pretty blue eyes look directly at me. "You're sure you want to live with me and a newborn?"

"I'm sure. Do you not want that?"

"I do," she whispers. "I'm so grateful you want to help me, but I worry about what you're giving up."

"Lennon, we've been through all this. This is what I want."

"But why?" she asks.

I could tell her it's because I love her, but I know she's not ready to hear that. She's not ready for anything romantic. She's not ready for a new relationship. I know that. But she does need my friendship. Above everything else, that's what I'm trying to do here. I'm trying to be there for her. So I answer honestly, just not with complete honesty. "You'd do the same for me."

She takes a deep breath. "I've decided to sell the house."

"What?" She loves this house. She grew up here. All her memories are here. This was not what I was expecting when she said she wanted to talk about me living here. I was expecting a reversal on her part, not a full-on commitment.

"It's too small," she says. "I won't have you sleeping on the sofa in the den for months and months. That's not right."

"Lennon, you could literally have that baby at any time. Now's not the time to pack up and move."

"But . . ."

"No."

"It's my house," she says. "I can do what I want with it."

"I know that," I say. "Just give it some time. Maybe six months or so."

"But you'll be on the sofa."

I want to tell her that if I'm not sharing a room with her by then, it's not the sleeping on the sofa that will do me in, it's the lack of any sexual contact. I don't even want to think about how long it's been.

"I'm not going anywhere," I say.

"Chase thought that, too," she whispers. "His last words to me were that he'd be back before I could miss him." A tear rolls down her cheek, and she quickly wipes it away.

"I'm so sorry," I say.

Silence fills the space between us. It's funny how silence can do that. How it can take up so much room. Steal all the energy. Zap any positivity away with ease leaving nothing but anxiety and fear in its wake.

"I fell asleep," she says so quietly I almost miss it. "I fell asleep while he was dying. I didn't wake up until the police rang the doorbell. I still remember the exact time. Two twelve." She glances toward the clock for a second. "I didn't even worry enough to stay awake. I was sleeping," she sobs.

"What was there to worry about? Lennon, you couldn't have known."

"I could have stayed awake," she says. "After all, he was out that night because . . ."

Her hand flies over her mouth, and her body begins to tremble. Enough is enough. I'm not sure if it's because I'm so fucking exhausted or because I know she can't move on until she gets this off her chest, but it's time to get this shit out in the open and off her heart.

"He was at some convenience store close to Alexandria, right?"

She nods.

"Really late at night?"

"Yes," she whispers.

"Was he working late and stopped on his way home?"

"No. He died on a Sunday. No work."

I sense she wants to tell me but can't find the words, so I keep going. If I just ask the right question, maybe she'll open up. "Was he out because he was doing something he shouldn't be doing?" That's the most tactful way I can think to ask if he was cheating on her, but the way Lennon's eyes bore through me lets me know there's not enough tact in the world to make that question okay.

"I didn't think he would," I say quickly.

"Chase would never," she says. "He'd do anything for me."

It hits me. "He was there for you?"

The tears that flow from her eyes let me know I'm right.

"He died because of me," she sobs.

"No, Lennon," I say, trying to wrap my arms around her, but she pushes me away.

"Yes!" she cries. "He died because he loved me."

"If he died loving you, and knowing you loved him, then he died a lucky man."

"How can you say something like that?" she screams.

She leaps out of bed, now crying and pacing back and forth, when she was just at the hospital a few hours ago. This can't be good for her or the baby. I need to calm her down. Maybe now wasn't the time for me to start asking questions. "I'm sorry I brought it up," I say. "You're supposed to be resting. Please get back in bed."

"I try every day to write to him or draw something for him. Yes, to say goodbye, but more to say I'm sorry. I'm sorry I wasn't a better girlfriend. I'm sorry that I read your messages when he asked me not to. I'm sorry for that night at the lake. I'm sorry I messed up our wedding day. I'm sorry I was asleep when he died. But I can't tell him I'm sorry. It's not working."

"Did you have a fight that night? Is that why he left?"

"No," she says, locking eyes with me. "He was so happy that night. It was the night I told him I was pregnant."

The room goes quiet. There's not a noise from outside. Neither one of us seems to even be breathing. It's dead silence. He died within hours of her telling him about the baby. This explains so much—why his financial affairs weren't in order and why Lennon didn't tell anyone before the funeral.

Getting to my feet, I step closer to her, but something about her posture prevents me from reaching out to her and taking her in my arms. "How'd you tell him?" I ask. "One of my buddies in the Corps, his wife sent him a box of blue confetti. Did you do something like that?"

"No," she says, shaking her head. "It's not like this was planned or anything. Things between Chase and I were good, but we'd tabled any decisions about marriage, the future, so getting pregnant was the last thing on our minds."

"You said Chase was happy, but were you?"

She sits down on the bed and wipes a few tears. "Yes and no. I mean, when I stared down at the positive result, I was so scared. I had no idea how Chase would react. He was very practical and responsible, so he was in charge of the birth control. I was really scared he'd be upset. Plus, we weren't married, and I just kept thinking about my mom and how she raised me alone. I'm ashamed I had those thoughts."

"I think you're being way too hard on yourself," I say, kneeling in front of her.

"It took me two days to tell him," she says. "Maybe if I'd told him when I first found out, things would be different."

"You can't think that way."

"I was nervous all weekend. He kept asking me if I was okay, but it wasn't until Sunday night that I told him. We were already in bed, the lights were out, and he leaned over, kissed my forehead, and told me good night. In the blanket of darkness, I whispered that I was pregnant." She draws a deep breath. "He sat up, flicked on the light, and asked me to repeat myself. So I said more confidently that I was pregnant."

She looks down at her lap, her hands folded across her belly. "And?"

"He cried," she says, looking at me. "I still remember his face. The smile, the tears. There wasn't a moment of anything other than pure joy."

I find myself smiling at the image.

"We both started laughing. He kept thanking me for giving him a family again. He promised me he'd spoil this kid rotten. He promised he'd make me happy, do anything for me."

To think I once hated this guy.

She bites her bottom lip like she's trying to keep the rest inside. Gently, I rest my hands on top of hers. "Like I said, we were laughing, being playful, and I told him I was going to hold him to that promise." Tears roll down her face, landing on our hands. "Teasing him, I faked like the baby and I were having our first craving. Willing to keep his word, he got up and grabbed his keys." She lowers her head like she's in confession. "I told him I was craving this fried chicken from a convenience store close to Alexandria."

I see the pieces falling into place.

"On our first date, we'd gone to some fancy place with tiny portions, so after, we were both still hungry. I saw the sign for fried chicken, and we pulled over and got some. Ate it in the car on the ride home, laughing the whole time. It was kind of an inside joke between us."

"You had no way of knowing."

"I wasn't even craving it," she cries. "Why did I let him go? Why didn't I stop him?"

This is why she won't ever let me go pick up food and insists on delivery. That day when she was pacing outside waiting for me, it wasn't because she was hungry. It was because she was reliving this. How could I have missed that?

"He wanted to go. That was his first act as a father. No way could you have stopped him," I say.

Her head collapses in her hand. "What will I tell this little girl? How will I explain to her that her daddy died because her mother sent him out in the middle of the night for a craving that wasn't even real."

"You're going to tell her that her father loved you and her so much he'd do anything for you both."

"But . . ."

"Chase was a smart guy. Don't you think he knew that the craving wasn't real?" She doesn't answer, but I know she knows I'm right. "He didn't go out to get chicken. He went out to prove to you that he'd be there. That he'd do anything you needed. He went to prove something to *you*."

"He had nothing to prove to me."

"Yes, he did," I say. "Be honest with yourself. He's the one who called off the wedding. He's the one that changed our friendship. He's the one that took your ring back. He's the one that you changed your life plans for. You would never have lived with him or had sex before marriage if it wasn't for him. He knew you well enough to know that those were compromises you were making for him."

She doesn't say a word, but I know I'm right.

"Chase needed to prove to you that it wasn't all in vain. That he wasn't going to walk out on you again. Because that's what he did after that night at the lake. He walked out on you. It was short-lived, but he still did it. And he needed to prove to you that he wouldn't do it again. That's why he went, not because of you."

She falls into my arms, and I hold her as she cries. Only this time, the tears feel different. I know they aren't the last ones she'll cry over Chase, but they feel like the most important ones.

These are her goodbye tears. The ones you cry when you are finally trying to let go. The ones that make room for someone else.

CHAPTER THIRTY-SEVEN

DUKE

"Your phone," Lennon groans, pushing my shoulder.

"Hmm?" I yawn.

"Your phone," she says again.

I sit up, rubbing my eyes, and look around for my phone. But it isn't here because I'm in Lennon's bedroom. As planned, we stayed in bed all day yesterday, and when I moved to go to the sofa last night, she sleepily asked me to stay.

Nothing happened. We slept. In fact, we'd still be sleeping if that ringing would stop. It comes again. "That's not my phone," I say, getting up. "That's the doorbell."

"What time is it?" Lennon asks without even attempting to open her eyes.

"Almost noon."

"I had to get up to pee like three times last night," she says. "This baby girl is right on my bladder."

The doorbell comes again. "I'll get it," I say. "Take your time getting up."

I look back at her one more time, lying in bed, the rumpled sheets where I used to be. Everything she told me yesterday has somehow made this morning seem different—brighter, lighter.

I rush to the door, my mom and dad both storming through it like the house is on fire. "What's wrong?" I ask.

They both scan me up and down, seeing my bed clothes, still half asleep. "Neither you nor Lennon were answering your phones," my mom says. "I've been trying to call you all morning to check to make sure she's all right."

"When you didn't answer," my dad chimes in, "your mother got worried."

Before I have time to explain, their eyes land on Lennon walking out of the bedroom, messy bed hair, yawning, sleep still rolling off her. Their eyes go back to me in a similar state, then to the sofa where they know I usually sleep but obviously didn't last night.

"Oh," my dad says, throwing me a look. "Morning, Lennon."

Lennon misses the look, saying, "Duke didn't tell me you were coming by."

"They got worried when we didn't answer our phones," I say.

"Two more minutes and your mother was going to break the door down," my dad teases. "Connie, we should go."

"You want to stay for breakfast?" Lennon asks. "Or should I say lunch?"

"No, no. We're going," my mom says, kissing me on the cheek and whispering, "Sorry."

She doesn't give me a chance to explain before my dad hugs me whispering, "We'll be more careful in the future."

Rolling my eyes, I'm glad that Lennon hasn't picked up on their silly theories. I follow them outside. The sun makes me squint my eyes a little. "Mom? Dad?"

They both turn. "Sorry."

"Stop acting like you interrupted the morning after," I say. "Nothing happened."

"If you say so," my dad says, smiling at my mom.

"At least we don't have to worry about you getting her pregnant," my mom jokes.

"You two are impossible," I say.

"Why can't they see it?" my mom asks my dad. "Iva and I could see how much they loved each other since they were little."

"I think they see it," my dad says. "They just haven't seen it at the same time."

"What nonsense are you talking now?" I laugh.

"Lennon was head over heels in love with you forever," my dad says. "But you didn't know it. Then she moves on, and you realize how much you love her."

"You both need to realize you love each other at the same time," my mom says.

Chuckling, I say, "I'm working on it."

"Work harder," my mom says, playfully pinching my cheek.

My parents are completely crazy, but it's nice to have their support. It's nice to be home and for more than a quick visit. I've missed them, living close.

Walking back inside, I find Lennon standing in the kitchen with a cell phone to her ear. She turns, smiling at me, and I realize it's not her phone but mine.

"Who is it?" I mouth to her, but she waves me off, continuing her conversation, laughing. If I didn't know better, I'd think she was flirting. But I've never seen Lennon flirt a day in her life. And if she has, it's so subtle that you'd need a microscope to notice.

"Yes, we'll be there," she says. "Me, too."

She hangs up the phone, handing it to me. "What was that all about?"

"Your phone was ringing," she says. "When I saw who it was, I figured I should answer."

"Well, who was it."

"Greggory," she says.

"Doesn't ring a bell," I say.

"Just because you all call each other by your last names doesn't mean you shouldn't bother to learn each other's first name," she says.

Whoever this Greggory is, he must be in the military, maybe at Quantico. I haven't connected with many people there, though. Then it hits me. "General Hale?"

Smiling and nodding, she says, "He and his wife invited us over for dinner tonight."

"And you said yes?"

"Of course," she says.

"You answered my phone when you saw it was him? And you're on a first-name basis now?"

She tosses me a smile. "I can call him back and cancel."

"You don't cancel anything with a four-star general," I say, closing the distance between us. "I was kind of hoping for another day in bed."

Her cheeks heat, and she looks away. "Maybe one with fewer tears?"

I shrug. "I'll take what I can get."

She laughs a little, stepping back slightly. "We'll have a signal. And if you need to escape tonight, I'll fake some labor pains."

"I don't think you had to bring flowers," I say to Lennon as we walk to General Hale's front door.

His house is a well-groomed brick colonial close to the base. Lennon smooths the fabric of her blue dress down over her stomach. She looks beautiful, much better than me in my jeans. "You look great."

"Thank you," she says softly, her cheeks turning pink.

I start to knock on the door, when it suddenly flies open. "Bang, bang, bang," a little gingered-hair boy says, before flying around us out the front door.

"Sorry, sorry," an older woman with long gray hair says, coming to our rescue. "I'm Peggy. Greggory's wife. You must be Lennon and Duke. Come in, come in."

Lennon holds out the flowers, and Peggy takes them, bringing them to her nose. "Aren't you a doll? Thank you."

"Bang, bang," the little boy appears again. "Got you, Grandma."

Smiling, she turns to him. "Grandma is wearing an invisible Kevlar suit—go attack Granddad."

"Did we get the time wrong, ma'am?" I ask.

"No," she says, leading us inside. The house is all open with the den and kitchen connected. Most of the furniture looks oversized and comfortable, not fussy, and there are pictures all over the walls and on the end tables. It's clear family is the center of their lives. "Our son called needing us to watch his kids. He has four boys."

"Four!" I say.

"Boys!" Lennon says.

Peggy smiles, pointing out the back windows where General Hale is on the ground being tackled by all four grandsons at once. "I try to get them to color or read, but they just want to play cops and robbers. I might be married to a military man, but I never let my boys play with toy guns, not even water shooters, but then one day, our oldest son picked up a pretzel. He couldn't have been more than three or four, and he picked up that pretzel stick and pretend shot me with it. It was then I realized I was fighting a losing battle."

"Lennon's having a girl," I say, patting her belly a little.

"Oh, how wonderful," she says. "Greggory and I had five sons, and now all the grandchildren are boys. What I wouldn't do for some frilly pink lace." She walks us out to the backyard. "I hope you don't mind the kids being here. We thought we'd grill out."

"We don't mind at all," Lennon says, answering for me like a wife would answer for her husband.

We walk outside. The backyard is huge, and the covered patio has a table and chair and a very nice-looking grill. General Hale grunts as one boy jumps on top of him. But he's smiling and laughing, and it's obvious he loves every second of this. Without thinking, I reach for Lennon's hand. When I look down at her, a confused little smile comes over her face, but she locks her fingers with mine just the same.

"So glad to see you again," General Hale says, limping over and kissing Lennon on the cheek.

"I keep telling him he's getting too old for all that horseplay," Peggy says, taking her place beside him.

"Too old, my ass," General Hale says, trying to recover his breath.

"Ass!" one of the boys laughs out.

"Greggory!" she scolds him playfully.

"Like he hasn't heard worse from you," he teases back.

She laughs. "Maybe I'll curse less when you retire."

"More likely you'll curse more," he says, wrapping his arm around her.

"Retire, sir?" I ask.

"Let's talk about that later," he says, catching one of the boys as they run by. "How about a little game of football?"

When Lennon said General Hale invited us for dinner, I didn't think we'd still be here at ten at night. We spent the afternoon playing ball in the yard while Lennon and Peggy visited on the patio. Every time I looked up, Lennon's eyes were on me. I don't know why. Sometimes she was smiling. Other times she wasn't. I'll have to pry later and see what they were talking about. The grandkids eventually left, and now we're all seated in the living room.

Lennon and I are on the sofa. General Hale is in a chair, and Peggy is sort of half sitting on the arm of the chair. She smiles down at him, some sort of invisible encouragement and strength coming from her, which seems odd considering who this man is.

He looks over at Lennon and me. "Some people think you get to be my rank by following all the rules and never stepping out of line. Maybe some do, but that's not me," General Hale says. "So when you approached me about a transfer, I knew it was out of the ordinary, but it didn't bother me. And it's going to bother me even less to move you to the top of the heap for the Nightwalks."

Wait, what did he just say? When I decided to become a Marine helicopter pilot, I never dreamed I get the opportunity to be a Nightwalk. General Hale did me one favor already, but this is beyond. I'm so stunned that I don't say a word. Lennon whispers to me, clearly not knowing what that means.

Very few from the squadron are selected to be Nightwalks. Not many pilots can say they've flown Marine One—that's the chopper that flies the president. Those select few are known as Nightwalks.

"You'd be one of the youngest," he says.

"I'm honored, sir," I say.

"I knew from that first day we met," he says. "You're perfect for the job." He glances over at Lennon, a small grin on his face. "And it will keep you in Quantico for a long while."

This time, Lennon reaches for my hand. "I can't thank you enough," I say.

"Yes, thank you," Lennon says, one hand on her belly, like her daughter is thanking him, too.

"It's us that needs to thank you," Peggy says. "What you did that day, saving my husband. Well, you gave us days like today. So many good years," she says, tearing up. They both look at each other. He wipes the tears from her cheeks. "I'm sorry," she says. "Please excuse me."

"Pegs," General Hale says, but she waves her hand at him, walking away.

Shaking his head, his eyes still in her direction, he says, "Sorry for that. She's having a hard time. I have cancer. Kidney."

I move to place my arm around Lennon, knowing this has to be like sticking a knife in an open wound. Her mom died of the same type, but before I can get my arm around her, she's up off the sofa, her arms around him—this man she barely knows.

I hear her whisper that she lost her mom, and his arms tighten around her. Then he pulls back. "Peggy's angry. Wants me to have treatment. It's stage four."

Lennon scoots back beside me, but all of us are now leaned forward, closer to each other. "My mom lived for almost four years," Lennon offers.

"But how did she live?" he asks.

"She was here," Lennon says. "Got to see me graduate college."

"You sound like my Peggy," he says. "I've fought for our nation my whole life. Now I just want to enjoy the fruits of that work. Time is precious. I want to roll around on the ground with my grandsons as much as I can."

"I understand," I say, rubbing Lennon's back. I know she also understands why he's not having treatment. But understanding his logic and accepting it are two very different things. She'd give anything to have more time with her mother, with Chase.

Lennon reaches out, taking his hand. "I know I'm young, and I wish I didn't have the experience to give you this advice. But I do. I lost my mom. It was slow. I lost the father of this baby. It was quick. So let me offer this. You have time. Time to tell her how you feel. Make sure she knows. Don't wait. Otherwise, she'll spend her life without you wondering."

His eyes go to me, getting to his feet, and so do we. "I'm retiring. But I wanted to repay my debt to you. To give you two a chance to have what Peggy and I have shared."

I don't think we said more than two words the entire car ride home. I know General Hale's diagnosis hit a little too close to home for Lennon. And I know Peggy's reaction hit too close as well—facing losing the man you love. Lennon's barely touching the other side of that grief. Tonight brought it all back.

Lennon's advice to him was solid—to let his loved ones know how he felt. I wonder if Lennon would give me the same advice. Would she advise me to tell her how I feel?

Staring up at the ceiling in her den, my pseudo bed doesn't feel so comfortable tonight, and I have to be up early. First day reporting for duty, and I can't be a zombie. I feel even more of a responsibility to be on my game. General Hale stuck his neck out for me. And to think he's nominated me to be a Nightwalk? That's an honor that very few men and women can claim.

"Duke." I hear Lennon say, but it doesn't sound like a scream or yell. It's more like her regular voice, like she's just hoping I'm awake and hear her.

Throwing my blanket off, I walk toward her bedroom door. It's cracked open, so I push it a little more. Her face is already looking my way. She holds her hand out and quietly asks, "Sleep with me?"

Shocked as shit is the emotion that comes to mind, but she doesn't need to ask me twice. I know she doesn't want to be alone after such upsetting news. I head toward her, and she scoots over a little, holding the blankets up. It's not like we haven't done this before, but usually, we're on the sofa, or it's happened by accident.

Lying down, I'm not quite sure what to do. Do I hold her? Do I give her space? Do I rip her clothes off and make love to her? Before I have time to decide, she rolls to her side—her head resting on my shoulder, and her pregnant belly being braced against my body.

I wrap my arm around her, and she cuddles closer to me. We lie that way for a long time in silence. It's natural to be next to her, holding her. I wonder if it feels the same way for her? I wonder if I should tell her how I feel? There are moments, like now, when I think I should, when I think she might be ready, but I fear if I screw this up again, I won't get another chance.

Next time I tell her I love her, I want it to be perfect. I don't want to do it out of selfishness or fear of losing her, like at the lake. I want it to happen naturally, and when it does, I hope and pray she feels the same way.

She shifts slightly. I know she hasn't fallen asleep because her breathing hasn't slowed. I let my fingers comb through her brown hair, trying to soothe her anxious mind and heart.

In the cover of darkness, she takes my hand, locking our fingers together, whispering, "Don't ever do something like that to me. Promise me you'll never stop fighting."

Hope fills my heart, and I hold her a little tighter. "Promise."

CHAPTER THIRTY-EIGHT

DUKE

The first day is never easy. I was up at the crack of dawn and on the road to Quantico, trying to avoid the traffic. Lennon offered to get up with me, but no one should get up before seven unless they have to. Besides, she looked too damn beautiful asleep under the covers when I left her. No matter how the rest of the day goes, waking up in Lennon's bed at her invitation makes this day perfect.

Outside the base aircraft storage facilities, I'm met by my commanding officer. A female colonel who once was a Nightwalk herself. She's probably in her late fifties, pretty, and I bet she took a lot of shit because of it. I'm dressed in my military fatigues, but she's in her officer's uniform with a shit ton of chest candy which doesn't have anything to do with her chest size but the number of ribbons and medals she dons.

"I read your file," the colonel says. "And General Hale speaks highly of you."

"Thank you, ma'am," I say, standing at attention with my eyes focused straight ahead. A Sikorsky VH-3 bird waits on some pavement not far from me. Otherwise known as Whiter Tops, these helicopters are designed especially for presidents.

"I'll judge myself," she says. "I don't like being told what to do. Which you might find odd since taking orders is what the Marines is all about."

Well, shit. General Hale had good intentions, but there's a protocol to becoming a Nightwalk. You have to work your way up. Only four or five pilots are assigned to Nightwalk duty at a time. I'm stepping on a lot of toes here. Which is becoming more and more obvious by the size of the crowd gathering around us. No soldier would just stop his duties, so I know she must've arranged their presence. They've all come to see the FNG, that's military code for fucking new guy, in this situation me, fall on his ass. Something tells me I'm about to be made an example of.

"Let's see if you're as hot shit as you think you are," she says, motioning to the bird. "Take her up."

"Ma'am?" I ask, my eyes darting to her. I quickly correct my focus when she glares at me.

"Is that a problem?" she asks. "You are a Marine Corps pilot, aren't you?"

"Yes, ma'am."

"Then what's the problem?" she asks sarcastically.

I hear some snickering from the gathering crowd. She knows damn well what the problem is. That beast costs at least a couple of million bucks, and never in my entire career have I flown that type of aircraft.

"No problem at all," I say, cocking my chin up.

"Good," she says, eyeing the squadron. "Take her for a little spin. Then bring her back down and land her in the field on that puck."

Fuck me! A puck is basically a little disk that you land a helicopter on when there are no runaways. The most famous one being on the South Lawn of the White House.

"What are you waiting for?" she asks.

"Who's my co-pilot?" I ask.

She just smiles. "This is a solo mission."

Walking toward the bird, I half expect her to call me back. There's no way she's going to let me take this helicopter in the air. It's worth more money than both of us will ever make in our lifetimes combined. When I reach the bird, I look back, waiting, but she simply stares at me. Holy fuck, this is happening.

Taking a seat, I see more buttons on this thing than any other bird I've flown, and I feel my heart start to race as if my whole world revolves around this moment. If I blow this, I could not only wreck a valuable machine, but I could also ruin my shot here.

And I have to be here.

Lennon.

Taking a deep breath, I close my eyes for a moment, picturing her face. Sailors find their true north, pilots follow the horizon, but for me, Lennon is my compass, the guiding force of my life. She's what drives me, what centers me, what gives me purpose.

Before I know it, I'm in the air with the base below me. When most people think of helicopters, they think of the sound of the blades whipping through the air, but this baby is quiet. I could carry on a whole conversation without any trouble and no need for headsets.

I glance down at the squadron below, all watching me. Part of me wants to see what this baby can do, knowing she can go one hundred and fifty miles per hour. She's designed to fly if her engine goes. And I'm dying to take her to her limits, but I don't. Instead, I spot the puck in the field.

This is the real test. Flying and landing are very different. And as a Nightwalk, I'm going to be asked to land on one of these in front of the whole world with cameras watching. There are no second chances. I'd be a disgrace to the whole Marine Corps.

Obviously, this is my first time landing here, so I make sure to check my surroundings for any trees, wires, or anything else that could get in my way. The White House has surrounding trees, so that will be a consideration in the future.

Normally, you'd want to know the size of the surface you'll be landing on compared to the size of the chopper, but I'm going to have to eyeball this. The colonel sent me in blind. I'm sure this is why she didn't give me a co-pilot, either. She wants to see how good I am at thinking on my feet in high-pressure situations.

Perhaps the most important thing to consider when landing is the wind. If you get that wrong, you can land pretty hard, into the ground, and no one wants that. Here goes nothing.

If I hope to ever do this for real, I have to do it now. There's no getting distracted by the monuments I'll fly by or the magnitude of my passenger. Slowly, I start to ease her down to the point where basically, the aircraft is hovering over the ground. The wind from the blades kicks up dust, whipping the flags around. The power is exhilarating.

Patience is the trick here. You can't rush the landing. If I didn't have patience before, I have it now. These past few weeks with Lennon have given me that. Definitely can't rush that landing, either. Now I go ever so gently, and finally she lands, so lightly there's barely a bobble.

As I power her down, I can hear their roar, their flood of praise, the men of my new squadron, whom I've never met, cheering for me.

Before I exit, I take a second. I hope this means I've earned my spot and that when I tell Lennon *goodbye never*, it's real.

A normal day on base is your typical eight to five. When you're on a mission, things are different, but I expect regular workday hours for now. My schedule for the foreseeable future will be logging lots of airtime, familiarizing myself with my new bird, testing various systems on the choppers, and developing and learning their tactical maneuvers.

I pull into Lennon's drive about half past five. The traffic wasn't bad, and I might have been speeding, missing her.

Used to be, we'd share our days over emails or the phone, but now we get to do it in person. When I open the front door, the smell hits me right away, taking me back to our childhood. "Lennon?" I call out, walking toward the kitchen.

She turns to me, smiling, a little apron covering her very pregnant belly. "I cooked," she says proudly.

"Chicken spaghetti?" I ask, remembering when her mom used to make it for us as kids.

"To celebrate your first day," she says. "It was always your favorite."

"Thank you," I say, wrapping one arm around her and kissing the top of her head.

She smiles up at me, and I feel myself fall a little more in love with her. But also with this life. This is what I want. Not her cooking, although that's nice and appreciated. But coming home to her. That's what I want—to know at the end of the day she'll be there, and I'll be there for her.

CHAPTER THIRTY-NINE

DUKE

I'm not sure how the pregnancy seems to Lennon, but it's going quickly for me. She's already thirty-five weeks, and we have to get Lamaze done. So this weekend, we are doing a crash course at the hospital. Apparently, two days is all you need.

Over the past few weeks, Lennon and I have fallen into a little rhythm. We work during the day, then spend our nights and weekends together. We even share a bed at night, although we don't talk about that.

I wouldn't call us roommates, but I wouldn't say we are "living together" in the relationship sense, either, so I'm not sure what we are. I am quite sure that I can't keep this up forever. It's getting harder and harder not to kiss her or tell her how I feel. I wanted to give her time after Chase, but I'm not sure how much time is enough. She doesn't cry like she used to, so that's a good sign. But her signals are all over the place. Add in the fact that she's about to give birth, and I'm confused as fuck.

It's been a long week. They seem to have me on the fast track. This weekend is the Lamaze class, so I'm hoping our Friday night can be a whole lot of nothing. I'm home a little later than usual, so it surprises me when Lennon's not here.

Pulling out my phone, I check to make sure I didn't miss a text or call from her. You can't be too careful when dealing with a pregnant woman. I live as though she can go into labor at any second even though I know she has five more weeks until her due date.

No messages. I start to dial her number when the front door

opens. Lennon's turned around, waving to someone as she walks in. Her hair is wet, and she's wearing nothing but a bright pink bikini and flip-flops with a bag slung over her shoulder.

"Hey," she says, dropping the bag to the floor.

My eyes scan over her body. I don't care how pregnant she is. My dick pulses against my pants because she's practically in her underwear. I can't decide what looks better, her tits or her ass.

She pulls her hair up, tying it in a messy bun. "Summer just barely started, but it's already so hot. Brinley and I went to the lake. She was off today, and I'm almost done with the book, so we had a girls' afternoon."

Like a complete idiot, all I can say is, "Okay."

"I think this baby girl makes me feel ten degrees hotter than everyone else."

She's definitely hotter than everyone else. Always has been. A knock on the door interrupts my ogling her. Lennon opens it up, and Brinley holds out one of my button-down shirts. "You forgot this," she says to Lennon.

Lennon takes it from her, turning to me. "Hope you don't mind that I borrowed your shirt. It was the only thing I had to use for a cover-up."

"Don't mind," I say, my throat suddenly dry.

"Thank God you got waxed earlier, or there would have been a situation happening in that suit," Brinley says.

"Brinley!" Lennon shouts, glancing at me.

"It's Duke!" Brinley says like I'm not a red-blooded American man.

"You're the one who got me the gift card for the wax!" Lennon says, laughing. "After you told me that horrible story about that woman in the emergency room who gave birth and vividly described how you didn't think she had ever shaved in her life."

"If you like your OB/GYN, you don't want to do that to her," Brinley teases.

"Get out!" Lennon says, laughing and playfully pushing her out the door.

"Bye, Duke," Brinley calls out to me as the door closes on her.

Lennon turns back to me, and I can't help but smirk. "Don't say a word."

"About what? The wax or your barely there bikini?"

Her mouth drops open, and she throws on my shirt, trying to cover up. "Stop it."

I chuckle. "Think I'll go take a shower. A very cold shower."

"We're going to fail Lamaze class." Lennon giggles, lightly elbowing my stomach. We're on the floor sitting on a mat with a few other expectant couples, but I think we're having the most fun.

The instructor is an older lady who hasn't smiled one time. I thought having a child was supposed to be a happy occasion, but apparently, it's an occasion for handing out brochures, showing overly graphic birthing videos, and making weird noises with your partner.

The instructor glances at us, explaining the next position. So far, Lennon's been on her side, on all fours, and now she's between my legs. "All these are sex positions," I whisper in her ear.

She laughs again. "You're bad."

"It's been a really long time since I've been bad," I admit, my cock hard and erect and pushing against my shorts. I'm sure she can feel it, but since her ass is between my legs, I really can't help it.

She looks back over her shoulder at me. "How long?"

"Longer than you," I say with a grin, gently rubbing her bump. "Now pant."

She laughs. "You mean, breathe?"

"I'd prefer you pant." She laughs so loud, then covers her mouth when all the other couples stare at us. "Sorry," I say to everyone. "Keeping her relaxed as instructed." I can't see her face, but I can feel her smiling in my arms.

"Let's take a five-minute break," the instructor says, probably on the verge of kicking us out of class.

I get up then reach down, helping Lennon to her feet, but we end up in a little hug. We stand there staring at each other, smiling like damn fools.

"I bet he's still having sex with his wife," one of the other pregnant women scolds her man as they walk by.

Lennon and I both burst out laughing. "If they only knew," she whispers. "Vows of chastity over here."

"I never took a vow," I say, winking at her.

"That's right," she says. "You never even tried to hold out. Who was your first? What was that skank from high school's name?"

"I never told you when or who I lost my virginity with," I whisper.

"Well," she says, throwing a sassy hand on her hip. "Since you know mine, I think I should know yours."

"Nope."

She shrugs. "Doesn't matter. I know it was her."

"You know nothing."

"Tell me," she says, poking my shoulder.

"Still waiting for the right woman," I say.

She rolls her eyes. "I'll get it out of you eventually."

"Probably so," I admit. "Eventually, I'll have to tell you a lot of things."

Her head tilts, her pretty little lips curving up. Just then, the same sexless pregnant woman walks by again. This time, it's her following her husband, but she's still nagging him. "I heard if you have sex, the baby will come quicker."

Lennon's lips close together in a tight line, trying to contain her laughter. I raise a hopeful eyebrow at her. She shakes her head at me, but something about the smile on her lips is wickedly naughty.

∽

I look down at the small suitcase Lennon has open on the bed, packing for the hospital. The Lamaze nazi sent the fear of God through her, saying that she should've had a bag packed already. So as soon as we got home, Lennon started.

"That side is for you," Lennon says, pointing at the small cube of space she's left open for me. "Pack for four days. Usually it's just two nights, but if I have to have a C-section for some reason, then it could be up to four."

"Okay," I say. "But I'm sure everything will be smooth."

She nods, but gone is the playful woman of earlier. She's on a mission. And a mother on a mission is only to be listened to and agreed with. "I don't have nursing bras," she says, throwing her hands up like that's the end of the world.

"I'll write it down, and you can get them tomorrow," I say. "I didn't know you planned on doing that."

"Breastfeeding," she says. "Why wouldn't I?"

So I don't like the word breast. It reminds me of fried chicken. I much prefer tits. "I just hadn't thought about it," I say. "I envisioned myself feeding the baby at night for you."

She stops what she's doing and turns to me, taking a deep breath. "I'm happy you're here."

Opening up my arms, she falls into my chest. "If you forget something, I'll get it for you. Or my mom will. Or Brinley. It will all be okay."

"I need you to promise me one more thing," she says, and I prepare myself for more orders from her, hoping they're not as morbid as the last ones. "When she's born, they might need to take her out of the room to weigh her and clean her up. No matter what, I don't care if something goes wrong with me or not, you stay with her."

Looking down into her eyes, I say, "I won't ever leave her. You have my word."

CHAPTER FORTY

DUKE

I haven't seen Lennon all day. She was in her office when I got up this morning and hasn't come out at all that I've seen. Since it's the weekend, I'm off. So I cut the grass, went to the grocery store, worked out, and stopped by to see my parents, but it was getting late in the afternoon, and I felt like I should check on her.

When she works, she can lose track of all time, all meals, and I never want to distract her, especially when she's on a tight deadline and the baby's due date is just a couple of weeks away. She hoped to be finished by now, but she continues to make small edits to her illustrations. Still, a small break won't hurt.

Lightly, I knock on the door before opening it. "Lennon?"

"Five minutes," she says, not looking up at me, which is a good thing because there's no hiding how much I want her right now. She's wearing a black bra, no shirt, and an old pair of cotton overalls covered in paint splatter. It's the sexiest damn thing I've ever seen, and suddenly, I can't wait a second longer.

"Now," I say.

"Just sending it off. It's . . ." She stops midsentence when she looks into my eyes. "What is it?"

"You," I say, my hands flying wildly in the air.

"What?" she says, looking down at herself.

"First, you strut around the house in a bikini. We share a bed every night, and now I find you sitting there in your underwear. Are you trying to kill me?" She laughs a little, giving me the most confused look. "Fuck!" I say, storming out of the room.

"Duke!" she calls out, her sweet voice making me halt quicker than any military order ever could. Her hand lands on my shoulder, my back to her. "What was all that? Talk to me."

I turn around, my eyes landing on hers. My chest is rising and falling quickly. The muscles in my body are tight with need. My heart's been waiting so long—containing my love for her. I have to tell her how I feel. Even though this might blow everything up, I can't hold it in for one second longer.

"Are you ready?" I ask. "Because what I have to say can't be unsaid."

She steps back a little. I've envisioned this moment a thousand times, and it never took place in her hallway. She looks me right in the eye. "I'm ready."

"I messed this up before, Lennon. That night at the lake, I . . ."

"The lake?" she says like she barely ever thinks about it. "You still feel the way you did at the lake?"

"Still, always, and forever will," I say. Her breath catches, seemingly surprised by that. And it's completely charming. "Lennon, what do you think that night was about for me?"

She moves away from me like I'm the most dangerous living thing on the planet. "Wanting what you can't have."

"No," I say, closing the distance between us.

She looks down, her head shaking. "But I'm pregnant with another man's child. You can't . . ."

"I do," I say, cupping her face in my hand. "I want you. It's always been you. It always will be you. I love you."

Her blue eyes lock on mine. At this moment, I can't read her and am not sure what to say or do. Is she preparing to kick me out of the house? Tell me she only wants to be friends? Have I screwed this up just like I did at the lake?

Then her lips crash into mine. Both previous times we've kissed, I've kissed her. Third time's a charm, I guess. I wind my hand in her hair, taking control. Her mouth parts slightly, and I stop for a moment to look at her, the desire in her eyes, the heat radiating between us. Keeping my eyes on her mouth, I lean in, feeling her body tense in the best way. I hesitate, making her wait, making her want, like she's made me wait all these months—years.

Gently, I nibble her bottom lip, and a little moan escapes from her gorgeous mouth. Then I kiss her gently, finding her tongue eager for mine. Slowly, our tongues dance around each other's before I trail kisses down her neck.

She moans sweetly. "Don't stop."

"Never," I whisper, flashing her a wicked smile.

She pulls me back to her lips, and my hands start to roam like they have a mind of their own. First, they slip up her back, pulling her closer, then one hand slides to her neck, the other cupping her tit in my hand, finding her nipple under her bra.

"Oh, God," she cries, grabbing my wrist. "Duke."

My head snaps back, hoping she's not making me stop. Her blue eyes are wide. I can see her breathing heavily.

"My water just broke!"

Lennon glances at me as Brinley and my parents surround her hospital bed. They all met us at the hospital. Between them, the nurses, and the epidural guy, Lennon and I haven't had more than a minute alone. She was already four and a half centimeters dilated when we arrived, so they moved pretty quickly getting her in a room and getting her pain meds, although Lennon said she wasn't feeling a thing.

I've been sitting in a corner watching the machine that monitors her contractions as everyone else monopolizes her. She flashes me a small unsure smile. I wonder what she's thinking. Does she regret what happened? Or does she want it to happen again?

"Do you think you could go get Duke something to eat?" Lennon asks them. "We missed dinner, and no telling how long this will take."

"Since you can't eat, I'm not going to eat in front of you," I say. "And I'm not leaving you for one second." Lennon throws me a frustrated look. Clearly, I missed her hint to get me alone. "But maybe you should try to get some sleep while you can," I say, giving my own hint to our guests.

"He's right," Brinley says. "We should let them rest."

My parents hug and kiss us both then everyone goes to the waiting room. I promise to keep them updated. When the door closes behind them, I turn to find Lennon's eyes on me. "I thought they'd never leave," I say.

"Why'd you want them to leave?" she asks, a flirty tone to her voice.

"So I could do this," I say, cupping her cheek with my hand and placing a sweet kiss on her lips.

"I like that you touch my face when you kiss me," she says, placing her hand over mine.

"I was afraid that maybe you were having second thoughts. That maybe you weren't ready."

"I didn't know I was," she says.

I look around at her in a hospital bed, about to give birth. "I know my timing sucks again," I tease, and she smiles.

"This might be the last time we are alone for a while," she says, raising an eyebrow. "I feel like we need to . . . I'm not sure . . . figure things out, I guess."

Flashing her a grin, I say, "We already live together."

"Why do I get the feeling that was your plan all along?"

"Oh, I have a lot of plans," I say, leaning down and kissing her again.

She places her hand on my shoulder, stopping me. "No sex for at least six weeks after you give birth," she teases.

My body deflates. What the hell kind of rule is that? That seems pretty arbitrary to me. Who decided on that timeframe? Playfully, I lift the hospital blanket up a little bit. "We still have a few hours then."

She giggles. "You're impossible."

Running my fingers through her hair, I say, "We can take things as slow as you want. I just couldn't hold in my feelings any longer."

She takes my hand and studies it, slowly intertwining our fingers. "When you came back for leave and found me at the cemetery." She looks up at me, the question in her eyes.

"I never stopped loving you, Lennon. Not for one second. I came back, hoping for a chance." I gently place my hand on her belly. "And when I saw you were pregnant, I fell in love with her, too."

Her eyes fill. "All those times you were being flirty, I had no idea. I thought you were just trying to make me smile."

"Now that you know," I say, my voice coming out dirty. "What are you going to do about it?"

"I'm sure I can think of something," she says, pulling me into a kiss.

"Another big push," Dr. Ashley says. "I can see her head."

"Don't look," Lennon screams at me, gritting her teeth and bearing down.

"I'm not." I laugh.

She stops pushing, taking a few deep breaths. "I swear to God if you look, I'll never sleep with you. Never!"

The nurse and Dr. Ashley exchange a look. "Must be the drugs," I say to them.

"Duke!" Lennon cries out.

Her head is right next to mine, so I'm not sure why she screamed my name so loud, so I just wipe her forehead with a wet rag. "Right here," I say, her eyes locking on mine.

"It's your fault this happened!"

"My fault! How is this my fault? I wasn't even there when this happened, remember?"

"You kissed me, and my water broke!" She grits her teeth at me as she pushes some more. "Your fault."

"Sex is supposed to bring on labor. I must be a damn good kisser," I say, and she bursts out laughing.

A little cry fills the room.

"I don't think I've ever delivered a baby with a mother laughing before," Dr. Ashley says, peeking over at the little girl wrapped in a pink blanket in Lennon's arms. "That has to be a good sign," she says, patting Lennon's arm. "Try to get some rest tonight. I'll see you tomorrow."

The door closes behind her, and I join Lennon in admiring her baby girl. She's been weighed—seven pounds even. Measured—twenty inches long. Hair—bald. Eyes—blue. All ten fingers and all ten toes counted. Everyone has visited already. Everyone wants to know her name, but Lennon hasn't settled on one, or at least she isn't saying.

"I love her," Lennon says. "It's this overwhelming, I'd die for her feeling."

"I know it," I say, grinning at her.

"She has Chase's toes," Lennon says. "He had these long skinny toes."

"I hope she's a better athlete than he was?" I tease.

Lennon laughs. "But good with numbers like him."

"We'll make sure she has all the best parts of him."

Lennon looks up at me. "I hope she learns how to love from you."

I feel my throat tighten and my eyes fill. "I know Chase is her father. But I'll be her best friend."

"I l . . ."

"Let's see if we can get her to latch," a nurse says, barging inside and interrupting our moment.

Lennon looks up at me, and I say, "I'll wait in the hallway."

"Stay," she says, pointing at a little sofa in the room. "Just sit over there."

I do as she asks. Pulling out my phone, I scroll through the pictures I've taken of Lennon and the baby today. I find the one my mom took of the three of us and make it my screensaver. I make sure to keep my eyes averted from what she and the nurse are up to. Besides, Lennon doesn't want the first time I see her naked to be like this. I respect that, but I can't close my ears when the lactation nurse starts talking about milk supply, cracked nipples, and something called rooting behavior.

"Why won't she do it?" I hear Lennon cry.

"Some babies take a few times," the nurse says in the calmest, most reassuring voice.

"I don't like to think about her hungry."

"Your milk hasn't even come in yet," the nurse says. "Why don't you let me take her to the nursery for a few hours? You rest. Then I'll bring her back to you in a little bit, and we'll try again."

"But I thought she could sleep in here with us," Lennon says with a sob.

"The baby stays in here," I say without looking up, my voice direct with an air that the nurse better not mess with me.

"Of course," the nurse says. "Oh honey, don't cry."

I go to Lennon instantly, and I don't care if her tit is hanging out or not. But she's already back covered up. I look at the nurse, who has the kindest eyes, and feel bad that I snapped.

"This is my first task as a mother, and I'm failing," Lennon cries.

"No, you're not," I say.

"I am."

"I'm sorry, but I'm not going to let your success or failure as a mother be wrapped up in whether or not your tits produce enough milk or your nipples are the right shape."

Lennon bursts into a little laugh, and so does the nurse.

"That's pretty good," the nurse says. "Can I use that?"

"Absolutely," I say.

CHAPTER FORTY-ONE

LENNON

I'm in that state of sleep when you are waking up, but you don't want to be awake, so you just lie there, eyes closed, unsure what's real and what's not. Did I really have a baby a few hours ago? Was this all a dream? That kiss with Duke was so good it had to be a dream. Am I really a mom? Moms are supposed to know more and have more answers.

Did I really just push a human being out of my body? Dear God, I don't even want to know what my vagina looks like right now. Has it gone back to normal, or is it still big enough to fit a large piece of fruit through?

Chase.

My heart grows heavy, even on this, the happiest day of my life. He will never see her, hold her, smell her. She will never wrap her fingers around his or know his smile. Her first taste of coffee won't be with him. He won't walk her down the aisle one day or wipe her tears after her first heartbreak. Her life began with loss. She will always know it.

A tear rolls down my cheek, but I don't move to wipe it away. Sometimes, we are too quick to do that—to try to rid ourselves of tears. Some tears need to be cried. Their journey needs to have a start and a finish. It needs to travel down your face, making a path on your skin, until its trail ends, and it falls to the ground.

The journey of our tears might be long or they might be short, but either way, they need to be given time to complete. Duke's given me that. He's been there for the journey of my tears. He hasn't rushed it. He simply stayed beside me.

"You let me know if I'm doing this wrong, okay?" I hear Duke whisper.

Not willing to move any other part of my body, only my eyelids flutter open. Through the darkness, I see him on the little hospital sofa with my daughter tucked safely in his arms.

He didn't hold her all day. No one held her except me or a medical professional. It was pretty late when she was born, and everyone kept their visits brief, but I should've had Duke hold her at least. Although, he never asked to. Still, there he is, having his own private moment with her. The one I'm spying on.

He leans down a little and whispers, "I'm Duke. The voice you've been hearing. I'm not your daddy, but I wish I was."

How did I not know how he felt? Brinley tried to tell me, but I didn't believe her. Or maybe I wasn't ready to believe her. All these months, he's been in love with me but kept it to himself—putting his feelings aside to allow me the time and space I needed. He's not the same boy who kissed me then made out with his ex. He's not even the same man who kissed me at the lake and ruined my wedding. This man knows what it means to really love someone.

"I love you. It took me a long time to tell your mommy that, too long," he tells my daughter.

My mom was wrong about love. You don't need a man to love you more than you love him. It's not a contest. We aren't love-sick teenagers sitting on the phone saying I love you more, no I love you more to each other over and over again.

Chase loved me. It was safe, steady, secure, the exact thing my mom wanted for me. Maybe it was how I needed to be loved at that time of my life. Chase never scared me. His love never frightened me.

Duke scares me. I can't lose him. And love can get messy. Friends falling in love can get even messier. The way he loves me is the kind of love that flies across an ocean to be with you. The kind that stands with you when your mother is dying. The kind that loves my daughter when other men would go running for the hills.

"We have to get you some hair," Duke whispers. "So you can wear ribbons like your mom used to."

I giggle, giving myself away.

Duke looks up at me. "Sorry we woke you. She was fussy. I wanted to let you sleep."

I watch him slowly get up like he's holding precious cargo. Carrying my daughter, he walks toward me, and my heart aches. I feel like it's coming back alive after a long, long sleep. It hurts a little, but it also feels warm, sweet.

He moves to hand her to me, but I shake my head, simply glancing at her sweet little face, her eyes lidded, dozing off in his arms. He's grinning down at her. "I can't believe she came out of you," he says.

Placing my hand on my stomach, I say, "I kind of miss my big ole belly. Is that weird?"

He shrugs, unable to take his eyes off her. "I didn't know it was going to feel like this," he says. "I know in my head she's not mine, but my heart doesn't care about the biology."

"Look, Duke, she's doing it!" I whisper scream, not wanting to scare her off my breast, which she's finally taking.

"Oh, now I can look?" he teases, taking a seat beside me on the bed.

I don't know what made me try again this morning, but I'm so glad I did. I think the nurse was right, and once I relaxed, it happened.

"Is it wrong that I'm jealous?"

"Yes," I say with a smile.

"So you're not going to let me try that?"

"You pervert! No!"

He laughs. "Have you decided on a name yet?"

I shake my head. Duke doesn't know it, but he's hit a sore spot.

"No matter what you decide. I'm going to call her Duchess," he jokes, but I don't laugh. Sharply, I turn my eyes away from him.

"Lennon?"

"I can't decide on a first name because I don't even know whose last name to give her," I say, the tears starting to flow. "I mean, I don't have Chase's last name. We weren't married. But it would feel weird to have a different last name than my baby. But I don't want to do what my mom did to me either—never knowing my father's last name."

"Shit," he mumbles. "I hadn't considered that."

"Why does everything have to be hard?" I ask, looking down at her. "Naming her shouldn't make me sad."

"Can I suggest something?"

"As long as it's not Duchess, then yes."

"I know it's not my place to name Chase's child." He takes a deep breath. "Especially when I hope at some point she'll carry my last name."

"What did you say?" I ask, my eyes darting to him.

"I'm not asking you to marry me now," he says, holding his hands up. "But consider yourself warned that it's coming."

I can't help it when I start laughing. "You're warning me of an impending marriage proposal."

"Yes," he says, the biggest smile on his handsome face. "And no, I'm not going to tell you what needs to happen before I ask you, how I'm going to ask you, or anything of the sort. I would, however, like to know if you're going to make me wait to take you to bed until marriage."

God, this man makes me crazy happy. "You'd do that?"

"You always said you wanted to wait."

I throw a glance at the baby girl in my arms. Obviously, that didn't happen.

"You took a detour, but if you wanted to be back on that road, then I'll ride along with you."

"And if I don't?"

"Then you better mark your calendar for five weeks and six days from now."

I just laugh. "I thought you had a suggestion for naming this little girl."

He looks down at her, running his finger along the skin of her tiny hand. "Arden."

"Chase's last name?"

His steel-gray eyes find mine. "It's kind of perfect. Lennon could be a last name. People call me by my last name. She'll fit right in."

"Arden," I whisper.

"This way, no matter what her last name is. Yours, mine," he says, raising an eyebrow. "Or God forbid, her husband's one day, she will always carry her father's name."

CHAPTER FORTY-TWO

LENNON

Looking down at Arden in my arms, it's hard to believe she's already a month old.

The past month has been a blur—a happy, exhausting, overwhelming blur. It amazes me that you have a baby, and they just send you home. You might not have ever changed a diaper before, but suddenly, you have a poop machine at your fingertips. Somehow, you just figure it all out. It helps that I'm not alone in this either. Duke brings humor and fun to my most stressed-out situation.

That was more than evident when breastfeeding didn't come easily to me. When she finally latched on at the hospital, I thought things would go smoothly, but I was wrong. My milk supply was almost nonexistent. My natural inclination was to blame myself. I spent so much of my pregnancy sad. I figured my boobs were sad, too, and what little milk they did have was probably spoiled with sadness. It was hard for me to let go of my dream of nursing my baby, but when Arden was down a whole pound at her first-week checkup, I killed that dream real quick. She's been on formula since and is doing great, now a roll of perfectly beautiful baby pudge.

Placing her down in her crib, I look at the clock. Duke will be home any minute. He's been back at work for a couple of weeks now. He hates that Arden naps around this time every day because he wants to see her when he gets home. But her afternoon nap gives him a chance to unwind before our nightly routine of diaper changes, bath time, and feedings.

I hear the front door open. He's always extra quiet when he

comes in from work. Tiptoeing out of her room, I meet him in the den. My body tingles at the sight of him in his uniform. Clearly, I'm feeling better after having Arden.

We have a pretty good routine worked out, and it seems like I'm finally shaking off some of the guilt and sadness of the past year. "She out?" he asks, running his fingers through my hair. Smiling, I nod, knowing what's coming. He takes my chin, pulling me to his lips. We'll get to the "how was your day" and "what do you want to do for dinner" portion of the greeting, but this always comes first.

Untucking his shirt, I run my hands up the muscles of his back as my tongue slowly strokes his. Kissing is the extent of our sexual activity. I just had a baby. When she sleeps, I sleep. Duke's working and helping with Arden, so he's tired too. Still, I know he's anxious for more. He never says it, but he doesn't need to. His dick seems to be hard twenty-four seven.

"Missed you," he says quietly.

Running my fingers through his hair, I look into his gray eyes, and he smiles, but it's tight-lipped. Something's wrong. "Bad day?" I ask.

He steps away from me. "Let's talk later. Arden will be up soon."

"We have at least thirty, maybe forty minutes," I say, reaching for his hand. His head turns to me. He's always been there for me. He basically has seen me back from hell. Whatever is wrong, I want to be there for him. I step up to him. "How about we talk in the bath?"

His eyes heat. He knows I'm not cleared from the doctor yet, so this is coming as a shock, I'm sure. I'm shocking myself. I've had a baby. My body isn't exactly the same, and Duke is a perfect male specimen of muscle, but I can't hide from him forever.

"Do we have to talk?" he asks, a naughty grin on his handsome face.

"Yes!" I say. "Just give me five minutes."

Walking toward the bathroom, I see him start to undo the buttons on his shirt. Suddenly, my confidence wanes. Why did I suggest this? He's never seen me naked. I close the bathroom door, placing the baby monitor on the counter. Then like a total chicken, I start the tub water, pouring in lots of bubble bath. Making sure the entire tub is full, I quickly undress and hop in the water just as Duke opens up the door. He looks down at me submerged in the bubbles.

"Tease."

I don't take my eyes off him as he slips off his shirt, biting my bottom lip a little at the sight of his perfectly cut abs. "Close your eyes," he says, grinning. "If I can't see you, then you can't see me."

I shake my head, refusing.

"I'm shy," he says with a smirk.

"No, you're not."

"Fine," he says, sliding his pants and underwear down at the same time. "See what you're missing."

Holy crap! He's hard and freaking huge. I immediately avert my eyes, and he chuckles at me, sliding into the tub opposite me so we're facing each other. "Lennon, you know I think you're sexy as fuck."

I glance up at him. "My body's not the same," I say. "You never got to see me in my prime."

He reaches for me, pulling me closer. "If it was better than this, I don't think I could've handled that."

"You haven't seen anything yet."

"I've been imagining for years," he says, grinning.

"Perhaps you won't have to imagine much longer."

"Two weeks," he says, a hopeful look in his eyes. "Maybe I'll ask my parents to watch Arden that day."

"I'm not sure I'm ready to leave her with anyone," I say. "But maybe if it's just a couple of hours."

"I'll need more than a couple of hours," he says with a smirk.

He finds my foot under the water, starting to rub. "This tub is supposed to be about talking, not flirting."

He draws a deep breath and then looks directly into my eyes. "I want to always come home to you and Arden. Always."

"I like that thought," I say, smiling at him.

"I have some decisions to make," he says.

"Okay."

"Being a pilot is my career," he says. "It's what I do."

"I know."

"My initial commitment of five years is almost up. I have to let them know my plans. In fact, I should've done it already. They are investing a lot of time and resources into me being a Nightwalk. I've been avoiding doing this, but I have to decide how many more years to re-enlist for."

Somewhere in the back of my head, I knew this, but I guess I didn't want to face it, but here it is, naked and opposite me in the bathtub.

"Because there aren't many of us helicopter pilots, I can do what I want. A year, two, five. But I have to tell them something."

"I understand."

"I didn't want to make the decision without talking to you."

My heart misses a beat. I know he said he loves me. I know he's been by my side, but I don't know that I felt like we were a team, like we were in this together until this moment.

"Nightwalk duty is twelve to fourteen months typically. So I probably have at least two years here at Quantico, but after that, I don't know. I could be assigned anywhere in the world. Could be Stateside, could not be." His gray eyes stare at me. "I need to know if you'd come with me. If I got transferred, would you come with me? Are you willing to do that?"

I've lived in Montclair all of my life except for that brief infancy prison stint. Would I want to take Arden all over the world? Moving every few years, away from my friends, Duke's parents? What about my career? I guess I could do that anywhere.

"I know it's a lot to think about," he says.

"What if I don't want that for Arden?" I ask.

He doesn't blink. "Then I'll get out. Do something else."

"No, you love being a helicopter pilot."

"Not more than I love you and Arden."

"Duke," I whisper.

"I'm not going to leave you and her here while I'm stationed somewhere else. That much I know."

The way Duke loves me is overwhelming. Chase loved me, but it never felt all-consuming like this.

"You said you're pretty sure they'd keep you at Quantico for at least two years."

"There's no guarantee," he says. "If the country goes to war, then all bets are off, but otherwise, I think I'm pretty secure here for that long."

"Why don't you sign for two more years," I say. "We can re-evaluate then."

"But we're agreed," he says. "We stay together."

"Together," I say, leaning forward and sealing it with a kiss.

CHAPTER FORTY-THREE

LENNON

Arden goes to bed between eight thirty or nine every night, which means that Duke and I go to bed between eight thirty and nine. She usually gets up twice a night, once around midnight and then three or four. If she's up when Duke gets up for work, he feeds her, changes her, and puts her back to sleep so that I can get a few more hours. I'm not back to working yet, and frankly, I am not sure how that will work. I guess I'll work when she naps, but we'll cross that bridge when we get to it. Although, I do miss it. I find myself doodling, showing Arden, talking to her about all the different colors in the world.

But for now, I'm excited when I get showered and dressed and can toss a load of laundry in. Duke's parents have been an amazing help, and Brinley stops by a couple of times a week too.

If the past year has taught me anything, it's that no matter what my plans are, life has its own. So no amount of worrying will make one damn bit of difference.

After putting Arden down for the night, I walk into the master bathroom to get ready to put myself down for the night. Why did Duke and I both bother putting clothes back on after our bath? That is going to cost me precious minutes of sleep now.

I see Duke standing at the lone sink. When I remodeled, I should've gotten double sinks. He turns slightly, his toothbrush hanging loosely from his mouth, but it's what he's holding in his hand that has my attention.

Quickly, I snatch them from him. "Where'd you get those?"

He spits and rinses. "They were right here on the counter. When did you go on birth control?"

"Last week or so," I say.

"You didn't think to mention it? Because I could have saved thirty bucks," he says with a little grin, walking over to the nightstand and pulling out a box of condoms that I had no idea were there. "Military has taught me to always be prepared and plan ahead."

Laughing, I ask, "When did you buy those?"

"Last week," he says, raising an eyebrow. "Guess we're both on the same wavelength."

He plants a soft kiss on my lips. "I left things to Chase before, and look what happened," I say. "I wanted to be extra careful. Don't need any more surprises."

"Fine with me." He tosses the box of condoms in the trashcan and then tackles me to the bed. "I know we have to wait a few more weeks, but there's a whole lot of other things we can do for warm-up."

I feel my skin heat and a few butterflies in my stomach. I want to be with him. I know he dreams about being with me. I just hope his dream isn't better than reality. I wiggle out from under him, but his hand lands on my waist. "What's wrong?"

"Nothing. I'm tired."

His eyes bore through me. My attitude coupled with exhaustion, and sexual frustration make for trouble, and he huffs out of bed, heading for the bathroom.

"Where are you going?"

"Take a shower."

"We already took a bath."

"I need to jerk off," he snaps. "Okay! Do I need to wait two more weeks to do that, too?"

"You do that in the shower?" I ask, trying not to laugh at him.

"Every damn day."

"How long has this been going on?" I ask, giving him a small smile.

"Almost since day one," he says, his voice thawing out. "Haven't you noticed that you're going through more shampoo since I moved in?"

My lips purse together, and so do his, both of us bursting into laughter at the same time. "Sorry," I say, taking his hand. He sits down on the bed, pulling me into his lap.

"Is this more post-pregnant body crap?" he asks.

"A little," I say. "But it's not just about my body. It's about Chase."

"I hate that he was your first," Duke says softly.

"I know that," I say. "That's why I can't talk to you about this."

"It should have been us. Your first time."

"I wanted that," I confess quietly. His eyes dart to mine. "That day at the lake, you said it should've been you and me. I thought the same thing for years."

"But you went to Hawaii with him."

We both know that's where I lost my virginity with Chase. We don't have to say it. I hate thinking about anything bad related to Chase. You're not supposed to speak ill of the dead. "It was about a ten-hour nonstop flight from DC to Hawaii. He didn't say a word to me the whole flight." I can feel Duke's muscles tighten under me. "Somewhere around the seven-hour mark, he took my hand. I think that was his way of letting me know it would be okay, but he just couldn't get into it all on an airplane."

"Don't make excuses for him," he says. "He asked you to come. He should've treated you better than that."

I nod, remembering the guilt I felt on that plane. I thought about Duke more than I should have. Yes, most of it was disguised as anger, but I'd just lost the most important person in my life. At the time, that role should've been Chase's, but it wasn't. And it ate me up inside. I tried to deny it, to focus only on Chase, but Duke was always in the back of my mind.

"You can imagine. We get there. Exhausted from the flight, from our fight. Everyone kept referring to us as Mr. and Mrs. It was supposed to be our honeymoon. The room had a gorgeous view and only one bed."

"I'll never be able to go to Hawaii now," he says as a joke, but I know there's truth underneath.

"It was a difficult week," I say. "Chase was hurt. Jealous."

"It was one kiss," he says. "That you stopped."

"It wasn't just the kiss," I say. "He hated how close you and I were. It bothered him. I didn't realize it until that trip. He saw you as the guy who strung me along. Only wanting me when I was with someone else. No matter how much I tried to explain. He didn't believe me."

"So you had sex with him to prove something, to show him he was the one. Because you convinced yourself he was."

Maybe he's right. I'm not entirely sure. But this isn't about that.

"I believed he was. I did love him."

"What happened?" he asks.

"I waited so long to sleep with someone for the first time, but it wasn't how I thought."

His gray eyes fly to mine. "Did he hurt you?"

"No, nothing like that," I say. "He was very sweet. It was nice."

"Nice? Sweet?" Duke repeats. "Those aren't adjectives I'd normally use to describe sex."

I raise my eyebrow at him. I've just given him all the information he needs to understand how sex was with Chase. It was pleasant, but I knew something was missing. I think I knew it the whole time we were dating. His kiss never rendered me speechless like Duke's did, but I told myself that was okay. That he loved me in other ways, important ways, and that was enough. That's what my mom always said I should look for.

The fact that I never had an orgasm with him was something we could work on. After all, I was the inexperienced one. Maybe it was me.

Six months is the sum total of my sexual experience, and it wasn't even adventurous or passionate. Hence, my nerves now. And now

I'm also a mother to a newborn to boot.

He stands, forcing me to stand, too. "Don't you know how sexy I think you are?"

My head shakes.

His steel-gray eyes hold mine. His thumb glides across my mouth. "Sexy." Subtly, I bite my bottom lip, and the cutest little smirk crosses his lips. "You have to know how sexy you are."

Again, my head shakes.

He takes a step back, looking me up and down. "Strip."

My jaw drops. Maybe it's his military background, but I find myself wanting to follow his order. Besides, I can't hide from him forever. Unable to stop myself, my hands start to move, unbuttoning my jeans and sliding down my zipper.

He unbuckles his belt and the top button of his pants, now hanging deliciously from his hips. My eyes lower to the band of his black underwear. Slipping my hands under the sides of my jeans, I wiggle them off in the most unsexy manner possible. When I stand back up, I pull my shirt down so it covers everything to my upper thigh. Suddenly, his hands are on me, grabbing the sides of my panties and forcing them down. Before I have time to think, he has me hoisted up, my legs wrapped around him, his hard dick hitting just the right spot.

My head tosses back, and a loud moan falls from my lips, "Oh, God."

The rest of our clothes fly off in a flurry, and it's not until he lowers us to the bed that I realize I'm totally naked in front of a man for only the second time in my life.

"We can't," I whisper. "Not for a couple more weeks."

"I know," he whispers back. "But I want to see you, feel you."

His hands slowly slide up my body. It's stupid to be so nervous. I'm naked in front of him. All he has to do is lower his eyes, but he doesn't. He only looks at my face, waiting for permission. I nod a little, and he leans back on his knees, his eyes slowly roaming my body. I feel my nipples peak and the muscles between my legs tighten. His hand reaches out, sliding down the curve of my waist.

"You're so fucking beautiful."

He lowers himself beside me, pulling me to him, my back to his front. "I have to touch you," he says, his hand slipping between my legs.

"Oh," I groan as his fingers stroke me.

His other hand slides to my breast, playing with my nipple, overwhelming me. His hands are driving me crazy as he kisses my neck, and I can feel every long inch of him against my ass.

"That pussy's gonna come for me," he growls.

His hand starts to move faster over me. I've never felt anything like this. It almost hurts but in the best possible way. I feel myself spreading wide for him, wanting him inside me. Just when I think I can't take it one second longer, I explode, my whole body quaking in his arms. It was just that easy—easy for me to let go with him, easy for him to know what I needed.

He flips me around, wrapping my arms around his neck, and slowly kisses me, his tongue playing with mine, igniting the fire between my thighs again.

"You have more for me, baby?"

"Yes," I pant.

He doesn't waste a second before his head is buried between my thighs. "If I can't fuck you with my cock, then my fingers and mouth will have to do."

"Oh, my God," I cry, my legs falling open, welcoming him. "Please make me come," I beg. "Please, please."

He chuckles slightly, sending shock waves through my body. Gently, he pulls my thighs to his shoulders, planting a featherlight kiss on each. My muscles clench together, wanting nothing more than to feel that delicious wave from my orgasm roll over me again.

"Impatient," he says, slowly teasing me with his tongue. I don't mean to, but a frustrated growl escapes. "Demanding, aren't you?"

"Duke," I moan.

"I love it when you moan my name," he says, kissing me between each word.

"Duke," I breathe out.

He rewards me by sucking down on me hard. My whole body is tense, wanting him and only him. The only thing I can focus on is what's happening between my legs. This is so new. I think men stay focused on their penis most of their lives, but not women. We often don't pay enough attention to what we want, what we need in that department. But right now, I'm solely focused on it, the tension building in my body.

His tongue moves expertly around me, knowing when to lightly lick and knowing when to suck down harder. The ride is incredible. This is what this is supposed to feel like. I always was skeptical of people who are sex addicts, not quite believing that's a real thing, just an excuse celebrities use when they have affairs. But holy hell, I'm a believer now.

My muscles clench over and over again, and I'm aware that I'm thoroughly fucking his mouth, and I don't care. Right then, he gives me one long hard suck, and I lose control. My head arches back, my legs tremble, and I scream, "Duke!"

"Shh," he whispers, planting light kisses against my folds, making sure to take every last bit of my orgasm from me.

I look over at the baby monitor, praying for her to stay asleep. It probably will earn me a one-way ticket to hell to pray not to have our fun interrupted, but I do it anyway.

Duke kisses his way back up my body until he's lying beside me. He just did all kinds of naughty things to me, but I still feel my face blush.

"I had no idea," I whisper, "it was like that."

He smirks at me, his hand wandering back between my legs. "You have a nice little on button down there. Just got to know where to find it."

I can't help but giggle. He always puts me at ease. It's just one of his many gifts. "Where's your on button?" I flirt.

"I'm more of a stick shift," he says with a laugh, pulling me on top of him. His eyes roam my face, his fingers playing with my hair. "You are so beautiful, Lennon. I imagined moments like these so many times, and the real thing is better than my wildest imagination."

"I love you," I say. The words float from my mouth as if I've said them before, been saying them my whole life. Maybe because I have—in my head, in my heart, I've said those words to him thousands of times.

"And here I thought there could be nothing better than you calling my name when you come," he says, flashing me the most wicked grin. "This is so much better."

We both laugh, but a few tears roll down my cheeks. Rolling to his side, he wipes them away, leaning in to kiss me. Our tongues meet, and a low rumble comes from his throat. The sound is pure desire. I can feel his dick heavy, resting on my inner thigh.

I roll to my back, and he's on his knees straddling me. His body is one hard piece of muscle, tanned and toned, and all mine. He looks at me naked beneath him, and I take him in both of my hands. His jaw clenches. From the look on his face, it looks like it's been a really long time since a woman has touched him like this. He told me as much, but I don't think it registered until now.

Using both hands, I stroke him. "Lennon," he groans.

I know what he means about the name thing because I love hearing him say mine with such need. Inspired, I angle myself to a more seated position, place one hand on his tight ass, and guide him to my mouth.

"Fuck!" he moans as I slip him between my lips.

Let's just say that Duke has nothing to be shy about in the penis department. God was very generous to him the day he passed out dicks. But I'm determined to handle him, every long hard inch of him, until he reaches the back of my throat.

He watches me take all of him. And I can almost hear him praying not to finish quickly. We've waited so long. It's a double-edged sword. On the one hand, you've waited so long you are desperate for each other. And on the other hand, you've waited so long you want it to last forever.

I slip him out of my mouth, stroking him, giving him one long lick up his shaft. "Don't hold back," I whisper, peeking up at him. Keeping my eyes locked on his, I slide him back in my mouth, moaning a little.

He grabs my hair, holding it back, and his hips start to thrust. I can tell he's close.

"Lennon," he grunts.

I give his balls a gentle tug, and he releases. Guess that's his off button.

Naked in the darkness, I lie in his strong arms. We've been this way for hours. But I know it's about to end. I know Arden will wake up any minute for her first feeding of the night, and the afterglow of our little warm-up session will be over. It was well worth the loss of sleep.

His finger lightly slides down my body, between my cleavage, down my stomach. "So beautiful."

I've never been a woman who thought she was pretty. Not that I think I'm heinous, but just average, I guess. Nothing special, but hearing those words from Duke, they make me believe. Well, at least they make me believe that he believes what he's saying.

Reaching up, I play with his dog tags, admiring him. "We should get dressed. Arden will be up soon." He responds by kissing me.

I get out of bed, searching for some clothes to throw on. When I turn back around, Duke's totally naked down on one knee, holding out a simple silver band with a round diamond in the center. My heart thumps loudly against my chest. What's happening?

"Oh, my God! What are you doing? Get up!" I say in shock.

He laughs. "No, I'll stay down here all night if I have to."

I can't do much but stare. My voice is gone. This isn't the first proposal I've received, but it is the first one naked, and the first one where the man was on one knee.

"You can't be too shocked," he says. "I did warn you it was coming."

"We're naked!"

"I told myself as soon as you admitted you loved me, that I'd ask you. And you said it tonight."

I look down at him. "I do love you."

"Then marry me," he says. "You are all my good days. You've been there."

"All the bad ones, too," I whisper, a few tears starting to fall.

"Those, too," he says softly. "I want to be there for every good and every bad day for the rest of your life. Marry me."

CHAPTER FORTY-FOUR

LENNON

The diamond on my finger glistens in the morning sunlight as I walk into the den. It's been two weeks since he asked me. Everyone is thrilled for us. We haven't set a date or talked about any plans yet.

I can't believe I'm engaged. Honestly, when I lost Chase, I thought that was it. I thought I'd have the life my mom had—my daughter and me, and that would have to be enough. To get a second chance at love is not something I ever expected.

I was born on the floor of a jail cell, for goodness' sake. If those prison guards could see me now. They probably would've never bet on me succeeding in life or having a healthy relationship—not after my start. But I do. Even after all the ups and downs that my life has taken, I'm happy.

When I told Brinley about the engagement, she screamed so loud I had to hold the phone away from my ear, and when she saw the ring, she actually did a little happy dance. But her reaction was nothing compared to Duke's parents. Connie and Charlie cried. Both of them. I hadn't expected that, so of course, I cried. They were so happy they couldn't speak. They simply wrapped me in their arms, holding me so tight that I thought they might never let go. I thought they had forgotten about Duke altogether until his dad laughed out, "It's about damn time," and pulled him into the embrace.

I hope my mom and Chase are up in heaven doing their own little happy dance for us. I know neither one would want me alone or unhappy, so I pray they are blessing us from above.

Stopping in the doorway, I see Duke is back on his old bed, my sofa, only this time he's got a sleeping buddy. Arden is nestled into his chest. They are both out like a light. Even as they sleep, he has both arms around her, protecting her. Her little head rests right where I know she can hear his heartbeat. He loves her. And I know he can love her enough for himself and for Chase.

Smiling, I walk to the kitchen, the smell of coffee greeting me. It's silly to make coffee every morning, but somehow, it helps me start the day off remembering Chase. I want Arden to know him as best as she can. She'll have Duke in her life, and he understands that she also needs to have Chase in her life as much as possible. That's one reason our relationship works. He respects the role Chase had in my life and the role he will continue to have because of Arden. He doesn't fight it. If he did, this would never work.

It's just one of the many reasons I love him.

Walking back into the den, I sit down on a chair, admiring how perfect they look. Duke—handsome and strong. Arden—angelic and sweet. I wonder how long they've been like this.

I wasn't awake when he got home. Apparently, he could be called up for Nightwalk duty any day, and there was some special training he needed to complete last night. He told me not to wait up even though yesterday was my six-week checkup, and I'm now clear to resume all activities. Well, there's only one that Duke is concerned about. I tried to wait up for him, but after Arden's first feeding, I dozed off.

Still, he arranged for his parents to babysit Arden today. It's the first time I'm leaving her with anyone other than Duke. I'm slightly nervous about that, but it's just for a few hours. We won't be far, and they are coming here so she has everything she needs and will be in familiar surroundings. I might be overthinking the whole thing, but as a first-time mom, I think I'm allowed.

"Hey," he whispers, smiling at me, his dimple sneaking through.

"How was last night?" I ask.

"Fine," he says softly. "Practiced some formations." He must see my confusion because he then says, "When you fly the president, you fly in a five formation. So with other birds. Four of them are decoys."

"I don't like the idea of you as a decoy."

He removes one hand from Arden, holding it out to me, and I take it. He twirls my engagement ring on my finger. "Prepare yourself for my parents," he says. "They keep asking for a date."

I scoot down off the chair and onto the floor, so I can be closer to him. He runs his hand through my hair. "I don't want to cheat them or you out of anything, but I planned the big wedding before, and . . ."

Arden makes a little noise, and he adjusts her slightly. "You don't want a big wedding?" he asks.

"Not really. What do you want?"

"To marry you," he says.

Rolling my eyes, I say, "If a big wedding is important to you, then I'll do it."

"I honestly don't care."

"I think your parents will care. You're their only child. I think they are going to want a huge ceremony."

"What do you want?" he asks.

"Elope?"

"Where?" He grins.

"You pick," I say.

"The lake," he says, his eyes soft. "Just me, you, Arden, my parents, and Brinley."

"When?" I ask.

"I'm out of leave for the year. Used it all up when Arden was born," he says. "January?"

I can't help but laugh. That's only a few months away. "Perfect."

I stand at the threshold of my front door, kissing my baby girl goodbye. Autumn hasn't officially arrived yet, but a cool breeze blows, hinting that it's on the way. The hem of my dress blows slightly. I haven't gone out much since Arden's birth, so I decided to dress up a little. "We'll be back in two hours," I say.

"Six," Duke whispers to his parents.

"You said a couple of hours," I say, throwing Duke a look.

"Take as much or as little time as you want," Duke's mom says.

"We won't be gone that long," I say.

"First time we left Duke," Mr. Charlie says. "Connie threw up in the car. Worked herself up into such a fuss."

"I didn't throw up," she says, shaking her head at me in the most reassuring way. "I merely dry heaved."

"Maybe we shouldn't go," I say, looking up at Duke.

"But I have your birthday present ready," he says.

"Huh? Our birthday isn't for a few more weeks."

"Got done early," he says, urging me out the door a little more.

"We won't stay gone long?" I ask him.

"I'll bring you home as soon as you're ready," Duke says, placing his hand on the small of my back and waving to his parents as he pushes me toward his truck.

I twirl out of his arms, my dress whirling with me, and start back for the house. "I should change her diaper before . . ."

He captures me. "I did that."

Still staring at my front door, he ushers me into his truck, and we drive away. Immediately, I pull out my phone. "I'm just going to text them and remind them that she likes the pink blanket better than the gray one."

Just then, my phone dings, and I hold it out for Duke to take a glance. It's a selfie of Arden with his parents, wrapped perfectly in her pink blanket. Giving me a little grin, he places his hand on my leg as we drive through town.

"I feel like a part of me is missing," I say. "Is that weird?"

"Not at all," he says. "I felt the same way when you were pregnant, and I had to leave you to go back to Japan. I was leaving two parts of myself behind. You and her."

"Thank you," I say. "For making me do this. For whatever this surprise early birthday gift is. For putting me back together again."

He takes his eyes off the road for a second and winks at me. "I didn't put you back together. I just reminded you that you were strong enough to do that all on your own."

I lean over as far as my seat belt will allow and kiss his cheek. He deserves so much more than a kiss on the cheek. If not for him, his love, his patience, I would probably still struggle to get out of bed every day. The guilt and grief still overwhelming me.

"You gonna tell me where we're going?" I ask.

"You'll know soon enough," he says.

"Has to be the lake," I say with confidence.

He simply grins at me. Leaning my head back, I stare at his handsome face. How many times did I have this exact view as a teenage girl? Only then, I'd quickly turn away if he caught me staring. It feels like we've come full circle. I guess that teenage girl knew more than I thought. She was right. Duke and her would end up together. The road was rockier than she thought, though.

Duke makes a familiar turn, and I look back. I was sure he was taking me to the lake, but he's heading somewhere else. It can't be where I'm thinking. What birthday gift could possibly be at a cemetery? He didn't buy us matching plots?

Duke has always been a good gift giver, but I'm not so sure about this. He parks his truck, looking over at me.

"I wanted to blindfold you, but thought it might look weird to blindfold you and walk through a cemetery. So the blindfold will have to wait for later," he says, smirking at me.

"This is hardly the place to celebrate our birthday," I say.

"Trust me," he says, walking around the truck to get my door. Slipping my hand in his, I let him lead me up the path I know too well—the path where Chase is buried. I've walked it so many times that I know exactly how many paces it is up the hill and how many trees there are. For the longest time, the walk never seemed to get any easier, but today it is. Because today I'm not walking it alone. "I had to give you your gift early because otherwise, you'd see it when you visit Chase."

He nods his head toward Chase's grave. My hand flies to my mouth, and my eyes fill with tears. I cannot believe he did this. Chase's headstone was a sore spot for me. For months and months, I agonized over if it was right, if I did the right thing. We weren't married, so no one knew I was pregnant. I had no idea how to memorialize him. And with the one-year anniversary of his death looming, I was still struggling with his epitaph.

Falling to my knees, I outline the letters with my fingers. The words *Loving Father* now engraved into the stone under the infinity symbol. As I lean my head on the stone, my tears fall to the ground. I've shed many tears at this spot, but these feel different. They're not happy tears, but they're not sad either. Somehow, they feel final. They feel like I'm done. I know I'm not. I know I will never be done grieving him. Grief is lifelong. I know I'm going to have to grieve him with Arden. But these tears are tears cried because I'm ready to move on.

I turn around, looking at the man I'm ready to move on with. He's stepped back a few paces, giving me space. He has his hands in his pockets, and when his eyes meet mine, he offers me a small shrug and smile, as if this was nothing when we both know it was everything.

Kissing two fingers, I lay my hand on those words, get to my feet, and walk toward my future.

CHAPTER FORTY-FIVE

LENNON

Duke hasn't let go of my hand since we left the cemetery. As we drive through Montclair, I'm still stunned he thought to do something like that for me, for Arden. The way he loves me always is a surprise, and I'm not sure why.

When he squeezes my hand, I realize I haven't said anything since we left the cemetery. "Do you want to go home?" Duke asks, probably assuming I'm worried about Arden.

"No," I say. "Turn in here."

He glances at me. "Here?"

I nod at him. Montclair is not a big town. We have plenty of hotels, but if you're looking for a four- or five-star luxury place, you're going to have to drive a distance, and frankly, I don't want to waste the time. So a clean three-star hotel will have to do.

He puts the truck in park, turning to me. I know he thinks we can do better than this. I know he wants our first time to be special, so before he can say anything, I say, "It reminds me of the place we spent my prom night."

Leaning toward me, he grins. "I'm not going to let you fall asleep this time."

"Doubt you would've let me fall asleep then if you knew I had condoms in my bag."

His jaw drops open. "You're shitting me."

"Nope," I say, planting a soft kiss on his lips. "We're wasting time."

Laughing, he hops out, gets my door, and has us at the check-in desk within seconds. We don't have a reservation, but they have a room. Duke doesn't ask a single question before slapping down his credit card. We don't volunteer that we'll only need the room for a few hours. Don't need them thinking this is an affair or, worse, that I'm a working girl.

The desk clerk starts to tell us about the hotel amenities, but Duke grabs the key. "The only amenity we need is the bed," he whispers to me.

I wouldn't say we run to the room, but it's a fast-paced walk, for sure. Before he even has the room key inserted, he pins me to the door, kissing me. He hoists me up, my legs wrapping around his waist. If there are cameras in the hallway, there is no doubt what we are here to do. We both laugh as he opens up the door, carrying me through.

"Shit," he mumbles, and I turn my head, seeing two double beds.

"We don't need much room," I say with a smile.

He smiles back at me. We've waited too long for this moment to let anything dampen it. It doesn't matter where we are or what kind of bed it is. The only thing that matters is us.

Taking me down to the bed, he covers my body with his. "I love you," he whispers.

"Show me," I say.

Slowly, his fingers start to unbutton my dress. He takes his time, undoing each button, revealing more and more of my skin. I stand, and he slides it off my shoulders until it drops to the floor. Slipping off my sandals, I'm in nothing but a white lace bra and matching panties. He lifts his shirt over his head, then slides his fingers underneath the straps of my bra. I feel my heart rate speed up, and my panties soak under the gaze of his gray eyes. He unsnaps the button on his jeans, standing there without a shirt, his muscles bulging.

"Duke," I say, only it comes out in a needy moan. I can hardly believe this is finally happening.

A naughty grin comes to his face. And I know this is going to be fun. One look from him, and I know I'm in for the ride of my life.

I crash into him, and he rips off my bra and panties. I slip my hands under his jeans, sliding them down. His mouth moves over mine to my neck, fast and furious. Somehow, I'm back on my back. He forces my thighs apart with his, settling between my legs. I've never wanted anything more in my life than I want this man inside me right now.

He slows down as his dick is poised at my entrance. His eyes lock on mine. This is the moment I know he's imagined a thousand times. This is the moment I wanted for so long—wanting him to love me, wanting him to see me as more than a friend. I might not be handing him my virginity like I imagined, but I'm handing him my heart, my future, my daughter's future.

He reaches down, gliding his tip inside me. His eyes clench shut. "Shit, that's tight."

I've had a baby, so I'm not sure how "tight" things are now. The more logical explanation is that he's very well hung. I feel my body stretching, opening, making room for him. Slowly, he slides himself inside me until he's buried deep. He doesn't move right away. I think we're both a little shocked that this is finally happening.

"I want this to be good for you, baby," he says, starting to move.

"Make me come like this," I pant.

He pins my wrist over my head, increasing his speed. Our hips grind together, over and over again. A shot of pleasure shoots through my body every time he hits just the right spot. We find our rhythm, and I clench my muscles around his length. He groans a little, his eyes on fire. He reaches down, pulling my leg to his hip, thrusting harder. "You feel so good," he says through gritted teeth.

Suddenly, I flash to Chase. I don't want to. I don't want him in this bed with us, but I don't want a repeat of those experiences either.

"Please don't finish yet," I whisper.

Duke's eyes pop open, and he slows down.

"Never," he says, leaning over and kissing me sweetly. "All you should be thinking about right now is how hard you're going to come for me."

I nod.

"Say it," he says, thrusting his hips harder. "Tell me."

"My pussy's gonna come for you," I whisper.

"Again," he demands.

"My pussy's gonna come."

"Uh-huh," he says, moving faster.

"It's gonna . . ." A heat burns between my legs, an ache so primal and needy that I feel like I'm going to lose all control.

"Let go," he orders. "Come all around my cock."

The heat explodes, coursing through my veins, until my whole body quakes, my vision going bright white. My head whips side to side, and every muscle tightens and releases all at the same time. He has given me orgasms before, but this is different. This came from somewhere else. I've heard that some women can't orgasm through sex. For a long while, I thought that was me. I feel sorry for those women. Because this is freaking unbelievable.

My body still trembling, I open my eyes. Duke is still inside me, slowly slipping himself in and out, riding the wave of my orgasm with me. He pulls me up, so we are sitting, forcing himself deeper. I'm surprised when the faint glimmer of need between my legs is awakened again. From the look on Duke's face, he's not surprised at all.

My head tosses back, his mouth finds my breasts, and the pleasure shoots between my legs again. How is this possible? I want more. I just finished, but I want to come again. But I want to give him pleasure more. I want to make him feel as good as I do. I want to watch him come undone. Gently, I push his chest, forcing him back, so I'm on top, riding him. His eyes spark. My breasts push against his chest as I move my hips. He moves my hair back with one of his hands, watching us move together. His other hand holds my ass, and I kiss him, my tongue stroking his.

I sit up, giving him a better look. Gone are the insecurities about my body. It's impossible to feel anything but good with this man between my legs.

"Fucking gorgeous," he groans.

His hands on my hips, he helps lift me up and down. My body stretches to take the length of him. The muscles in his arms flex. He watches the way our bodies connect, move, and bites his bottom lip.

"Oh, God," I cry, so close, on the verge again.

"Don't you dare hold back," he demands, smacking my ass. "Give it to me."

"Yes!" I scream, my body bucking.

He sits up, pulls me tightly into his chest, thrusts, and comes right along with me. "Lennon!"

Naked, he holds me, our bodies still connected. I feel his breath in my hair. He whispers, "I love you."

He said the same thing when we started. I guess that's how Duke and I are and always have been. We start and end with love.

CHAPTER FORTY-SIX

LENNON

"What a big girl you are!" Mrs. Connie says, making a silly face at Arden. She came with me to have Arden's three-month pictures taken. Arden's wearing the cutest dress with the number three embroidered on it.

She's lying on her stomach, showing off her tummy time skills. Mrs. Connie's laying on the floor, too, making faces, just out of the frame of the photographer. My baby girl is hamming it up, smiling, laughing. She's gotten so big already. She still doesn't have any hair, and her fat rolls are multiplying daily. I love her more than I ever thought possible.

I'm not the only one. Duke's parents constantly dote on her, offering to watch her for us. Mrs. Connie even made a playroom at their house so when we are over there, Arden has toys and a place to nap.

Secretly, I motion to the photographer to snap a photo of Connie and Arden together on the floor. She does so much for us. It will be a nice thank-you gift.

My cell phone rings in my purse, and I step away slightly. It's Duke.

"Is the photo session over?" he asks, his voice distant.

"Almost," I say.

"Call me when it's over," he says.

"Your mom is with Arden. I can talk now."

He exhales deeply, saying, "General Hale passed away this morning."

General Hale's widow, Peggy, is in her black dress, moving around their house, talking with guests, and receiving their hugs and well wishes. She buried the man she loved. I know how that feels. I might be the only one here who has the slightest knowledge of how she feels, what she's going through. What she's about to face.

I remember Chase's funeral, doing the same things, offering meaningless smiles to all the well-meaning guests. I wasn't fine. I acted like I'd be fine, just like Peggy's doing now. But tomorrow, fine will be out the window. Fine will be replaced with fear, anxiety, and worry. Fine will turn into a sadness so deep you don't know what to do. The simplest tasks will feel like mountains. Walking and talking will leave you exhausted. Fine becomes praying for sleep, so you don't have to think. Peace is an ideal, something you had once, but can't believe you will ever have again. The once happy emotion of love transforms into a pain so deep that you can't even think about the other person. All the happy times hurt too much to think about.

Love becomes pain.

Pain is love.

I see Duke walking toward me with a plate of food in his hands. He's wearing his dress blues uniform and is easily the most handsome man in the whole state of Virginia. "You should eat something," he says, and I shake my head, watching Peggy. She's the one who should eat something. Her eyes catch mine across the room. We are now members of the same club, our pain recognizing each other. We don't offer each other stupid small smiles. We know better. Then she gets pulled into the arms of a mourner.

I'm transported back to the day I put Chase in the ground. The one-year anniversary of his death is only days away. I'm not sure how many people hugged me that day, but the one touch I remember is Duke's hand resting on my shoulder at the cemetery. It was the only thing that felt real about that day. I never told him that.

"Lennon," he says softly. I turn my eyes to his but can't think of anything to say. "I know this is hard for you."

"It's hard for me. This is impossible for Peggy."

"I wasn't with you those first weeks after Chase died. I don't know how you were or . . ."

"Most of it is a blur," I say. "I hardly left the house. Getting out of bed was exhausting. I only ate because I knew I was pregnant and had to. It wasn't pretty."

"In your emails, you never said how bad things were," Duke says.

I shrug. "Some pain is too hard to put into words."

"Is that why you've been so quiet?" he asks. "The pain is too hard right now."

"I'm all right," I say, trying to convince myself and him.

But something is brewing in my soul, brewing in my heart, and I don't like it.

What the brain tries to forget, the heart never will.

I startle awake, sitting up in bed, my heart pounding, a thin sheen of sweat covering my skin. My eyes fly to the clock just like they did one year ago. Two twelve in the morning, that's when the police came to my door.

This is the exact moment I learned Chase was dead.

Goose bumps radiate over my body. Why couldn't I sleep through this memory? I hear stories of people who have lost loved ones, dreaming about them. I've never had one dream about Chase. Not one. Why not? Did I not love him enough to dream about him? But I've relived this moment over and over again. I used to cry in my sleep a lot, but it wasn't ever because I was dreaming about Chase. It was always about this moment. The moment I learned he was dead.

My hand flies to my mouth, trying to contain my cry, hoping that only the darkness can hear it, not wanting to wake up Duke, asleep next to me. Curling my legs under me, I wrap myself in a ball, resting my head on my knees.

I will myself to stop shaking, but my heart is right back at that moment, the moment I learned the father of my baby was dead. I wish I could say that I handled the news with grace, but that would be a lie. I collapsed into the arms of one of the officers. I don't even know what his name was, but he was the only reason I stayed on my feet.

At some point, I must've given them Brinley's name and number because she showed up at my door in her pajamas. I didn't tell her I was pregnant that night. I didn't tell her for weeks and weeks. There's something that happens when tragedy strikes. I recognized it in Peggy. It's almost like you go into work mode or autopilot. You know things have to get done, funeral plans, notifying people, and somehow you do it. You might not even remember doing it. You certainly don't know how you have the strength to do it, but somehow it all happens.

My body trembles again, and I can't decide if I feel hot or cold. It's all too much. The anniversary—General Hale's death. Since his funeral, I haven't been sleeping or eating well. Concentrating on anything other than death has seemed impossible.

"Lennon," Duke whispers in the darkness. He sits up slightly, placing his hand on my back. On reflex, my body flinches. "Are you feeling sick?" he asks, and I shake my head. I can't think. There are no words to explain what's happening. He moves closer, placing his hands on the side of my face. My body is so full of tension that I think I might snap in two. "Jesus Christ, you're ice cold and sweating."

"Bad dream," I half-lie.

"No wonder," he says, stroking my hair. "You've been in a funk for days."

"Chase. Died. Today," I say, my teeth actually starting to chatter.

His gray eyes look off in the distance. It's not that I expected him to remember the date, but he does, and he seems to be thinking back to those early days, too. "Today is the anniversary."

"Right now," I cry. "Two twelve."

He looks at the clock then back at me. Duke scoots in behind me, cradling me to his chest. "I got you."

CHAPTER FORTY-SEVEN

LENNON

I feel hungover. Only I didn't get the night of fun binge drinking. Who knew panic could give you a worse hangover than alcohol could ever dream of.

My body feels heavy and tired as I sit at my desk. Overall, the author and publishing house were thrilled with my vision for the emu book. I just have a few edits to make, nothing major, and they've been very understanding and respectful of my maternity leave, but I need to get this done. So when Arden naps, I work. Lucky for me, she still naps a lot. And Duke has been a dream about helping out at night and on the weekends so I can work.

This isn't a long-term solution. Ultimately, I know I probably need to hire someone to come in a few hours a day so I can work. Since I'm my own boss, I can pick and choose which projects I take and how busy I want to be.

Since Duke is living here now, I wanted us to split the bills down the middle. That's the way Chase and I did it. Honestly, it felt a little more like roommates than I liked, but he was the money guy. Duke, however, is a little more old-school. He hates my paying for anything. But I still do. He doesn't need to cover my health insurance. We don't fight much, but that one got pretty heated. He only relented when it occurred to him that as soon as we get married, he'll add Arden and me to his policy with the Marines.

Still, I like working, and while I know that Duke would support me being a full-time stay-at-home mom, I'm not ready to do that. Perhaps in a few years, if we give Arden a baby brother or sister. But

Duke and I haven't even talked about that. We were both only children, and the one thing we always agreed on was that we didn't like it. Maybe that's why we became so close.

The baby monitor lights up, Arden's cry filling the room. Guess my work is done for the time being. I walk into her nursery, and as soon as she sees my face, she smiles. She smiles and laughs a lot now. I think babies were designed to do such cute things because it makes the exhaustion worth it.

And I need her little smile today. I wonder how long she'll be able to smile on this day. How many years until she realizes that this is the day her father died? When that realization comes will it steal her smile?

A quick diaper change, and we head outside. The fresh air will do me good. Arden loves being outside, and the weather today is mild, a perfect hint of fall. I don't bother putting her in a stroller. I love holding her as we walk. Duke does the same thing. We both like to have her close, stroke her soft skin, talk to her about the world around us.

We walk around the block. I point out birds singing, dogs in neighbors' yards. She's only three months old, but I talk to her just the same. And everyday, I make sure to tell her about Chase. Some days, I describe the way he looked. Other days, I recite some multiplication tables because I know he'd love that. Normally doing those things makes me happy, but today I'm sad.

I haven't recovered from my middle-of-the-night breakdown. I'm not sure what I expected on the anniversary of Chase's death. I knew I would be sad. I knew old memories would come rushing back, but things have been so good the last few months. I've been so happy with Arden and Duke. I guess I expected that happiness to buffer the grief more than it is.

I kiss Arden on the top of her head, holding her close. Her sweet baby smell lifts my mood. We round the corner, heading home. Tires squeal behind me, and I quickly turn around, seeing a car speed past me, coming to a scratching halt right in front of my house. "Mr.

Charlie?" I whisper, hurrying my pace. Then I see Mrs. Connie get out of the passenger side. They start toward my front door, but as if they sense me, they stop, their eyes turning to me. The fear in them shoots all the way down the street like a missile aimed at me.

My head shakes, and my legs go weak. My heart fears something is wrong, something bad has happened. "Lennon!" I hear Brinley. Somehow she's beside me, her car pulled up on the curb.

I look back and forth between her and Duke's parents, holding Arden tightly to my chest. "Have you heard from him?" Mrs. Connie asks, rushing to me.

"Who?"

"Duke," Mr. Charlie says, ushering me to my house.

"I saw on the news and rushed over," Brinley says, placing her arm around me.

"What news?"

"You haven't seen the news?" Mr. Charlie asks.

I look at Mrs. Connie, tears running down her face. "I was working, then Arden woke up from her nap, and we came out for a stroll."

Brinley takes Arden from my arms. "There was some kind of explosion at Quantico."

The explosion was a helicopter crash. That's what the news is reporting. Apparently, the base is on lockdown so information is hard to come by.

A helicopter.

They won't say whose helicopter. They won't say if anyone is dead.

A Sikorsky VH-3 helicopter like the one that flies the president. That's the kind that went down. That's the kind Duke flies.

Mrs. Connie gasps. "There's more than one of those, right?" she asks, looking at Charlie, stunned staring at my television.

"At least five," I say, my voice coming out like a robot. "They use them as decoys."

"Was Duke flying today?" Mrs. Connie asks me.

I shake my head. "I don't know."

"Think," Mr. Charlie says. "Did he say anything?"

"I don't know!"

"Try his phone again," Brinley says to all of us. We've each tried him at least fifty times. It goes straight to voicemail.

"Where's Arden?" I ask, needing to hug her.

"Asleep," Brinley says.

"I can't do this," I whisper.

I can't sit here and wait. I can't hear this news. I can't do this again. I can't lose him. I can't. I just fucking can't! Closing my eyes, I think back to the morning, the way he kissed Arden's head as he said goodbye. The way his lips felt on mine as he kissed me goodbye. Was that the last one?

No! Stop it! He's not gone. He's fine. He has to be. No way could fate be so cruel to take Duke from me on the same day she took Chase. That's not possible. No one is that unlucky in love.

But I haven't heard from him all day, not since he left. Up until Connie and Charlie sped down my street, I'd have said the day was passing pretty quickly, even though I was exhausted, but now each minute feels like a day, each second, an hour.

And there's nothing to do but wait. I can't bring myself to do dishes or laundry. I can't bring myself to get up from this sofa. I don't want to think about anything but Duke, about him walking through that door again. He's fine.

"Why hasn't he called?" Mrs. Connie asks. "He has to know we're worried."

We all look at her. Reality hitting us. Dead men can't call.

"Maybe he lost his phone," Brinley says. "It's got to be chaos over there."

"Of course, that's it," Mrs. Connie says, but Charlie and I look at each other. He nods at me, his way of telling me not to lose hope. But life hasn't taught me to hope. Everyone told me to keep the faith when my mom got sick. Hope screwed me then. Just like it screwed me when it took Chase from me. I'd hoped for a good man. I found Chase. Then hope said, "oh wait a minute, let's knock that girl back down again." So hope can go screw itself. I'm not hoping Duke is alive. I am fucking willing it so.

My cell phone rings on the table, but I don't reach for it. It's turned over, so I can't see who's calling, and I'm not sure I want to know. That could be the call that changes my life—again.

"Answer it!" Mr. Charlie says, but I don't move. I'm frozen.

Brinley grabs it. "Hello." Her eyes go to me, and she smiles, "Duke, it's Brinley. I'm going to fucking kill you."

"Sorry I scared you," Duke says, coming out of the shower, a towel around his waist. "They locked down the base. We couldn't use our phones. They weren't sure if it was a bomb or what at first."

I really don't care. He's explained it to me a hundred times since he first called. One of the pilots had some sort of seizure in the air. Totally unexpected, had no medical history of seizures, and the helicopter went down. Somehow everyone survived the crash, but the pilot is severely injured. Duke didn't know him well, but the entire squadron was pretty shaken up by the incident.

"Hey," he says, sitting down beside me on the bed. "I'm okay."

"I'm not."

"I know it's been a rough week," Duke says.

General Hale died, we had a funeral, it's the anniversary of Chase's death, and for a few hours, I thought Duke was dead—rough week doesn't begin to cover it.

"It's been a wake up call," I say.

"What does that mean?" he asks.

"Nothing," I say.

"Don't do this, Lennon. Don't shut me out. Go within yourself."

Even when Duke and I weren't talking those few months after he kissed me at the lake, I knew he was alive on this Earth somewhere. There was a comfort in that. I don't want to be in a world without him. Leaning in, I lightly kiss his lips. He responds by kissing me back, a little harder than I kissed him, but still soft and sweet.

His kiss is asking if I want more. Slowly, I scoot back on the bed, removing my clothes as I go until I'm laid out naked before him. His gray eyes search mine, like he's not quite trusting what he's seeing, but he still sheds his towel, settling on top of me.

"I'm happy you're home and safe," I whisper.

"Staying right here," he says with a smirk, gliding himself inside me.

If only he could keep that promise.

Naked, I'm wrapped in Duke's arms. He made love to me soft and slow. The endgame of sex is the orgasm, but Duke never makes it feel that way. Instead, he makes it feel like every second is the most important, every move the one that will take me to the brink.

Carefully, I lift his arm, wiggling out from his embrace. He's asleep, but I've just been laying here, an overwhelming sense of relief, and enjoying what it feels like to be next to him, memorizing it. I didn't do that enough with Chase. I can't remember the last time he kissed me. I'm sure he did when I told him about the baby, but I can't remember it.

I'm not going to make that mistake again.

Slipping on a T-shirt and a pair of panties, I head toward the door, stopping for a second to look back at him. I could've lost him today.

I could lose him every day.

That's just the reality of life. Each day is an opportunity to lose someone we love. I know how dark that sounds, but it's true. Normally, we just choose not to think about it. But with everything that's happened lately, it seems life is forcing me to take a hard look.

Walking to the kitchen, I take a seat at the table, staring at Chase's coffee pot. It's hard to remember what his voice sounded like, his laugh.

I could've lost Duke today. Somewhere a woman is sitting beside the helicopter pilot who was injured today. She could be his mom, his girlfriend, a sister, or his wife. But it's not me. Not this time.

Am I next?

Everyone thinks love is a blessing, but what if it's a curse.

What if love has only brought you pain, heartache, destruction?

Would you do it again?

Would you take that chance?

I stare at that coffee pot and know the answer.

CHAPTER FORTY-EIGHT

DUKE

Yawning, I rub my eyes, reaching over to pull Lennon closer, but she's not there. When I glance at the clock, I know there's only one reason for her to be out of bed—Arden—but I didn't hear her cry, and it's much too early for her to be awake.

Throwing on some sweatpants, I walk down the hall to Arden's room, doing my best to be quiet. If she's sleeping, I don't want to wake her. A sleeping baby is a precious gift. And if Lennon is trying to get her back to sleep, I don't want to disturb them. That would not be good.

The door to the nursery is cracked, and I peer in. No Lennon, and I can hear little Arden breathing softly. Quietly, I continue searching for Lennon. I would've thought our little romp in the sheets would have sent her off to peaceful dreams, if not dirty ones. Guess I need to up my game.

I find her sitting at the table in the kitchen, her back to me. I found her like this many mornings when I first moved in, trying to find a way to say goodbye to Chase. As I get closer, I realize she's preparing for another goodbye—her engagement ring, no longer on her finger, but resting in the middle of the table.

"Why's it off?" I ask, my heart pounding.

"I can't marry you," she says softly, not turning to face me.

My heart pounds faster. She didn't just say those words. I misheard her. Crossing the room, I stand opposite her.

She doesn't stand, simply looking down at the ring. "You could've died yesterday."

"I wasn't anywhere near the accident."

Her blue eyes look up at me. I don't like what I see in them, the determination.

"Maybe not yesterday, but what about today or tomorrow?"

"Lennon," I say, kneeling beside her. "No one is guaranteed a today or tomorrow."

"No," she says. "But we don't have to tempt fate. And every day you go to work, fly that helicopter, you are taunting death."

"Chase was a freaking math nerd and look . . ."

"I know," she cries. "Look what happened. He was the most stable, safest guy in the world, and he died."

"I'm not reckless," I say.

"I can't. I can't be with someone who might die. Who'd risk that. I just can't do it. I can't live in that fear."

I'm on my knees in front of her. If I thought begging would help, I'd do it. "Would you give up the time you had with Chase to have him alive but never be with him?"

She looks me right in the eye. "Yes."

"You wouldn't have Arden."

"That's not fair," she says.

I motion to her ring. "Neither is this."

"Please take it back," she says.

"No, you had one man take a ring back from you. I won't ever do that. In my heart, you are already my wife."

"Duke," she says, starting to sob.

"You love me?" I ask.

"You know I do."

"Then why are you doing this?"

"Maybe if you go away, then I can stop . . ."

"You can't," I say. "I tried to stop loving you. Not being with you didn't make me love you any less. Hell, I was across the world from you, and my love never lessened. Not one bit."

She whispers my name, her voice pleading with me. "I can't."

"What about Arden? Think of her."

"I am thinking of her. She's already lost one father. I can't have her lose another. That's why it's best we do this now before she falls any more in love with you."

Anger burns in my chest. I can't believe she's actually doing this. After everything we've been through and how long it took us to finally be together, she's just going to throw it all away.

"So that's what you want to teach her?" I bark. "Don't love anyone because everyone dies anyway!"

"I'm not . . ."

"That's even more fucked up than the stuff your mom put in your head."

"Don't you dare talk about my mother!" she snaps, getting to her feet, and I do the same.

"Why not? It was her good advice that landed you with Chase in the first place."

"Get out!"

"Not a chance."

We stand there in her kitchen toe-to-toe. I'm much taller than Lennon, but she doesn't back down, glaring into my eyes. She's angry. That's good. At least she's feeling something and not hiding behind her fear.

"I'm not leaving," I say through gritted teeth. "You'll have to change the locks while I'm at work and throw my stuff on the lawn. And even then, I just might pitch a tent in your front yard!"

She doesn't even crack a smile. My charms aren't working this time. "I don't know how to make this any more clear to you. I can't do this. It's over. Goodbye."

"Never," I say. "I don't accept that."

"You don't accept that?" she asks. "You are impossible!" A loud cry floats through the house. She throws her hands up. "Now you've woken up the baby."

"I'll get her," I say.

"No. She's *my* daughter. I'll get her."

Her words cut right through to my heart. That's hands down the most hurtful thing she could say to me, and she knows it. I reach out and take her elbow. Her eyes ripple with tears. "That's how you want things to be?"

She doesn't answer, and I release her and watch her walk away.

CHAPTER FORTY-NINE

LENNON

I just did the worst thing of my life. I hurt him on purpose. God knows I've done wrong things before, but nothing like that. Nothing so mean, so cold, so callous, so cunning. Nothing to intentionally inflict pain on someone—someone I love.

But he was being so stubborn. I knew he wouldn't let me go. I knew the only way to make him was to strike hard and with malice.

Picking up my crying daughter, I hear him storm through the house. I'm not sure if he's packing his bags or just throwing a fit. The front door slams. He left. He's gone.

I stand there, holding her, both of us crying. It's not that I expected him to understand. I doubt most people would, but yesterday hearing the news that a helicopter was down, my life stopped. It felt like Chase all over again. Actually, it felt worse, even more unbelievable.

He's fine. But I'm not. A hole opened up inside me. I thought it was closed. But I was wrong. It feels even bigger than before. It's consuming me.

I'm scared. I absolutely hate feeling like a coward, but I'm scared. Scared to love him. Scared to lose him.

My mom lived her life without a man. She was happy. I can do the same. I have Arden. I look down at her in my arms, her eyes lidded and heavy.

A dark thought enters my head, or maybe it's just my heart trying to shake some sense into me, but I think about how much I love Arden. That doesn't scare me. Of course, every parent fears something might happen to their child, but that just makes you hold them closer, not push them away.

Should I be holding Duke closer?

No, I did the right thing. His job is simply too dangerous. I should have considered that long before. His chances of being killed are higher than say the average person. It's different. Heck, he's about to start flying around the leader of the free world. There are more than a few people worldwide who'd like to take a shot at them. And Duke would be right in the line of fire, or be drawing the fire as a decoy. He's literally paid to take a bullet for someone else.

I have to protect my heart. Arden's heart. I don't want that phone call. I don't want to stand at another grave or have to hear gunshots saluting him at his funeral. I don't ever want someone to hand me the folded flag once draped over his casket.

It hurt to do what I did. It will always hurt, but with time maybe . . .

My heart whispers to me again: You know you'll always love him. God forbid he does perish in the line of duty. It will hurt worse to lose him if I never really take this chance with him.

No! I shake my head. I made my decision. It hurt like hell doing it. I have to be strong, even if I am a coward at love.

Gently, I lay Arden back down in her crib. I don't know how long I held her for, way past when she fell back asleep. Lightly, I run my fingers over the blanket Mrs. Connie had made out of Chase's old shirts. I can't help but wonder what he thinks of all this.

Does he think I'm making a mistake? Is he happy Duke won't be around to raise Arden? Or would he rather Arden have a father figure, even if it's a guy he hated?

Sighing deeply, I grab the baby monitor and head toward my bedroom. I don't usually nap when she naps anymore, but I'm exhausted. I doubt I'll be able to sleep now, but I don't have the energy to do anything.

I see Duke's clothes still hanging in the closet. Obviously, he just wanted to get the hell out of here. Away from me, a crazy, sad person. It's not that I expected him to move everything out today or anything, but in situations like this, it's best to rip the bandage off quick, not prolong the pain.

Wiping my cheeks, I head to bed, wanting to hide under the covers for the rest of the day. I have a newborn, so that's not going to happen, but a girl can dream.

Right now, all I want is my pillow.

My eyes land on it, and my heart stops. It can't be. It's not possible.

Lying there are a stack of letters, wrapped in an old faded red hair ribbon, weathered by the sun.

He kept it. All these years.

At first, I don't pick them up. They feel like an old antique that will fall apart if disturbed. A small folded-up piece of paper is on top. I recognize the paper. It's from a pad in my kitchen. Gently, I reach for it, unfolding it.

I promised you I'd give you back this ribbon someday.

Lightly, I touch the ribbon, thinking of my mom, how she always made them. Remembering the day Duke removed it from my hair, how much I wanted him to kiss me. It was our first big goodbye.

Every goodbye letter I've ever written has been to you. Is this our last goodbye?

Tears rush down my cheeks, and I reach for the stack of letters. Years in the military, and I'm the person—the person he wanted to give his last goodbye to. Slipping one out of the ribbon, I see the date was from shortly after he arrived in Japan. I feel my heart open as I start to read his words.

Dear Lennon,

I've been talking to you since we could talk. Sent countless letters and emails over the years. So what do I put in this—the goodbye letter.

What haven't I said to you? What words are left unsaid?

So much.

If there's one person in this world who doesn't know how I feel about them, it's you.

I could've died today. The who, what, where, and why of that statement aren't important. What's important isn't even that I didn't die (although I'm happy as fuck I didn't). What's important is that I could've died, and you would've never known how I felt about you.

In the middle of a storm of bullets around me, I saw your face. I suddenly wasn't worried about my own life. I only thought of you, getting back to you, telling you . . .

I love you, Lennon.

I hope I get to look into your eyes and say those words to you one day, but if I don't. If next time I'm in a dogfight, I lose, I need you to know that while I might've died young, I had a full life because it was full of love for you.

Even if you didn't know.

You are the only person getting a letter like this. My parents know I love them. If they need a reminder, please tell them. But it's you that needed to know you were loved. I have never said that to any woman (besides Mom), and I won't ever say those words to any other woman but you.

If this letter ever finds its way into your hands, I hope those words can also find a way into your heart.

This might be a goodbye letter, but love knows no goodbyes.

Goodbye never—love forever,
Duke

CHAPTER FIFTY

LENNON

Tears streaming down my face, I don't need to read letter two or three to know I've just made the biggest mistake of my life. What is wrong with me? What in the hell have I done?

I love him.

There are loves, and then there are LOVES. Shouty cap loves. The ones that stand the test of time. Defy the odds. That's what Duke and I have.

You don't throw away that kind of love just because you're scared. He had to be scared out of his mind that day, but it didn't make him push love away. It made him want love even more.

I'm so stupid. I've been so dumb. I let fear and sadness get the better of me. That's not who I am. I'm jail baby. I smile at that thought. I was born tough. I walked around most of the early part of my life with people whispering behind my back. It bothered me, but it didn't consume me. I've let this fear and pain consume me.

Grabbing my phone, I rush toward the den. Shit, I can't go after him. Arden is here and asleep. Screw it, if there was ever a time to wake a sleeping baby, it's now. Doing a one-eighty, I start toward her room, only then realizing I don't even have pants on, still dressed in a T-shirt and panties.

Okay—pants first, then get Arden, then go get my man!

Wait! My ring! Running to the kitchen, I find it still resting on the kitchen table. Gently, I pick it up, my eyes landing on the coffee pot. Right then, the pot turns on, the automatic timer starting the morning brew, the smell of coffee beginning to fill the air. I think

Chase just gave me his blessing.

Smiling, I rush toward my bedroom. Dear God, please let him forgive me!

I'm like a madwoman searching for socks and shoes. Still pulling on my pants, I fly into the hallway, coming to an abrupt halt when I hear the doorknob.

"Duke!" I cry out, running toward him. He catches me in his arms. "I thought you left."

He pulls back, gives me a little grin, his dimple popping out, and says, "No. I just went to buy a tent."

I laugh, tears streaming down my face. His lips land on mine, and just like that, I'm wrapped in his strong arms. The thing about Duke and me is that no matter distance, time, anger, or grief—beside him is where I've always felt I belonged. I tilt my head up to look at him.

"You got my letters?" he asks softly.

Nodding, I say, "I'm so sorry. For trying to push you away. For hurting you."

"Shh!" he whispers. "You're not getting rid of me that easy. I promised you I'd always fight. I promised you I'd never leave Arden. And I won't."

"Goodbye never," I whisper.

EPILOGUE
ONE YEAR LATER

LENNON

"Dudu Dudu," Arden squeals, toddling over to the television and smacking the screen with her hand. She's wearing a bright pink tutu that covers her diaper. It was a gift from Mrs. Connie. I'm not sure who is having more fun picking out clothes for Arden—me or Connie. It's dangerous how fun it is to shop for a baby girl.

"Yep," I say, squatting down next to her and pointing at the helicopter poised on the South Lawn of the White House. Poor Arden thinks that every helicopter we see is Duke. But in this case, she's right. I recorded his last landing, so I could replay it for Arden when she misses him. He's not actually flying the president today. God, that's so weird to think about. My husband flies the leader of the free world.

We got married this past January. I wore a simple white dress. He wore his dress blues. As planned, the ceremony was small, at the lake with just a few friends and family. A fresh snow covered the ground. I held Arden as Duke slipped the wedding band on my finger, and he gave her a locket that holds a picture of Chase. She's too young to wear it, but it meant the world to me.

"Dudu Dudu," she says again, smiling.

I can't help but giggle. Duke and I had many conversations about what Arden should call him. Dad, Daddy, Papa, Duke? In all ways but biology, Duke is her father. Chase is, too. But you can't explain that to a baby, and I didn't want to deny Duke or Arden the title of father and daughter. So I suggested she just call him Daddy. He would never admit it, but he teared up when I told him that's what I wanted.

Still, for all our planning, Arden calls him *Dudu*. She somehow combined Duke and Dada into what essentially sounds like she's calling him a slang term for poop. We both cried the first time she did that from laughter, which was probably the wrong reaction to have because it stuck, and she's called him that ever since.

I'm sure she's not going to go off to college calling him baby talk for shit, so we've just gone with it for now. It's one for the baby book.

Arden and I both hear his key hit the lock. Duke walks through the door with a huge smile on his face. She takes off, her little droopy diaper not slowing her down at all. I get up, feigning like I'm racing her, and she laughs in delight. We do this every night when Duke comes home. I always let her win.

He picks her up, lifting her high in the air, and she giggles as he kisses her belly. "Dudu missed you," he says. Then he holds open his free arm, pulling me to him, kissing me, and giving my booty a hard squeeze. "Missed you, too."

Gone are the days of Arden being asleep when he gets home. Now she's awake until her bedtime, around seven thirty. It gives us all a few hours of family time before she's hopefully out for the night. Sometimes, Duke takes over, and I use the time to work. But Charlie and Connie have been helping me out during the day a few times a week. That gives me time to work, too. They used to watch her here, but as she's gotten mobile and louder, they take her to the lake, the park, their house. It's been a blessing to have them so close. Not sure how we will get on if Duke ever gets transferred from Quantico. They joke they will just move with us. I don't doubt them.

"You want dinner duty or Arden duty?" I ask Duke, knowing which he'll choose.

Honestly, I don't mind either way, but I have her to myself most of the day, and he doesn't—so he always chooses Arden over cooking.

Carrying her, he follows me into the kitchen. Duke installed child locks on all the cabinets but one. We made that Arden's cabinet. It's got old pots and pans, play cooking stuff. Mostly she throws it around, makes a lot of noise, and pretends to feed him. He sits on the floor with her, and she knows the drill, opening up the cabinet.

I start preparing dinner, listening to Duke and Arden. It's not like she can hold a full conversation, but she's got a great vocabulary for her age, and I swear she understands everything we say. She knows her basic body parts—eyes, ears, nose, toes. She can tell me when she's tired, hungry, and even some names for food. She was always a pretty easy baby, but being able to communicate with her makes things even easier.

"Two!" she screams, and I look over.

Duke's got two fingers up in the air. "Yep," he says, smiling at her. Then he takes his hands, hiding them behind his back. She tries to look around him, but he won't let her. She giggles, and then he dramatically brings his hand back around. "How many is this?" She holds up one of her fingers, mimicking him. "One," he says. "That's how old you are."

"No," she pouts, using one of her favorite words. "Two."

"No," he says gently. "Arden is one."

"Two!"

Duke scoops her in his arms, looking at the coffee pot that still rests on our counter. "Chase, dude, I'm trying," he says. "But she might not be a numbers girl."

Peering into Arden's room, I see Duke rocking her. He has Chase's blanket draped over her, and he's telling her some story about our high school baseball team. It's one of the few stories he has about Chase, so he tells it to her a lot. His eyes catch mine, and he grins. I know he'll be putting her down soon, so I tiptoe down the hallway to our room.

It's not late. We no longer go to sleep when Arden does, but we usually end up in bed, or the shower, or the tub. I mean, we are still newlyweds.

Standing in the bathroom, I slip off my jeans as I hear Duke close the bedroom door. "She's asleep," he says, coming up behind me. I reach for my birth control pills and some water. He lowers his head to my shoulder, gazing at my eyes in the reflection of the mirror. "Maybe don't take that tonight."

My mouth falls open. We haven't talked about having other children in any real way. And I certainly didn't know he ever thought about it. Arden was a complete surprise, so I do like the idea of planning this time around. Still, I laugh, half-thinking he's joking. "Arden is only fifteen months old."

"Which means she'd be two when her little brother is born if you get pregnant right away," he says with a grin.

I turn around to face him. He slides his arms around my waist. "You're serious?"

I don't think I've ever seen a bigger smile on his face than at this moment. And from the feel of things, he's more than ready to start trying right now.

"That would mean, probably two in diapers at the same time," I say, a whirlwind of thoughts going through my mind. "And we don't have another bedroom for a baby. And you might be getting transferred around that time. I'd hate to have to change doctors mid-pregnancy or give birth in a strange place."

"So that's a no?" he asks, smirking.

"It's a have-you-thought-about-all-that?"

He picks me up, hoisting me up on the counter, my legs wrapping around him. "I have," he says, starting to kiss my neck, his fingers toying with the edge of my panties.

"Mmm," I moan, lifting his shirt over his head. "And you still asked?"

"'Ask and you shall receive,'" he says.

"I don't think you should quote Bible verses with your finger doing what it's doing."

He chuckles, giving me a long, slow kiss. "Let's make a baby."

I'd like to have his child, give Arden a sibling, something neither Duke nor I had. And I love the idea of being happy through the whole pregnancy this time. Duke is a great father. Thinking about how I'd tell him makes my heart skip. I thought that would scare me, given what happened with Chase, but I only feel overjoyed and blessed at the idea. Maybe I am ready.

"Well, it's not a terrible idea," I flirt.

"It's the best idea," he says.

"A boy?" I ask, sliding down his pants.

"I'll do my best."

ALSO BY PRESCOTT LANE

The Right Side of Wrong
Ryder (A Merrick Brothers Novel)
Knox (A Merrick Brothers Novel)
Just Love
A Gentleman for Christmas
All My Life
To the Fall
Toying with Her
The Sex Bucket List
The Reason for Me
Stripped Raw
Layers of Her (a novella)
Wrapped in Lace
Quiet Angel
Perfectly Broken
First Position

ACKNOWLEDGEMENTS

To my friends and family who listen when I'm excited with a new book idea—You are the same ones who wipe my tears when I hit a roadblock, think I won't finish, and ignore my curses. Your pride and encouragement fill my heart and help my fingers type.

To anyone who has ever picked up one of my books—you are a dream maker. You probably just thought you were passing the time, looking for an escape, but every person who turns one of my pages is helping me make my dreams come true. Thank you. This is me sending you a huge hug.

To the team at Grey's Promotions—thank you guys for organizing my release, keeping me on track, and sharing my book.

A special thanks to Lori Jackson for her cover design. You absolutely crushed it!

Jenny Sims at Editing 4 Indies, thank you for correcting all my grammar, commas, semicolons, and overall helping my words be pretty.

To Hilary Chapman, thank you for loving my words and always being willing to help.

Finally, thank you to Michelle Rodriguez, for always saying "YES." Not only are you the best beta reader in the world, but you have a huge heart. I value your support so much.

Until next time,
Hugs and Happily Ever Afters,
Prescott Lane

ABOUT THE AUTHOR

PRESCOTT LANE is originally from Little Rock, Arkansas, and graduated from Centenary College in 1997 with a degree in sociology. She went on to Tulane University to receive her MSW in 1998, after which she worked with developmentally delayed and disabled children. She currently lives in New Orleans with her husband, two children, and two dogs.

Contact her at any of the following:
www.authorprescottlane.com
facebook.com/PrescottLane1
twitter.com/prescottlane1
instagram.com/prescottlane1
pinterest.com/PrescottLane1

Made in the USA
Coppell, TX
12 September 2023